Praise for *THE IMPROV*

"M.J. McDermott writes in two voices. One is the bright, hopeful and funny college student she certainly was, and the other is the news professional, mother and woman she has become. In *The Improv,* she returns back to that girl and that time, but writes through the prism of a woman who understands how a place of learning and joy can also be a place of confusion and pain. *The Improv* is the kind of book people always say they are going to write. Kudos to McDermott for getting over her stage fright, and putting one of her life's dramas out there."

~ Nicole Brodeur, Columnist, *Seattle Times*

"M.J. McDermott has written a chilling account of the college theater experience. Based on a true story, *The Improv* works like a 'whodunit' although in this case, it's a 'whatwasdone.' McDermott sustains an air of mystery and foreboding that makes *The Improv* impossible to put down once you've started reading."

~ Alice Kaderlan, Award-Winning Arts Journalist for *Crosscut.com, KUOW, Seattle PI*

"Too many college theatre directors abuse their power and violate their actors, as do those in other competitive arts where the fear of 'being cut' can cause participants to sacrifice their own moral compasses. I worked briefly in the real setting that inspired this work and can testify to stunning improprieties. M.J. McDermott has done a wonderful job of telling the truth, with humor and humanity, while protecting other victims from further embarrassment. I hope this book will cause more young artists to stand up and speak out."

~ Robert Barton, Professor Emeritus, former Acting Program Head, University of Oregon, author of *Acting: Onstage and Off, Theatre in Your Life, Life Themes, Voice: Onstage and Off, Acting Reframes, Style for Actors*

"As a recent graduate of a university theatre program I stayed up till the early hours reading this novel as it genuinely reflects the thoughts that penetrate a budding artist's mind – how far will one go to reach a character and where does ~~one draw the line in bringing~~ in real life to your work?"

~ Addie Keller, Actress

"With what has come to light about Penn State regarding Jerry Sandusky, Joe Paterno and all who knew of ongoing predatory sexual behavior but kept silent or dismissed the allegations, *The Improv* is a very timely book. While our concern tends to focus on the youngest of children who are abused, there is plenty of evidence that similar crimes take place in other academic / teaching environments as well, couched as 'games' or 'improv' and implicitly sanctioned by institutionalized power structures. For young adults there is perhaps less sympathy but an equal need for speaking out. M.J. McDermott deftly illustrates the thin trapeze line that young actors navigate between trust and betrayal, creativity and repression, youth and adulthood – as her very real characters grow up in ways they could never have anticipated. A good read indeed."

~ Perry Norton, PanRight Productions

"I thoroughly enjoyed this book for so many reasons – but one of them for me was the fact that it took me back to my own college days and life in the college theatre department. . . . I was totally taken in by the characters and what they were experiencing as they dealt with someone who was a mastermind at manipulation. I found myself caring deeply what would happen to these people. . . . Thank you for sharing this story with me, and with the world. I believe there is much to be learned from reading this book."

~ Bill Berry, Producing Director, 5th Avenue Theatre, Seattle, Washington

"Improvisation, when used respectfully, can be a very powerful and useful tool, as it allows the actor to genuinely and spontaneously experience and express a large range of emotions, especially those that they usually repress. If not used respectfully, it can be psychologically damaging. *The Improv*, based on the author's experience in college, unveils for us what can happen when this process is misused by an ambitious and unscrupulous professor. Like improvisation itself, the story reveals itself in surprising ways, taking us on an unpredictable and exciting ride."

~ Susan Warner, M.A., R.C.C.
Family Therapist, British Columbia, Canada

THE IMPROV

M.J. McDERMOTT

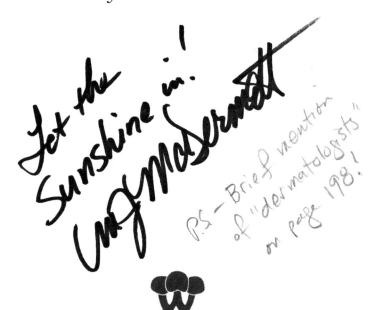

Let the Sunshine in!
M.J. McDermott

P.S. — Brief mention of "dermatologists" on page 198!

Wooded Isle Press
Seattle, WA

Published in the United States of America

Lyric permission for The Improv *by M.J. McDermott:*

AQUARIUS, GOOD MORNING STARSHINE, HAIR, I GOT LIFE, LET THE SUN SHINE IN, MY CONVICTION , SODOMY and **WHITE BOYS (all from "Hair")** Music by GALT MacDERMOT Words by JAMES RADO and GEROME RAGNI, © 1966, 1967, 1968, 1970 (Renewed) JAMES RADO, GEROME RAGNI, GALT MACDERMOT, NAT SHAPIRO and EMI U CATALOG All Rights Administered by EMI U CATALOG (Publishing) and ALFRED PUBLISHING CO., INC. (Print) All Rights Reserved. Used by Permission.

Happiness
From YOU'RE A GOOD MAN, CHARLIE BROWN
Words and Music by CLARK GESNER
© 1965 JEREMY MUSIC INC.
© Renewed 1993 MPL MUSIC PUBLISHING, INC.
All Rights Reserved
Reprinted by Permission of Hal Leonard Corporation

Library of Congress Cataloging-in-Publication Data

Copyright © 2013 M.J. McDermott
All rights reserved.
ISBN: 0-9844898-4-3
ISBN-13: 978-0-9844898-4-8

Wooded Isle Press
2400 NW 80 Street, #272
Seattle, WA 98117
woodedislepress.com

For the Drama Majors.

NOTE

This is a work of fiction, but it is based on something that really happened to me when I was an undergraduate in college. Characters' names have been changed. Some characters are composites or completely fictional. I have sought the approval of important characters. Some parts of the plot are completely fictional.

For more, please read the Afterword or visit: www.mjmcdermott.com.

M.J. McDermott

Im-prov, *n.*, **1** improvisation; specif., a skit or act in which the actors improvise a situation **2** the art or technique of doing such improvisations

To create characters, one must build background.
And one of the tools we use is improvisation.
~ Harvey Keitel

CHAPTER ONE

Margo bowed hand-in-hand with Rob McCall, the hunky captain of the football team. She closed her eyes and told herself to cherish this moment. It was curtain call of the final performance of Shakespeare's *Much Ado About Nothing*. She and Rob were the leads – Beatrice and Benedick. For a few more magical moments, Margo was a star. She looked and felt sexy. Her boobs bulged miraculously over the tight bodice of her blood-red Elizabethan gown. She wished Rob would put his arm around her tiny corseted waist.

The curtain came down and she opened her eyes. Rob had already let go of her hand saying, "See you at the cast party," over his shoulder. His green tights revealed every muscle as he jogged off stage.

"I see you looking!" Friend and fellow actress Jen rested her head on Margo's shoulder, sharing the view of Rob's exit. "Smartest thing they ever did was put that man in tights. You two gonna get it on at the cast party?"

Margo sighed. "Perhaps ours was merely an infatuation of the stage. Even if it ends here and now, I can always say I kissed the captain of the football team in college."

"Wouldn't you rather say you slept with him?"

"Shut up, Jen."

Margo forced a giggle as they made their way off the stage and down the circular stairway to the dressing rooms below. It was a precarious maneuver in the hoop-skirted dresses. Despite their friendship, Margo had never told Jen that she was a virgin.

1

"Oh, when will I ever have the lead in a Shakespeare play again?" She and Jen entered the harshly lit beehive of the dressing rooms. The men were high-fiving each other and trotting off into their room as costume crew members shouted instructions. Kathleen was taking pins out of her wig as she pushed the door to the women's dressing room open, squealing something hilarious to Brandy who was right behind her.

Margo stopped before going into the dressing room after them. "I don't want to get out of this dress. I love this dress."

"Cut it out. At least you had a lead. And it's all because you had a nose job over the summer."

"Which I paid for myself, after slaving in offices for three summers instead of enjoying some goofy drama camps, like other people I know."

"Well bravo, sister, because that's the reason snooty Dr. Stockerton cast you. He loves a pretty lady." Jen moved Margo out of the way, pushed the door open, held it open for Margo and curtseyed to her, saying, "And that's why I'll only ever be a lady-in-waiting in his majesty's fucking kingdom. Not pretty enough. And I can't wait to get out of Ursula's humble frock." She untied her apron and tossed it over the costume rack where it hung like a rag. "I'm never auditioning for that fox-faced persnickety hypocrite again!" She assumed a classical pose with cocked wrists, pursed lips, and a bogus British accent, "As Hamlet said – Speak the speech, I pray you, as I pronounc'd it to you, trippingly on the tongue." She rolled her r's with great exaggeration. The other two girls stopped to watch her.

Kathleen applauded, "That's a spot-on Stockerton!"

Jen continued with a sonorous, if nasal, voice, "It takes intelligence and years of training to perform the classics – Shakespeare, Molière, the Greeks."

Kathleen took up the game, standing on a chair to make her pudgy petiteness more imposing, "Working from the outside–in, we achieve artistic greatness through posture, poise and diction."

"But if you're a woman, you'll never get anywhere without a pretty face and great tits!" Jen bowed with her arms out to Margo. Kathleen jumped off the chair giggling.

Margo pushed Jen away. "My tits are not great, they're just average."

Jen looked down at her own chest, "And like Fanny Brice in *Funny Girl*, my 'incidentals are no bigger than two lentils.'"

"C'mon Jen, you are uniquely attractive."

"Stockerton called me a horse last night."

"Son of a bitch."

Suddenly there was a loud knock on the door and the girls shrieked, grabbing clothes to cover themselves up. Ellen Graham, the costume mistress, poked her head in. "Okay Ladies. How are we doing?" She struggled in with a cardboard box and a blue plastic bin that she dropped on the floor.

"Put the bum rolls in the box, the farthingales on the floor in the corner, and the corsets in this container."

"Just hang the dresses?" Kathleen held up her gown.

"You know, bring 'em over here." Ellen plopped her hefty grandmotherly frame into an old armchair with padding showing through holes in the upholstery. "I'll rip out the pit pads right now."

She pulled half-glasses and a seam ripper out of her apron pocket, took the gown from Kathleen, turned the bodice inside out, deftly tore the sweaty underarm pads from the dress, and tossed them into a trash can. She handed the dress back. "Hang it on the rack and I'll get the dresses off to the dry cleaners tomorrow. Next!"

Jen untied the donut-shaped bum roll from off her hips and threw it like a Frisbee into the box.

"Score!" She pumped her fist in victory, snatched up her lady-in-waiting frock and dropped it unceremoniously into Ellen's lap. "Here you go, Ellen. Good riddance!"

"What? I'm hurt." Ellen acted offended. "Didn't you like the dress?"

"I loved the dress. I just hated the part." Jen turned to the other actresses and raised her hands in the air. "Hey – let's give Ellen a big hand for her excellent work. Another brilliant achievement from the Goddess of Costumes!"

Margo applauded and shouted, "Hear, hear!" She thought she saw the grumpy granny grin a little as she worked the seam ripper on Jen's pit pads.

Ellen took off her glasses and wiped them with a corner of her apron. Was she crying? "You know, I'll do this later. Just hang the dresses. And finish up! The sooner you get this done, the sooner you can get to the cast party." She went to the door, then stopped and turned around, "Ladies, it's been a pleasure. I wish you the best in your future acting careers. I'd better go check on the men." She turned and stomped out of the dressing room.

Jen smiled. "Was she getting emotional?"

Margo was hanging up her dress and held it out one last time. "She really is a marvelous costume designer."

"Speaking of future acting careers, who's auditioning for *Hair*?" Across the room, the beautiful Brandy was already dressed in her party clothes. A hot pink puffy sweater fell to mid-thigh over shiny black leggings. She was bent over like a dancer, zipping up her black and silver boots, while her thick and bouncy raven-colored curls cascaded off her head and just about touched the floor.

It sounded like an innocent question, but Margo knew Brandy was fishing. Typical. The curtain is barely down on one show, and everyone is already plotting for the next.

"Going for your next lead, Brandy?" Jen asked, rolling her eyes behind Brandy's back.

"Why not? It's my last chance before graduation. And, you know, I'm more of a dancer and singer than I am a Shakespearean actress." She stood up and tossed her head back, shaking her hair out. It fell in fetching ringlets that framed her angelic face.

"Wasn't that your talent at the Miss Something County Pageant?"

"Yes. I sang and danced 'In My Own Little Corner' from *Cinderella*. In toe shoes. And I won Miss Juniper County. I almost won State too."

"Cool," said Kathleen.

Margo hated that she hated Brandy. Brandy was one of those women men lust after. She did have great tits, cover girl good looks and an effortless charm. Things just seemed to come easily to her. Margo had had the lead in *Much Ado*, but the role was a man-shunning tough girl. Brandy had been the lovely ingénue Hero. Type casting.

"So, who's auditioning for *Hair*?" Brandy asked, looking right at Margo.

The boisterous Jen saved Margo from answering the poisonous question. She removed the cap she'd been wearing, undid her own stringy, dirty blonde locks, flung them over her head in a mocking imitation of Brandy, and danced around singing badly while swishing her hair dramatically, *"Give me a head with hair – long beautiful hair – gleamin' streamin' something something something."* She stopped and made a face. "Guess I'm not auditioning. Can't sing. And I don't know the words."

Kathleen undid her frizzy red hair, used her fingers like she was lathering it up, making it wildly unruly, opened her elfish lips and squealed, *"Aquarius! Aquarius! Aquarius!"* Then she burst into giggles and declared, "Can't sing either! Plus, if my Irish Catholic parents saw me naked on stage, they wouldn't pay my tuition."

Jen had just taken off her corset and stood topless. "What's wrong with being naked?" She assessed herself in the full-length mirror. "Shit. I gotta lose a few pounds."

Kathleen put her hands over her eyes. "Ahhh! Put your shirt on!" She peeked out from behind her hands. "And no you don't! You're actually too thin, girl. I can see your ribs." Jen shrugged and reached for her clothes. Kathleen went on in a more serious tone. "Do you really think they'll do the nude scene?"

Buttoning up her blouse, Jen said, "Horrible Harry's directing it. You know they'll do that and more!"

"That man creeps me out. He looks like Orson Welles, in a bad hand-knit sweater with greasy food stains on it. And the little baby voice that comes out of those blubbery fish lips is just wrong."

Brandy took the center of the dressing room. "Dr. Harrison P. Adler directs the most provocative attention-getting shows at this university. He gets actors to reach parts of themselves they wouldn't get to with anyone else. Did you see *Oedipus* last year? It was breathtaking. His shows are electric and beautiful, and, yes, pretty sexual. I would kill to work with Harry."

Kathleen waved her hairbrush at Brandy. "And now he's directing the most sexually explicit musical in Broadway history. Have fun, Brandy! The guys will love seeing you all naked up there."

Margo reached behind her back and began to fumble with the laces of her corset. Brandy floated across the room to help Margo, pushing Margo's thin mousy-brown hair out of the way.

"So? You didn't answer, Margo. Are you auditioning for *Hair*?"

Margo was uncomfortable with Brandy being behind her back where she couldn't see her. She hesitated, "I think so. I mean, yeah, sure, I'm auditioning."

"Aren't you worried about Harry?" Kathleen asked.

Jen peered at Kathleen with squinted eyes. "Okay, Kathleen, what have you heard?"

Kathleen moved closer to the other three. She spoke quietly with wide eyes. "Well, my older sister knew someone in Harry's *Jesus Christ Superstar*, and she said, in one improv, he had all the apostles stripped down to G-strings and slithering on the floor trying to touch Jesus where the sun don't shine."

"Men in G-strings?" Jen whistled. "Maybe I'll audition after all."

"There's more I could tell you." Kathleen opened the dressing room door a crack and peered out. She popped her head back in and shut the door quickly. "The men are coming! I'll tell you later."

There was loud pawing and knocking at the door and various male voices, "C'mon ladies, let's go! The cast party beginneth! What takes women so long?"

Jen yelled at the door, "We're almost done, you troglodytes! Go on ahead – we'll be there soon!"

The men grunted and made other animal noises outside the door. "Hurry up, girls!" one of them barked and their manly sounds drifted away.

Jen grabbed Kathleen's arm. "What else do you know? I've been in this Drama Department for three years and no one will say anything about what actually goes on in a Harry improv."

Margo said, "I've heard of 'bonding exercises,' 'dominance or status games,' 'body awareness movements.' That doesn't seem so bad. More like group therapy than theatre exercises."

"Right," said Jen, "I mean, I've taken two of his classes, and we did improvs but they weren't that big a deal. Supposedly, it's in his plays that things get really outrageous. Plus, Harry supposedly prefers doing his 'special' improvs with boys only."

Brandy said, "People who've been in his plays say it's all overblown."

"Then why don't they tell what happened?" Jen asked. "I think they're too embarrassed to admit what they've done."

From outside the door Ellen said loudly, "I'm turning the lights off, girls. Let's get going!"

Kathleen took a breath and sucked in her lips. "Okay, look, I'll tell you at the cast party . . . about the boy who killed himself."

CHAPTER TWO

By the time the girls got to the cast party, the men had the keg tapped and the beer flowing. They were hoisting red plastic cups, looking nothing like the 16th century gentlemen they had just bid farewell.

When Rob saw Margo, he raised his cup and sang off key, from *Much Ado*:

"Sigh no more, ladies, sigh no more,"

The other men joined in:

"Men were deceivers ever!
 One foot in sea, and one on shore,
 To one thing constant NEVER!"

The men "clinked" their cups together and nodded at one another. The girls suppressed their smiles and shook their heads.

"Then sigh not so, but let them go
 And be you blithe and bonny,
 Converting all your sounds of woe
 Into Hey nonny, nonny!"

Cheers broke out and the men slapped each other on the back.
Jen stepped forward and shook her fist at the men, "I'll give you a 'Hey

nonny nonny!' Where's my beer?"

More cheers as red cups were filled and handed to the women.

Margo took her cup with a smile, then looked for a place to put it down. "I wonder if there's any food."

"In the kitchen, Margo. I haven't had a chance to put it out. And thanks for coming." Carl had been the male equivalent of Jen in the play, third lord from the right. He had offered his off-campus apartment for the party. It was a big place and Margo guessed Carl had persuaded his roommates to be elsewhere this evening so he could impress his castmates. For a guy's apartment it wasn't bad. Shelves made of plywood and cinderblock, and lots of milk crates, but at least it seemed clean and organized in the dim light.

In the kitchen Margo dumped her beer in the sink and filled the cup with water. She saw three bags of Ruffles and a container of onion dip. She brought them out to the living room where the guys descended on her, snatching the chips and tossing the bags to one another before ripping them open and beginning to devour the contents. Carl took the container of dip, opened it and placed it on a beat-up coffee table.

Jen was lighting a cigarette while Kathleen sipped from her cup of beer. Margo caught their eyes and cocked her head toward the kitchen. Brandy was chattering happily in the middle of a group of guys, one of whom was pouring something from a bottle into Brandy's cup. She was oblivious to the other women.

Safely in the kitchen, Margo cornered Kathleen, "Talk."

Kathleen hesitated and took another sip of beer.

Jen filled the silence, "A boy killed himself over one of Harry's plays? I never heard that."

"That's what my sister told me. It was a long time ago, probably fifteen years now." She licked her lips. "After a rehearsal with Harry, a theatre major committed suicide. It wasn't really over Harry's play though. He supposedly had emotional problems and they said he was high on drugs."

"What was the play?" asked Margo.

"*Death of a Salesman.*"

"Spooky." said Jen.

The kitchen door swung open. "What's spooky?" The handsome and talented Rob McCall crouched over, squinted one eye, and became the hunchback of Notre Dame. "I'll tell you what's spooky – a party where all the women hang out in the kitchen. C'mon ladies, join the party."

Kathleen giggled.

"Wait a minute, Rob." Jen grabbed his arm. "You were in *Oedipus* last year. What do you know about Harry's plays?"

"Oh, hell, is that what you're talking about? Shit!"

"C'mon Rob, what're the improvs like?"

"For Crise sake. Okay, first of all, I'm not supposed to tell you because an improv is private, you know?" He said it like he was talking to kindergartners. "But I will tell you that it's no big deal. The improvs help you break through your inhibitions and shit. Don't worry about the improvs. Just know that if you're in a Harry play, you're gonna get great reviews."

Margo had to ask, "So are you going to audition for *Hair*?"

"No."

"Because you don't want to be in another Harry play?"

"No, because I don't do musicals – didn't you just hear me sing? Now let's get back to the party!"

He pushed them toward the living room where music had been turned up and the lights turned down. His hand lingered across Margo's backside until he tripped over the door jamb and he stumbled against her, his beer sloshing. *It didn't take him long to get drunk,* she thought.

There was a tappity-tap little knock at the door that was barely audible. Carl was almost at the door when it opened and in poked the exquisitely-coifed head of Dr. Stephen Stockerton. "Helloooo!" he crowed and he let himself all the way in.

Heads turned and Rob started to applaud with big loud athletic claps. Everyone joined in and there were some hoots too. Someone turned the music down.

Stockerton cocked his head to one side and pursed his lips while he shrugged his shoulders. Then he reached out and applauded the room with straight arms.

"He looks like a seal," Jen murmured to Margo.

"Noooo, noooo, the applause goes to all of yooooo!" Stockerton gushed. "It was a triumph. The finest group of actors I've ever directed!"

"I'll bet you say that to all your casts," came a witty retort.

"Of course I do!" said Stockerton. "And it's always true!"

Smiles and laughs and people started sitting down. Margo sat on a threadbare couch and Rob plopped down next to her, crushing her thigh. Then he sat forward and bellowed, "Speech! Speech!"

Stockerton appeared flattered, "Oh no! I'm just here for one beer, then I'm off to let you kids do what you will." Carl handed him a red cup. "Oh, thank you. Okay, I will give a toast." Cups were raised. "To the talented cast of *Much Ado* – may there be much ado in all of your future endeavors!"

"Hear hear!" Everyone drank.

Rob stood up, lifted his cup and spoke loudly, "And to the toughest director I've ever worked with. You're worse than a football coach! Thanks for helping a big dumb lug like me pull off Shakespeare."

Everyone cheered and drank again.

Stockerton laid a hand on Rob's shoulder and massaged it as he spoke seriously, "Rob, I cast you because I was convinced you could do it. You worked hard and achieved more than I'd even imagined. Bravo to you, young man. You are an actor."

Rob smiled proudly and made like he was going to shake hands with Stockerton, then said, "Hey! Come here!" and pulled him in for a bear hug. Everyone cheered again and drank again.

Stockerton was one of the three tenured professors in the Theatre Department and playing a lead in one of his plays was a coup. Margo had paid her dues with him for three and a half years before scoring Beatrice. She'd perched on a ledge on the proscenium arch high over the stage and tossed tissue paper hearts onto the finale of *The Boyfriend*; she had been Props Mistress for *Romeo & Juliet* (during which the actor playing Paris caught his sleeve on fire while carrying one of her torches, prompting the Stage Manager to joke over headset "Is Paris burning?" as Margo threw his arm into a bucket of water); and she ran lights for *The Tempest*, never quite getting a lightning effect right for the demanding director. Acting-wise, she'd suffered through his puffed-up professorship in "Speech for the Stage," "Style for the Stage" and finally "Styles of Acting – The Classics." And he had cast her only once before *Much Ado*, as a winged no-name fairy in *A Midsummer Night's Dream*.

Stockerton finally granted Margo a meaty part in one of his mainstage productions. She was grateful, of course. But throughout the rehearsal period, he never seemed satisfied with her performance, never once praised her or gave her much attention at all. He became interested only during dress rehearsal when he called her wardrobe "quite nice." She was left largely to her own devices, which was fine with her – until he actually screamed at her a couple of times for doing something he didn't like. Then, like the frustrated former actor he apparently was, he would show her how he would do it, rather than directing her to find herself in the Shakespeare. She felt like she was walking on eggs during the entire rehearsal period and was relieved to get to performances when audiences gave her the encouragement she longed for. He gave most of his directorial attention to Rob, who she supposed needed it more. He was a drama major, but the charismatic football player had a long way to go before becoming a believable Benedick. Under Stockerton's tutelage, Rob had achieved a solid Shakespearean performance. And now, as she watched Dr. Stockerton thumping Rob's muscular shoulders while being crushed in his embrace, Margo felt that maybe there was at least a shred of humanity in the man. Rob sure liked him anyway.

Rob let Stockerton go and the professor exhaled and checked his ribs as if to make sure they weren't broken. The men shared a laugh as Rob straightened out Stockerton's shirt and shrugged in a comic apology.

Margo smiled and shook her head, then watched Rob get another refill on his beer. He returned and stood talking with Stockerton and some of the other guys, finishing the cup of beer in rapid slugs. *Is that three or four?* Margo thought. *Shit, I'm counting his beers. Let it go. Let it go. Let it go. Why can't I just have fun?*

Jen tilted toward her. "He really is a great looking guy, Margo. And he's sweet. Look at him talking with Stockerton."

"I know."

Eventually Stockerton took his leave. The music was turned back up and cigarette smoke made the room look dreamy.

Rob plopped himself next to Margo again and laid his arm across the back of the couch near Margo's shoulders. She could feel his heat and smell his make-up. Margo glanced over at him. He was gazing at her with one eyebrow raised. Suddenly he sat up, grabbed her elbows and said, "Let's dance. This is my favorite song."

The Captain and Tennille's "Do That To Me One More Time" was emanating from the stereo. *At least it's not "Muskrat Love,"* Margo thought, hiding her grimace.

She couldn't have objected if she had wanted to. He was so strong he pretty much lifted her up. He lurched a little, but held her steady and eventually they landed in the middle of the floor where two other couples were gyrating, including Brandy and her *Much Ado* co-star. *How cute*, Margo thought, as Rob put his big biceps around her.

Margo knew people were watching. She was certain Jen was smirking.

"You're a beautiful woman, Margo," Rob growled.

Did you know that I've had a nose job? Margo thought about saying. She could smell his beer-soaked breath and she suddenly wanted to flee. *Shit! What is this panic? This is a handsome hunk who is holding me and nuzzling my neck. Why am I so terrified?*

Rob ran his hands down her torso. "Man, you didn't really need one of them corsets. You're pretty fit. I can almost put my hands around your waist." And he demonstrated. Margo held in her tummy. "And I love your shapely *ass!*" He palmed her buttocks and pushed his groin into her pelvis.

Okay! Nope. No. No. This isn't happening.

"I want you," he growled again and actually licked her ear.

Tennille finished up and Billy Joel took over. Rob danced a little faster, singing about how Catholic girls start too late. Margo doubted he knew how truthful the lyrics were. She tried to pull back. No luck. Rob still had his mighty hands clenched to her shapely ass.

"What?" teased Rob. "Where ya going?"

He pulled her closer. *Dang, he is strong!* It suddenly occurred to Margo that this man could actually rape her. She chastised herself for being so melodramatic, but found that she was being held in an almost painful embrace. Romantic it wasn't. She wanted to break free of him.

What's wrong with me? 22 and still a virgin. Is it just because I haven't found the right guy yet? Is it because all I do is study? Am I really waiting until I get married? Who does that anymore? It's 1982 for crying out loud. Heck, I'm really just a nerd with a nose job. If he only knew. I'm a fake fake fake. I have no life experience. How dare I think of myself as an actress? How the hell can I audition for Hair? Maybe I should just do it with Rob and get it over with. Consider it an acting exercise.

She tried to get into it and rocked with Rob and felt herself respond a little as he kissed her neck then finally let go of her ass to cradle her head in his big hands. He tilted her head back then gave her a tongue-filled kiss that practically suffocated her. She struggled not to gag.

I'm not feeling it. At all. I am now officially repulsed. I really hardly know this guy. He's pretty much drunk. He's just horny and I'm here. I've waited this long, I'm not losing my virginity tonight. Like this. To him.

Rob let go a little in order to take her hand and move it to his crotch where he encouraged her to massage his manliness.

Margo took advantage of his loosened grip to pull away and very gently say, "Rob, I'm really not interested."

Rob stumbled back a little – thrown off his balance and his game. "What?" he snorted.

"You're a great guy, Rob. But this isn't me."

"What the hell?" he bellowed. "What do you mean? The whole god-damned play you're gazing at me with those big brown eyes – asking for it! Begging for it! Don't tell me that was all acting."

"Well," Margo stared at the floor. "It kinda was."

"What the FUCK!" Rob sounded truly furious and Margo got scared. "What're you? Frigid? What're you? A lesbian?"

Margo stood perfectly still, mortified in front of her friends. And terrified that Rob was going to crack her across the face. Her panic was rising irrationally.

It was like the party was put on pause.

Then it all happened in a nanosecond. Rob spun around, grabbed his beer, shouted, "I'm getting the fuck outta here," kicked the crappy coffee table over, spilling Ruffles, onion dip and three beers onto the shag rug, and stumbled his way to the door, slamming it on the way out.

Carl fell to his knees on the floor in front of the mess. "Shit, shit, shit," he moaned as he picked up a leg that had broken off the coffee table. "My roommate is going to kill me."

Kathleen ran and brought a roll of paper towels from the kitchen. Margo snapped out of her paralysis and went to help clean up.

She was shaking all over and could only say, "I'm sorry, Carl. I'm really sorry." Then she looked up at the crowd that had gathered to watch them and said pitifully, "I'm really sorry everybody." There was Brandy, warm and womanly in her hot pink sweater dress thing. She was smiling at Margo in a benevolently sympathetic sort of way. As though she wished she could bestow her effortless beauty-queenliness upon her.

The words "frigid" and "lesbian" echoed in Margo's head. Hands gooey with onion dip, she no longer felt like a sexy star. She was plain old virginal teetotalling uptight boring ugly nerdy Margo again. What if she did get into *Hair*? There weren't enough hours in a rehearsal period to break through her truckload of inhibitions.

But if I ever hope to be a real actress, hell, if I ever hope to be a real woman, I think I need to work with Harry.

CHAPTER THREE

Harry sat behind a Formica table in a plastic and metal classroom chair that was too small for his prodigious ass. He had piles of resumes all around him, a yellow pad in front of him and three paper cups that had held coffee off to one side.

In the corner, a skinny acne-scarred pianist half stood and raised his hand. "Hey Harry, I need a smoke. I'll be back in a few. Okay?"

Harry peered up over his reading glasses and nodded. "No problem, Jimmy. Take your time."

Jimmy got out from behind the piano, stretched his back and left the room, giving Margo a thumbs-up as he closed the door.

Margo swallowed and tried to calm the gurgling in her stomach as she stood alone at the opposite end of the Black Box Theatre watching Harry's sausage-y fingers clutch a fountain pen that was making big swoops on the yellow pad. She had just finished singing "Easy to Be Hard," the emotional ballad of the female lead in *Hair*, and she could feel little hope flowers blossoming inside of her chest, fertilized by Jimmy's thumbs-up.

He's really thinking of me for Sheila! Oh God, is he really thinking of me for Sheila? She didn't feel that singing was her strong suit. But she'd been taking voice lessons in the Music Department and she was thrilled with how the song had come out of her. She always did have a loud voice, and singing the low-pitched ballad, she had felt her voice fill the small black room. And she knew she could *act* the part – a passionate peace activist and protester from NYU – better than anyone in the Department. Even

Brandy. But what did Harry think?

Harry put down his pen and picked up the information page that Margo had filled out when she auditioned the previous week. He looked up at her as if appraising her and Margo consciously sucked in her stomach and tried to appear confident. Then Harry looked back at his papers and she exhaled, letting her stomach back out.

She felt like that song from *A Chorus Line*, *"God I hope I get it!"*

She studied the top of Harry's head. It was mostly bald with a scruff of reddish/grayish hair that stood at awkward attention and was moving slightly by itself. She glanced around, wondering where in the world a breeze could be coming from in this stuffy air-tight shoebox of a room.

Suddenly, Harry's chair creaked as he sat up, leaned back with arms folded across his vast chest, and smiled with corpulent lips that were partly obscured by his walrus mustache. Out came that tinny baby voice, so odd coming from such an enormous man:

"Well done, Margaret Lee Laughton."

"Thank you, sir."

"No need for the sir. Just call me Harry."

"Sorry. Force of habit."

"Come again?"

"Military brat."

"Ah!"

"I used to have to answer the phone, 'Colonel Laughton's Quarters, Margo speaking.'"

"Wow. Is the Colonel still on active duty?"

"No. In fact, he retired within this past couple of years."

"Ah. So things are a little uncertain in the Laughton home?"

"Well . . . let's just say that I don't plan to move home after graduation."

Harry nodded and paused. Margo felt like she'd said too much. Nerves did that to her. *Shut up! Shut up! Shut up!* Harry spoke again:

"Margo dear, you have an impressive resume and you're an A+ student. You're a well-trained actress and singer. You could easily pull off Sheila."

Margo dared to smile a little.

"But, as you must know, in my plays, actors do more than just pull off a performance. I require actors to embody the characters they play. To become them on an emotional or gut level. You must be willing to let go and lose yourself in order to discover the essence and motivations of the character. And I wonder if you can do that."

Margo felt herself go cold from scalp to ankles. She suddenly felt entirely naked.

"You are a smart woman, intellectual. And oftentimes intellectuals do not make the best actors."

He paused. *Am I supposed to talk now?* Margo did not know what to say. But she couldn't stop herself from blurting:

"I think that's why your plays are so exciting, Harry. You're able to get actors to exhibit the rawness of their inner selves. Your plays are electric and passionate and touch the heart of what it is to be human. That's why I want to work with you. I want you to help me get out of my head and become that kind of actor." *God, I hope I get it.*

"You know, I enjoyed having you in my Advanced Acting Class. I do believe you're one of the few students to really get my Anthropological Approach to Acting. How accessing one's own feelings and sense memory is not enough. How truly great actors tap into the deeper instincts of all humanity. This way the performance hits below and behind the rational mind and seizes the subconscious or even pre-human consciousness we all share."

Ever the professor. I can play that game. "I love this theory," gushed Margo. "The example of *A Streetcar Named Desire* that you gave is perfect. How Stanley Kowalski throws hunks of meat to his pregnant female and is leader of his 'tribe' in New Orleans, bonding with his fellow males and demonstrating his dominance among them. He protects his future progeny from those who threaten him, ensuring his immortality by passing on his genes and his name."

Harry smiled like a proud papa, and said gently, "Yes, you get it. But understanding a theory is different from being able to do it. In my plays, I require my actors to go deeply into themselves to find these primal instincts. The improvs require profound trust and willingness to let go. My classroom improvs are just a taste of that, and I always found you guarded in those. Have you considered becoming a director or a teacher?"

Margo felt punched in the gut. *No! No! I want to be an actor. An actor, dammit. Not a director. Not a teacher.* She felt her eyes begin to tear up. *Shit! No. Don't start crying!*

Harry got up from his chair and swung his pear-shaped form from around the table. He waddled over to Margo and took her clenched fists into his pillowy hands. They felt like soft gloves stuffed with marshmallows.

"Margo, dear, let it go. This is what I mean. Don't hold on."

Margo felt a tear roll down her cheek.

"Tell me about your family."

This threw Margo off. She felt uncomfortable, vulnerable, holding hands with this strangely gentle giant. She wanted to protect herself, pull away, crawl into her shell and back out of the room. But she thought, *He's testing me to see if I can do it – let go and access my SHIT. Okay, here goes.*

She inhaled and went for it. "I'm the oldest child in a military family, like I said. We moved a lot when I was a kid. Always the new kid in a new school." She swallowed. "My dad used to drink a lot and he was, uh, rough with my mom. I used to have to take care of my younger brother and sister when Dad came home drunk." She paused, remembering being eight or nine and lying in bed with the covers pulled over her head, praying to fall asleep so she wouldn't have to hear what was going on in the bedroom next to hers, vowing never to get married because *No man is ever going to treat me that way.* "You know, I didn't even know you could be drunk and not violent until I got to college." She let go of Harry's hands to wipe her nose. "Anyway, my home life was, um, chaotic, so I lived for school. I loved school. So, yes, I'm a good student. An intellectual, okay? But I became an actress to break out of all that. And I can access my feelings, god-dammit, I am an actress. And I *am* Sheila – the strong student protester, fighting against 'The Man.' No one could play this part like me."

Harry nodded and smiled, then opened his arms and held her in a big fatherly hug. "That's my girl. That's what I wanted to see."

With her face buried in the folds of Harry's chest blubber, Margo made some embarrassing snorting sounds but eventually calmed herself. *Fuck you,* she thought, pulling away.

Harry continued to hold onto her upper arms. "Thank you for letting me see this part of you."

Margo nodded, thinking, *Weirdest callback I've ever had. Does this mean I have the part? Do I even want the part if it means more of this?*

Oh yeah, she wanted it. She needed it. And she was scared to death that she would get it.

CHAPTER FOUR

The cast list of *Hair* was undoubtedly up by now, and Margo felt caught in a little corner of hell, wondering if her name was on it. And if it was, was her name at the top, or somewhere in the middle, or among the collection of names in the chorus? One minute, she was sure she had gotten the lead. The next minute, she could practically see "Brandy Jennson" written on the cast list next to the word "Sheila."

Harry would be crazy not to cast Brandy as Sheila. She would look great in bell bottoms with a bare midriff and bare feet, her long ebony hair loose and so shampoo-commercial sensuous.

But I would bring passion and determination to the role. I would be more the serious student-turned-protester. I really "get" Sheila. Brandy would just "play" Sheila. Isn't that what Harry didn't want?

But Brandy . . .

She was trapped in Dr. Cimino's theatre history class, barely able to focus while he showed slide after slide of the ruins of Greek amphitheaters. Dr. C, the venerable head of the Theatre Department, had been at the university forever it seemed. Every year, students thought it would be his last year and he'd retire. Then every fall, he'd reappear, as joyful as a senior elf in Santa's workshop, with unkempt wisps of hair shivering around his impressive dome, and protruding from his pointy ears. No one knew exactly how old he was, but sometimes Margo wondered if the Greek amphitheaters had been fully operational when he was young.

Now slumped in her seat, Margo was drawing flower-power designs all over her notes. As Dr. Cimino chuckled at his own anecdotes about a trip to Athens he took a thousand years ago, Margo wondered again if she would be any good in a Harry play anyway.

As Harry had said, she was more of an intellectual "outside-in" actor. She preferred the words of the text to the emotions and instincts of the characters. She acted from her head and Harry's plays required acting from the inside-out, from the gut. She loved to analyze her characters, construct entire lives for them and write down details of their pasts in order to understand them. She did not feel as comfortable improvising scenes to get to a character's emotions. She liked having a script to go from.

It was scary thinking about doing improv with Harry at the helm. Margo liked to maintain control. She did not enjoy letting go. She didn't feel comfortable exploring without a map. And she wasn't sure she wanted gross Harry to be the one leading any exploration.

Despite his grossness, though, Harry held her spellbound. Margo found his opinions and scholarship intoxicating. He was one of the reasons she had abandoned science and declared herself a theatre major, dedicating herself to the most precarious of careers and art forms. She had come to college to study physics. Now, as she approached graduation, she was prepared to wait tables as she floated from audition to audition and class to class, worshipping at the altar of Thespis.

But would she ever be any kind of successful actress if she couldn't let go and tap into her inner self? There's just so much research an actor can do. At some point, an actor has to reach into her emotional life, her life experience.

What life experience? She had never taken drugs, never even drunk alcohol, and she'd never had sex. Barely kissed a guy. But she also didn't want to be sexual just to prove something. She vowed silently to herself that if she got Sheila, she would do her best, but would not let Harry get to her. She would do his improvs, do sexy stuff (whatever that would be), but would stop herself when she felt things were going too far. Hell, she was an actor, she could fake it!

Her stomach gurgled. She was actually contemplating faking her way through an improv! Shouldn't a real actor be willing and able to access all of her emotions and instincts – sexual and otherwise? Shit. She just didn't know. And for the moment she didn't care. She just wanted to know if she'd won the part of Sheila.

She only had to get through the rest of this god-awful theatre history class.

Blah-blah-Euripides. Blah-blah-catharsis. C'mon, Dr. C, wrap it up.

Finally, Dr. C turned off the slide projector. Finally, he announced the next reading assignment. Finally, he said good-day, and left the classroom.

Margo carefully picked up her books. She took a second to calm her heartbeat and breathing before taking that long walk down the dead-end hallway to the Casting Board. It would be a long walk back out again, facing those who would know one way or the other. She didn't want to look upset if she didn't get Sheila. She wanted to be able to congratulate Brandy with what appeared to be sincerity. She wanted to save her tears and her tantrum for later.

She was so focused as she left the classroom that she didn't see Jen until she just about walked right into her.

"Shit Margo, 'bout time he let you out! You'll never guess what I found!" Jen seemed to be bursting with news.

Margo felt her scalp prickle. She asked, "Have you seen the board yet?"

"The board? Oh, you mean the cast list for *Hair*?" Jen shrugged apologetically. "No, I forgot. I'll go with you."

"Great!" Margo lied.

Jen was excitedly pulling some papers out of her bag as they walked down the hallway.

"Check this out!" Jen waved the papers in the air. "I've been in the library all day and managed to find this article from the *Utterance*!"

"Article?"

"Here!" Jen showed her the copy of a microfilmed article from a back issue of the campus newspaper. The headline read, "DRAMA MAJOR DROPS TO DORM DEATH."

Jen was breathless. "It was back in '69. The guy was nineteen years old. His name was Scott Warren, and he was an ex-jock who had switched from business to theatre. His parents are quoted as saying he was having emotional problems with school and girls and they think he was doing drugs. He was rehearsing the part of Biff in *Death of a Salesman* with Harry earlier that same day. Afterwards, he went back to his high-rise dorm and jumped out of a 9th floor window."

"Shit."

"Read this part here."

Margo read as she walked down the hallway to the Casting Board, "Mike Matthews, another actor in the play, said that Warren had appeared fine at the rehearsal, which included an acting exercise called an 'improv.' The play's director, Dr. Harrison P. Adler, called the young actor, 'a rare talent. He will be sorely missed.'" Margo shuddered. "Shit," she said again.

"Congratulations," said Jen.

"Huh?" asked Margo, following Jen's pointed finger.

"You got the part. You're Sheila!"

CHAPTER FIVE

"**A**nd playing Sheila will be Margo Laughton who, as you know, just finished a splendid, indeed brilliant run as Beatrice in *Much Ado About Nothing*!" Harry said, smiling at Margo.

"Woo woo woo!" "Yeah!" "All right!"

This was the first time Margo had received hoots of approval when being introduced at a first rehearsal. It was also more praise than she'd gotten from Stockerton during all of *Much Ado*. She blushed with pleasure. And stole a glance at Brandy.

To her credit, Brandy smiled warmly at Margo. She'd been cast as the young and innocent Crissy and would get to sing the funny, sweet song "Frank Mills," about a not-so-innocent boy she had lost. Brandy would also be Dance Captain of the show.

Sitting in a big circle in wooden folding chairs on the floor of the Black Box rehearsal room was the cast of *Hair*, otherwise known in the script as "The Tribe." *Perfect for Harry*, thought Margo.

There were twenty-four cast members, all fairly clean-cut Reagan-era college kids, excited about the opportunity to do all those things they'd missed out on by being born too late – protest the Vietnam War, make love, turn on, tune in, drop acid, fun stuff like that. Since the cast list had gone up, the guys had started an unofficial contest to see who could grow their hair the longest in time for opening. Tony Zampino, a white guy with kinky-curly black hair, already had quite a 'fro going from simply combing out hair that was normally tightly curled up. He and the other guys in the cast were also growing beards or side-burns. The women with short cuts had resigned themselves to wearing wigs.

The first rehearsal began with a business meeting. Harry introduced the directors and designers to the cast.

First was Zoe, the long-necked, perfectly postured choreographer. With expansive gestures and a husky voice (*a smoker?* Margo wondered), she talked about the movement that she was envisioning for the show. A child of the 60s, she was excited about making her "era" come to life on stage. She adored the music of *Hair.* And she was visualizing athletic, explosive, sensual, daring choreography that summoned the passion of the decade. She had worked with Harry many times before, including *Jesus Christ Superstar* (*the one with the G-strung apostles,* Margo thought), and was looking forward to working with him again, she said. She also said she looked forward to working with Brandy who would be her "second in command." Brandy smiled and nodded. Finally, she'd be working closely with the set and lighting people to create evocative, pulsating tableaux (she said it with a French accent).

The set and lighting designers brought in their concepts and designs. The cast got excited when they saw the 3D mock-up of the set. There would be lots of levels and a sort of "jungle gym" look to the stage so that actors could climb and hang on pipes and platforms and ramps and ladders. They even suggested that at one point actors might throw ropes from the balcony and shimmy down them into the audience below. This would be a very physical production, they said, and the set had to enable that.

Also very exciting would be the use of slides which would be projected onto large screens behind the action. Margo was surprised to learn that her currently quiet campus had been a hotbed of protest during the Vietnam War. She had had no idea that the National Guard had set up camp on the main quad and that a curfew had been enforced with helicopters and German Shepherds. There were news photos of all of this, photos that would root the play with a sense of reality and literally bring it home for the audience.

Costumer Ellen Graham was next. She showed them designs she had painted on matte board. She said she was hoping for help with costumes. She asked the cast to go through their closets, their parents' closets, their older brothers' and sisters' closets, and to visit thrift stores for vintage clothes. She didn't intend to build costumes for this show as much as assemble them. As Ellen passed out a schedule for fittings, Harry reminded them that finding clothes in thrift stores, decorating old clothes, and so on, was exactly what the hippies of the 60s would have done, so assembling a costume could be an opportunity for a character exercise.

Margo thought she had a leather peace symbol necklace somewhere. As she wrote a note to search for it, she noticed that her hand was trembling. *I am really nervous*, she thought. And she looked around at her fellow cast members.

There was a high level of excitement in the room, that was certain, but it was more than just the thrill of the first rehearsal. She would be willing to bet that every member of that cast had received the same comment from parents when announcing the happy news that they had been cast in the play *Hair*: "*Hair*?! Are you going to be naked on stage?!" And that's what everyone was thinking at that moment: *"Am I going to be naked on stage?!"*

A darker question loomed too – what would the improvs be like?

Finally, Harry got up to give his director's speech. The students hushed and perched on the edges of their squeaky chairs.

In his rat-like voice, Harry congratulated everyone on their superb auditions and said he was excited about working with each of them and told them they were a Tribe. Every one of them had unique talents and he was excited to nurture these talents and find ways to make this Tribe function as though it were one flesh. Someone gasped at the word "flesh" and Margo suppressed a nervous grin.

Harry went on, and finally he said it . . .

"I know you are all wondering about the famous nude scene."

The Tribe seemed to collectively sit up straight and become one big ear.

"Well, let me explain," Harry continued. "The nude scene in the Broadway production was actually kind of silly, and it was optional for cast members. It was for effect only and did not advance the plot or help the action in any way. At that time in New York, there was a law on the books saying that anyone appearing totally nude on stage could not move. So, in the 'Hare Krishna' number at the end of Act I, the actors got behind a curtain, and took off their clothes. The curtain was raised and they stood there frozen like statues for just a few seconds while the audience gasped and the lights went out. Intermission. Big deal.

"Because the nude scene really had nothing to do with the story, we're not going to do it."

There was an audible sigh from the cast.

"At least not like the Broadway company did."

The room stiffened up again.

"In our production, only the guys will be nude, semi-nude; but they will appear totally nude from the audience's perspective."

The Tribe started to get fidgety, especially the men.

"During the Army induction scene, when the guys are being given a physical to see if they qualify for military service, all the men will be lined up with their backs to the audience. When the sergeant tells them to drop their pants, they will. They will be wearing G-strings, but to the audience, they will appear nude. They won't turn around until they put their pants back on, so the audience will never know."

Some of the guys were glancing at one another.

G-strings! Margo thought. *Jen will shit bricks when she hears this!*

Harry surveyed the group and said, "It's *Hair*, after all. We gotta give them some skin."

Everyone laughed; the women more heartily than the men.

"If any of you guys has an objection to doing this scene, you won't have to do it. We'll find something else for you to do at that time."

Margo knew right then and there that not one guy was going to opt out of the bare butt scene. Yep, they were already bonding.

"As you probably noticed from reading the script, *Hair* is not written with a lot of specific stage directions. In the original production, a lot of the structure and action of the play, as well as the characters' personalities, were achieved through improvisation. The actual lines and lyrics are merely a skeleton upon which to build the body of the play. Every production of *Hair* is different. Like other productions, we will be exploring the play and creating our own version of it with the help of improvs."

The room got very quiet.

"For those of you with little or no improv experience, you may feel vulnerable; it's a daunting process. It is up to us to create together a safe and caring space and community within which to explore our emotions and to stretch our concept of ourselves. The first and only rule I want to establish in this Tribe is that what goes on in here is private. What people say in here, what we do in here, is privileged information and we have to be able to trust each other and trust that what goes on in this room stays in this room. Are there any questions?"

Margo peeked around. She was sure there were questions, lots of questions, but no one broke the silence.

Harry coughed and then went on in his squeaky-hinge voice, "I want to emphasize the importance of this. People do not feel free to explore and reveal deep, even dark parts of themselves if they can't trust the group they're in. I want you each to consider whether you can keep the activities of The Tribe confidential. If you feel you cannot, please feel free to leave now, no harm done."

Silence. No one moved.

"Now, I don't expect you to be filled with trust just because I tell you to. Before we get into the heavy improvs, we will do some 'lighter' exercises to get to know one another better so we can feel more trusting of one another. This will help create a safe place among ourselves before we jump off into any darker places. But for now, I need to be sure – are we in agreement that this will be a safe place, a secure place, and that nothing that happens here goes outside these walls?"

The Tribe nodded solemnly. The silent pact. *So this is how it begins,* Margo thought.

Harry roared, "Okay! Let's read the play!"

The Tribe pulled out scripts and pencils and began a read-through of the play, including fumbling through the songs, and stopping periodically for some explanation from Zoe about movement or from Harry about concepts.

Margo allowed herself the luxury of scoping out her leading man. She knew Doug, having had a couple of acting classes with him, but she couldn't honestly say they were friends, and she was really surprised that he'd been chosen for Berger. First of all, she didn't know he could sing. There were other guys in the Department who had proven themselves as terrific singers in other musicals, yet they were relegated to smaller roles or hadn't been cast. Further, she didn't think much of Doug's acting ability. He was okay. An average talent. Certainly not dynamic. She wondered if he could pull off the charismatic Berger.

Then there was the issue of his sex appeal. Margo, for one, would never have picked him for a boyfriend, but that didn't mean much. Hell, she'd run screaming from the hunky captain of the football team. She was a nerd who hadn't gotten involved with any men in her four years at college. Sure, she'd had a couple of make-out sessions with, ironically, acting partners she was supposed to be in love with (like the guy who played Motel to her Tzeitel in *Fiddler on the Roof*, which made the wedding scene that much more romantic). But these flings never amounted to much. And she'd read some books. She was actually more attracted to a couple of younger profs who excited her with scintillating talk about whatever subject they were teaching, including an Anthropology T.A. who was passionate and so brilliant. Intelligence was a turn-on for her. Doug wasn't exactly an intellectual. He was fonder of partying than studying, she knew, having heard him once in a heated discussion about the ten greatest beers in the known world. She didn't know much about his love life, though she'd heard him boast about a conquest or two. She thought she remembered something about someone having broken his heart a year or two ago.

He was an okay enough guy, but she wasn't really attracted to him. She was disappointed. There were a couple of guys in the Department that she could definitely have developed a crush on, but Doug was not one of them. Damn, she thought, if I'm going to be in sexual improvs with some guy, why does it have to be Doug Mulloy? She didn't want to hold his hand, much less stroke his you-know-what.

She suppressed a giggle and sneaked a peek at his crotch, which appeared just fine in his tight Levis. Okay, she scolded herself, now who's turning a play rehearsal into a carnal opportunity?

Her attention returned to the script and she enjoyed the rest of the evening feeling herself begin to fit into the skin of a new character and feeling the connection and energy of a group of individuals becoming the community known as a cast – or in this case, a Tribe.

This was a Tribe of hippies in the East Village of New York City in the late 1960s. Margo was aware that *Hair* got famous for its angry, radical, button pushing intent on shocking the establishment. But on hearing the play read and sung cold, she was impressed with the innocence and optimism of these young people who had faith in Peace and Love, who were horrified of dying or seeing their friends die in an unjust foreign war, who loathed the uptight-ness and prejudice of their parents' culture, who celebrated Life and every part of the human body, and who fervently believed that their energy, their passion, their candor and their courage would usher in a new era of *"Harmony and understanding, sympathy and trust abounding – Aquarius!"* A couple of times during the reading Margo got teary-eyed. She was proud to be a member of the Tribe. She wanted to

"Let the Sun Shine In!"

"Take a rehearsal schedule with you as you leave the room," shouted Harry above the din of chatting and the scraping of chairs and the gathering of backpacks. "See you tomorrow!"

Margo took a Xeroxed schedule and studied it as she walked out into the hallway. It was a calendar with just about every day of the next several weeks filled in with words like Music, Dance, Men, Women, Run-through, and so on. Every weekday evening except Mondays there was a three-hour rehearsal. Saturdays and Sundays had huge blocks of times marked; four to six hours at a time. She had two panicked thoughts:

- *I will never get all my homework done; and*
- *We are going to get to know each other really well. How well?*

CHAPTER SIX

Margo loved preparing for a play rehearsal. Especially that first week of rehearsals, when everything felt so new and full of possibility. She put on comfortable clothes she could move in and did some stretching exercises in her room. Facing her window she did a side stretch, breathing out slowly as she noticed the budding branches of the trees that lined the crisscrossing walkways below. Students with backpacks were shuffling and jogging to classes, to the library, to dinner, to the dorm. A Frisbee flew by, of course. She could hear a group drumming. She marveled at how different she felt preparing to leave college than when she had first arrived.

She had shown up on campus as a nervous physics major. "The only female physics major in her freshman class!" chirped the giddy Chancellor of the University, who was a physicist himself. Because she'd been given an academic scholarship she had met the man when she first got there. She should have been proud and sure of herself. But she hadn't told him or anyone else that her heart wasn't really into physics.

During her entire first year of college, she felt like a fraud. Despite her scholarship, she did not feel special amid the 20,000 other students at the University of Northern Massachusetts who bumped her with their bikes and backpacks as she tripped along the paths made lumpy by the protruding roots of ancient oaks and maples with notices of band gigs and petitions stapled to their trunks. When she stood in the atrium of the physics building with its Foucault pendulum steadily swinging, she did not feel at home at all. Being the only female freshman physics major was not a distinction she enjoyed. It was a curse. She was ever the object of late adolescent gawking by the Future Scientists of America who acted like they had never seen anyone who wore a bra (or washed their hair, for that matter). One of them actually stalked Margo, leaving creepy notes for her to find, including one shoved under her dorm room door late at night.

While she had always enjoyed studying math and science, she found her college classes horrifying. The teachers spoke English so haltingly, with such thick accents (one East Indian, one Chinese), that their lectures were virtually incomprehensible. She suffered panic attacks in classes for the first time in her A-student life because she often had no idea what her teachers were saying. It wasn't the physics that was hard, it was the English. It was depressing not to adore school for the first time in her life.

Born into a conservative, religious, military family, little Margaret Lee was an introverted girl with few friends who had spent her childhood in fear of her father's alcoholic episodes. She loved school because it was orderly and logical, and the expectations were clear. She had an aptitude and passion for math. It was clean and logical. There were clear, unambiguous answers. Math became her favorite subject. Science was second.

She had been bitten by the acting bug in junior high when doing what amounted to a short stand-up routine about biodegradable detergents for the Earth Day play. For the first time, the nerdy little scientist got laughs and she felt something quiver inside. Fellow Ecology Club members patted her on the back and said things like, "I didn't know you could be funny!" "You were great!" "I didn't even know it was you up there." She was hooked.

In high school, she signed up for the toughest math and science classes, but also joined the Drama Club. In her first audition ever, she won the part of Martha, Helen Keller's black friend in *The Miracle Worker*, as there weren't any black kids in Drama Club. Margo began her acting career screaming and wrestling as Helen Keller tried to poke her in the face with a pair of scissors. It was her only scene in the play, but it was thrilling.

She put the science guys (and they were mostly guys) into two camps: (1) the arrogant jerks who took sadistic pleasure in sabotaging the computer programs of others (mostly by tearing the punched paper tape that held their BASIC code), and (2) the super shy and private dweebs who dropped their heads between their shoulders (like turtles going into their shells) and muttered curses to themselves when they found their computer coded paper tape shredded. Both groups lacked social skills and had no idea how to communicate their feelings with anyone, let alone a girl.

Margo's new drama buddies could also be put into two groups: (1) the boisterous show-offs who were always "on," usually funny, always talking too loudly and often using some foreign accent, and (2) the shy, sensitive kids who wore all black or clothes that were a little "off" on purpose. Both types reveled in their newfound relationships and adored discussing feelings and motivations and showering each other with adoration. They would hug each other profusely and read plays aloud while lying in each other's laps. It was not sexual; it was familial. They were simply delighted that they could be affectionate with each other. Perhaps they were all as touch-deprived as Margo had been.

She received her first kiss backstage before going on in the chorus of *Guys and Dolls*. The boy playing the handsome lead, Sky Masterson, had found out that she was about to turn sixteen. He said, "Break a leg!" Then he kissed her and declared, "Now you can't say 'Sixteen and never been kissed!'" Thus began her fascination with leading men.

Her self-esteem grew as she became more deeply involved with drama. In senior year she played Gypsy Rose Lee, and performed a confident striptease while singing "Let Me Entertain You." Granted, she didn't reveal more than her legs and her midriff, but she felt herself blossom into a woman before the eyes of an audience. Her leading man saw it too and asked her to the prom two weeks before the big event. That night, in the glow of the mirror ball, to the strains of the Bee Gees, their backstage fooling around developed into a major make-out session on the dance floor. Margo French-kissed for the first time that night. Their romance lasted the summer, but ended as he went off to Harvard and she trotted off to the local state university that her parents could barely afford.

Margo felt schizophrenic. Or metamorphic. By day, she was a mild-mannered and emotionless mathematician and scientist. By night, she emerged from her cocoon and evolved into a passionate and dramatic butterfly. She hardly cared about the science in her science projects. She won awards in science fairs because her presentations were dynamic and funny. She could entertain the judges.

On the other hand, the caterpillar held the butterfly back. She had trouble letting go of her head enough to feel and emote on stage. She judged herself mercilessly and couldn't be calmly present in the moment. She analyzed characters to death, sucking the life out of them in her struggle to regain the spontaneity and authentic emotion she could achieve at an audition or first reading, when she wasn't thinking too much.

She felt insecure in both worlds and when applying for college, Margo clung to a childhood vow made while watching Apollo 11 land on the moon. She decided to aim for astrophysics with perhaps a path toward being an astronaut. She told people that she picked her college for its cyclotron, not its theatre.

Eventually, though, she had to admit that, rather than be an astronaut, she wanted to play one on *Star Trek*. For a brief while she contemplated a double major in physics and theatre, but her campus was too large. UNM was originally an agricultural college and the science buildings were in the older main part of the sprawling campus. The newer theatre building was at the other end at the top of a hill. For an entire semester she arrived late and out-of-breath for her Stagecraft class because she couldn't get from physics to drama in the ten minutes allotted.

Finally, in the middle of her sophomore year, knowing that she would be letting people down, she walked to the Administration Building and changed her major. The following semester she did not take any science or math classes. It was a huge relief. When her West Point Cadet brother found out, he said with disgust, "What a waste of your brain." That stung. Margo couldn't make him understand that while she may have been good at science, she never felt at home among scientists. Walking into her first college drama class, though, felt like finding her people.

The truth was – studying acting was the most challenging thing she'd ever done. She'd never been so intellectually stimulated. She couldn't explain this to a physicist, but she knew that, like the physicist searching for the smallest sub-atomic particle, the actor searches for the smallest kernel of truth at the center of a character, the spark that ignites her humanity. Like the scientist, the actor is an explorer – breaking through layers to get to the heart or the nucleus, then presenting her discovery to the audience, the public, the world.

Margo immersed herself in her acting classes, her laboratories of self-discovery. She wanted to crack her sterile scientific shell and reveal the messy fragile spirit inside. Acting was harder than physics; there were blocks in the way, but she believed that if she understood herself and her own motivations, she could better understand the characters she would play.

At first, she felt stiff in trust exercises, but she learned to let go. At first, she was uncomfortable hearing about the inner lives of fellow students, but she learned to listen. At first, she had trouble breathing as she contemplated revealing herself to others, but she eventually learned to open up.

After weeks of trepidation, she finally got up the courage to tell her family's deep dark secret in an acting class. She sat on the floor hugging her knees and quietly talked about her dad's alcoholic violence. Then she put her head on her knees and sobbed. When the sobs subsided, she didn't want to raise her head and see the repulsion on the faces in the room. She finally dared to lift her gaze and saw what seemed like compassion. One by one, each of her classmates came over to her and held her, stroked her, and thanked her for her honesty. Divulging the family secret felt like treason, but for this she wasn't shunned. She walked around for days in a stupor of shame, but the wrath of God did not descend upon her. Instead, she felt like she had been set free.

Reflecting back, Margo saw her real development as a human being on or around the theatre. After four years of studying theatre, Margo had learned a lot about Aristophanes and Shakespeare and Molière and Shaw and O'Neill. But she also knew and accepted and loved herself, her innermost self and herself as an instrument of expression. She had emerged from her shell and had learned to trust and embrace other people. Figuratively and literally.

As she walked to rehearsal, she took time to admire the work of the university groundskeepers. The grass was freshly mowed and smelled great, the flower beds were perfectly weeded with blooms ready to burst. She stood in front of the neoclassic theatre building with its white columns and brick exterior and felt like her heart was about to burst. It was almost over – her college career. She wondered how her final show would complete her development and help launch her into her future. She went into a side door and headed downstairs to the Black Box Theatre which would be the main rehearsal space until the set was ready for them on the mainstage of the majestic 1,500 seat Hancock Theatre.

As the Tribe assembled for the second rehearsal of *Hair*, Margo flashed back to the first time her parents had come to see her in a production directed by one of the four young non-tenured theatre profs. It had been in the Black Box Theatre and, as Margo's mom walked into the room, she announced loudly enough that Margo could hear her behind the curtain: "Oh, I see why they call it the Black Box Theatre. The walls and the floor and the ceiling and the curtain and the platforms for the chairs are all black!" Then she heard her dad say, "Let's just find a seat."

Harry clapped his hands to settle everyone down and Margo's focus returned to the present. Harry congratulated them on a terrific read-through the night before and explained that they would start today with an improv exercise designed to encourage trust.

He said, "Before we begin our first hard-core musical rehearsal today, we're going to experience our 'greeting ritual.' Each of you is to make contact with every other member of the Tribe. When you meet each other, you are to hug and then share a brief personal something with each other. Don't make this your life story. Just hug, introduce yourself if you don't already know the person, and say something brief but meaningful."

"Can you give us an example?" someone yelled out.

"Oh, for instance, I could walk up to one of you," he walked up to Jackson, the tall, dark-skinned black actor with the stern face who was playing Hud, the militant leader of the small group of blacks in the Tribe, "hug you," he and Jackson hugged, feigning great affection, much to the delight of the Tribe who laughed and hooted, "and I might say, 'Hi, my name is Harry and my father is a Christian minister who thinks that my being in *Hair* will earn me seven million years in Hell!'" The Tribe laughed with approval.

Then Jackson said, "Hi, my name is Jackson and if my momma knew I was huggin' a white dude, she'd come in here and kick my ass, and your big fat white ass too!"

The Tribe erupted in appreciative laughter and applause. Jackson flashed a dazzling smile and bowed. Then they were off on their "greeting ritual" which Margo thought of as their first "love in."

As the hug fest began, Margo glanced up at Harry. He was perched on one of the folding chairs with his hands folded across his stomach. His ostrich eyes were alert and he watched the Tribe with birdlike twitches of his head. He was smiling with a paternal pride and Margo thought he appeared sort of sweet. *He's really fond of his Tribe*, she thought. Then she was tapped on the shoulder and hugged a little too enthusiastically by an eager Tribe member she barely knew.

Most of the cast were juniors and seniors and were used to trust exercises. Hugging their fellow Tribe members and telling each a "personal something" seemed familiar. Margo went around the room sharing biographical bits with her new family, her Tribe. She'd shared so much of herself over the years, the activity felt sort of rote. And she had trouble paying attention to the mainly mundane sharing of the others. A couple of people stood out: big-hair Tony Zampino, who was from Brooklyn and spoke with a sexy accent, told a hilarious story about growing up in a tough Italian neighborhood; and Andrea, a thin, light-skinned black woman who was an Early Childhood Education major said this was her first play. For the most part, however, Margo was just ticking off the people she'd hugged.

At last, she encountered Doug Mulloy, her Berger. They stood face to face for a moment, gazing into each other's eyes. Doug's eyes were very blue and Margo was startled by their clarity. Other features about his face were noteworthy and in an almost clinical way she took in his sculptured nose, genuine smile and dimpled chin which was just beginning to be hidden by the beard he was growing. Blond curls framed his face. He looked lionish as he reached out and gave her a firm hug.

They pulled apart and studied each other again, holding hands. While Margo couldn't repress her smile, she was tongue tied. Mercifully, Doug spoke first.

"I feel, uh, intimidated by you because I know you're really smart and a really good actress. I, uh, I've really admired you in the classes we've had together and stuff, and even though I don't feel I'm as good an actor as you are, I hope we can work together and really get the stuff in this play. I mean really do it. I think we can really be right together in this. This play scares me, man, but I think we can be great, you know? I think Harry is the greatest and I can't believe that I finally get to work with him. And I'm really excited to work with you on this play too."

Margo felt herself get hot with shame. She realized that her openness to the Tribe had been superficial. She was locked up in her head again – a scientist reporting to people, not a person relating to other people.

She said, "Thanks, Doug. I mean, I'm sorry you feel intimidated by me, and that you didn't feel comfortable talking with me. That makes me feel ashamed. Sometimes I can get arrogant and cold and cut people off. It's something I'm trying to change in myself. So thank you for being so honest with me. I have to admit that I'm a little scared doing this play too. But I think we can work well together and help each other. I think you're a good actor and I hope we can trust each other and get through this together."

She could barely breathe. Something had changed her perception of Doug Mulloy.

"Good," Doug said smiling. "Real good."

They hugged again and moved on.

Margo watched Doug out of the corner of her eye for the remainder of the exercise and noticed how he greeted everyone with sincerity and affection. She found herself liking him more and more. The other Tribe members appeared to like him too. Maybe he wasn't such a bad choice for Berger after all.

In one of her surreptitious glances at Doug, she caught another glimpse of Harry. His sweet fatherly expression seemed to have morphed into a gleeful, devilish guise, which made her think of an adolescent boy at a peep show.

CHAPTER SEVEN

At the first reading of the play, Margo realized how little dialogue there was in *Hair*, and why most people call it a "rock opera" – the whole play is mostly sung. The first Saturday rehearsal was devoted to learning the music. It was grueling, with the detailed assigning of singing parts and sight-singing of the music, so the shot-gun lyrics would fit into their complicated rhythms. Harry had pointed out to them how many songs there were – thirty, as compared to the fifteen or so in most Broadway musicals. Saturday's rehearsal would be a five-hour marathon.

Margo was anxious about learning and singing her songs. She knew full well that she would be singing them while dancing wildly. She could pick out the Tribe's trained singers. They were reading music fluently – like they were reading words. How did they do that? With perfect rhythm, right on pitch. She read music like the 10-year-old she had been when she took piano from Mrs. Morgan and quit after her first nerve-wracking recital. She knew she would have to take time on her own in one of those stinky piano closets in the Music Department and plunk out her parts over and over to make them sink in. She took careful notes in her score with that plan in mind.

In the assigning of bit parts, random phrases of music, and solo lines in songs, Tribal members gradually lost their feeling of equanimity and free love, and Margo saw greed and desperation in their eyes. She knew what people were hoping, because she'd been there – *I want a bigger part! Gimme*

*more to do! God, I hope I get that part! That's perfect for me! I have to get that bit . . .
Shit! How could he give it to her, to him?*

Harry, though not a musician himself, was functioning as musical director. He relied heavily on Jimmy, the grad student from the Music Department who had played for the auditions. He patiently played every part of every song, over and over, on a beat-up old upright piano etched with cigarette burns that had been rolled into the Black Box for the rehearsals. As individuals sang their solos, there were bursts of hoots and applause from listening Tribe members who were thrilled by the caliber of the voices assembled. This was a cast of gifted singers.

Terrorized and exhilarated, Margo anticipated Sheila's songs. Margo actually loved to sing and desperately wanted others to like her voice, and to like how she acted in her songs, how she emoted through them. She had spent many private hours singing songs from *Camelot, My Fair Lady, Brigadoon, Finian's Rainbow* at the top of her lungs. She loved the feeling and, in the privacy of her own room, she felt confident. She'd done some musicals in high school, but her college work had been largely straight drama. There were some fantastic singers in this cast and she didn't want them thinking, "How'd *she* get the part of Sheila? She can act it, but she just can't sing it!" *Well, this was how people supposedly felt about Diane Keaton in the original Broadway production of Hair,* Margo thought. *At least I'd be in good company!*

When the time came to sing "Easy to be Hard," her big ballad about the cruelty of lovers, she closed her eyes and relaxed in her chair, letting herself imagine that she was all alone in her bedroom – like she had done at the callback. Despite its tinny sound, the beat-up old piano filled the room with booming bass notes as Jimmy's talented fingers pounded out the familiar rockin' vamp that starts the song. Margo felt her voice come up from her abdomen, just like her voice teacher had instructed, and allowed her acting instincts to take over. She opened her eyes and stood up, putting her music book down and belting out the song with her legs firmly planted on the concrete floor. As she sang the last phrase, she deliberately glared at Doug/Berger with all the feeling of betrayal that the song implied. His mouth was open and his eyes were wide.

When she finished there was silence and she sat down, burying her face in her hands. Then her Tribe-mates begin to cheer, and those on either side of her patted her on the back. She glanced at Doug and he was smiling broadly and nodding as he applauded her. Harry called to her from his place beside the piano. "Come here, Sheila." She got up and walked over to him shyly. He gave her one of his big hugs and whispered in her ear, "You're going to be *won*derful." Margo was euphoric.

As she sat back down she realized how much she wanted these two men to value her work and her talent. She felt a little sick.

Four hours later, the thrill was wearing off. Margo was getting a headache from the pounding piano and from struggling to get her music down as much as possible. As the Tribe sang out the last strains of "Let the Sun Shine In," Jimmy suddenly stood up, gathered his music and tip-toed over to Harry. He whispered something to him and left. The Tribe members breathed a collective sigh and began to gather up their scores, scripts, pencils and highlighters.

But Harry stopped them. He had an assignment for them.

From now on, at the end of every rehearsal, there would be a gift-giving ritual. In order for the Tribe to bond and become closer, every member of the Tribe was to prepare and present gifts to other members.

"*Every* other member?" one of the Tribe asked with obvious fear that he'd have to buy 23 gifts with a severe shortage of funds.

"No, not *every* other member," consoled Harry. "Just whomever you choose. Some of you may bestow one gift; others may give five or ten. It's up to you."

"What kind of gifts? Are we supposed to buy them?" asked another of the Tribe.

"No, no, no," said Harry, "That's the point. These gifts don't need to be purchased. They can be things you already have, or things you can make, or things you can do for someone else. The idea is to think about someone and come up with a gift that is meaningful to that person. For example, if I knew that someone in the Tribe was a beautiful dancer, I might give him or her a feather I found from a beautiful bird. The idea is to learn something about someone and give a gift that is somehow symbolic or meaningful for that person."

The Tribe nodded.

Andrea raised her hand and said, "Then the person who got the feather could put it on her costume or in her hair, and wear it in the play, couldn't she?" Andrea had stunned everyone earlier in the day with a voice that rivaled Melba Moore's. She would be belting out the famous "White Boys" number and bringing down the house every night, Margo was sure. Harry smiled at her with that fatherly smile.

"That's right, Andrea. Wonderful! So, starting tomorrow, rehearsals will go like this: We will begin with a greeting ritual like we did today, going around the room hugging everyone and sharing something brief with every other person. This will last about fifteen minutes. Then we will have a short physical warm-up, which will become increasingly necessary as we begin dancing. Finally, at the end of the rehearsal, we will have our gift-giving ritual, also lasting about fifteen minutes, where various members of the Tribe will bestow a gift on one or more other members, explaining the significance of the gift."

The Tribe exchanged looks of why-not and what-the-heck?

"That's it. See you tomorrow. Good work, everyone. It sounds great!" Harry dismissed his Tribe with a proud smile.

As Margo gathered her things, a satisfied exhaustion came over her. She was pleased with how her singing had gone and, as she received small compliments from her castmates, she felt warm and wonderful. This was already more than a cast or even a tribe, it was beginning to feel like a family, a big happy family, and Margo could feel warm vibes beaming toward Harry from just about everyone in the room. She watched Harry hug Andrea warmly, and smiled. Yes, she liked the community, the Tribe, that he was building. Only his frequent use of the word "ritual" concerned her.

CHAPTER EIGHT

"**M**argo, wait up!" Margo was jarred from her contemplation as she walked out of the theatre building. It was Andrea, who was running to catch up with her.

"Girl, mind if I tag along?" Andrea asked, flashing her engaging smile.

"Oh, not at all." Margo said, squinting from the sunlight. "Hey, you have a great voice! I loved how you sang 'White Boys.' It's gonna be a knock out."

"That's a funny song!" She started to sing it, "*White boys are so pretty. Skin as smooth as milk. White boys are so pre-e-e-tty. Hair like Chinese silk.*" She jumped up on a bench and did a funky chicken thing as she sang and Margo laughed. "Speaking of white boys," Andrea said, jumping down, "That white boy of yours is hot, girl."

Margo almost forgot to walk. "What do you mean?" she asked, feigning nonchalance, "You mean Doug?"

"Don't give me that 'You mean Doug' stuff, you know I mean Doug and I know you are interested, girl! And why shouldn't you be? He's a fine specimen of a white male. Uh huh! A fine specimen. Just let go and enjoy it, girl!" She laughed at herself and raised her hand for a high five.

Margo slapped her hand like a white girl and felt embarrassed.

"Anyway," said Andrea, suppressing a smile, "That's not why I wanted to talk to you."

Margo regained her composure. "What is it then?"

"Listen, I ain't in the Drama Department and I don't know all the acting stuff you guys know. I only auditioned for this show because I like to sing and I heard they needed 'African Americans.' But, you know," she lowered her voice and leaned in, "I heard rumors about this Harry dude and now I'm beginning to wonder what I got myself into. You been in this Department for years and you been this big actress and all. I figure if anyone knows what to expect from Harry, it would be you. What the fuck is an improv anyway?"

Margo collected her thoughts. She coughed. "Oh, uh, it's an exercise that's supposed to get you in touch with your own spontaneous feelings and instincts so that you can translate them to a character."

"Uh huh. Stop the acting talk, girl. How do you do it?"

"You just pretend. It's like when little kids play house. One's the mommy and one's the daddy and they talk like the mommy or daddy and do what the mommy or daddy would do, using their imaginations. It's play acting, sorta. Okay, say you were to do an improv about the song 'White Boys.' You might build a scene where you pick up a white guy in a bar. You and the white guy would pretend to be in a bar and you would check him out and come onto him. Something like that. Then, when you sang the song, you'd have the memory and feeling of the scene with the white guy in your mind as you sang and it might help you. Does that make sense?"

"Okay, sure. You pretend so that you can get some feelings about your character that's not really in the script. Right?"

"Exactly," said Margo.

"Okay, that seems like no big deal. So what I wanna know is, are we in any kind of trouble? I mean, is any kind of weird shit gonna come down? How come so many people are talking all nervous about Harry's improvs?"

Margo felt queasy. "*Are* lots of people talking about his improvs?"

"Girl, where you been? It's like the nasty secret thing goin' around."

"Huh." Margo had no idea that the other actors were speculating about Harry's improvs. But of course they would all be wondering. It was the big mystery of the Department. It bothered her that no one in the cast had talked with her about it until now.

She approached the touchy subject carefully. "Well, see, there are a lot of rumors going around about Harry's improvs over the years. About how he's been able to manipulate people in improvs to do things they wouldn't ordinarily do, things they regret later."

Andrea was hanging on her words, "Like what?"

"Well, that's the problem. No one really knows for sure. Most of it's a long-standing rumor because no one who's been in a Harry improv has said exactly what goes on. Either it's so bad that they're too embarrassed to tell, or it really is no big deal after all and the rumors are just that, rumors." She chose not to mention the suicide of '69.

"You mean *you* don't know?" Andrea seemed incredulous.

"Sorry. I don't. I've never been in one of Harry's plays. I mean, he does do improvs in his acting classes, but they're no big deal. It's in his plays that the really wild stuff supposedly happens in improvs."

"So you believe it?"

Margo tried to sound matter-of-fact. "I don't know what to believe."

"But you're scared, aren't you? That it's going to get wild, or something."

"What have you heard?"

"Well," Andrea paused, leaned in again and spoke more quietly, "I heard that Harry likes mostly homosexual shit. And that is just too weird for me, let me tell you. If it gets to that kind of shit, or any other sexual shit, I'm outta here. I don't need to prove nothin' to nobody, not for no play."

Margo wondered who told her that there might be homosexual shit. And she was right. None of that "shit" had to be done in the context of a play rehearsal. And yet, there's all kinds of sexual "shit" in *Hair*, including homosexual "shit" and didn't the actors have to be prepared to play it?

"You know, though," Margo explained to herself as much as to Andrea, "Most movies today have explicit sexuality in them, including homosexuality, and an actor has to be prepared to deal with that kind of stuff."

"Oh, yeah, you actors are wacked. You'll do anything for your acting. I see it in that room. There are people in there who would jump into shit for Harry. He's like some guru to them or somethin'. But I'm telling you, that ain't for me."

They were silent for a moment as they walked through late afternoon sun.

"Listen," Margo said finally, "It probably won't get that bad. Another thing you have to know about actors is that they exaggerate. They love an audience. All the rumors are probably overblown."

Andrea thought about that. "Yeah, you're probably right. I mean, I like the man. He's funny and he's nice. He just don't seem like a pervert to me, you know?"

"I've been thinking the same thing. But I'm still worried about next Saturday where it says on the rehearsal schedule in big capital letters . . . "

"IMPROV!" they said together, looked at each other and laughed.

"Tell you what," Margo said. "Let's keep our eyes and ears open. If you hear anything definite, you tell me. And if I hear anything, I'll tell you. That way we can protect ourselves in case any weird shit does come down."

"Okay. That's good." Andrea was thinking. "But what about the men? I mean Harry's supposed to like boys. What if he does stuff just with them?"

"I don't know. I guess the men are going to have to take care of themselves."

"Shit, I seen the boys in this Tribe. They're all starin' at Harry with their tongues hangin' out. They'd do anything for him. Hell, they already agreed to drop their pants on stage for him!"

"I know. But what can we do? I think all we can do is watch out for ourselves. Plus, how bad can it be? I mean, Harry's still a teacher and director in good standing. If he was really bad, they would have stopped him a long time ago." Margo didn't sound convincing.

"Sure. I'm sure they would have. Good point. Okay." Andrea pointed at the building ahead of them. "Well, this is my dorm. Thanks for the talk. See ya."

"'Bye," Margo called after Andrea, watching her run up the stairs to her building.

When Margo reached her own dorm, she found something scribbled on the message pad on her door: "Your mom called. 5 p.m." Margo glanced at her watch. It was only 7; she might as well call her back.

She walked down the hall to the lobby where there was a row of graffiti-covered pay phones. Only one other student was using one and she was hanging up. Margo went to her favorite, the most private of the public phones, the one on the end. Above the phone some drama major from years gone by had scrawled, "'Love is merely a madness!' – Rosalind, As You Like It." Margo smiled whenever she read that. She put in her coins and called home.

A quivering voice answered, "Hello?"

The hair rose on Margo's neck. "Hi Mom? What's up?"

"Oh Margo, is that you?" her mom said in her Mary Tyler Moore trembling voice.

Margo knew the voice. It was the one she used when she was scared and had been or soon would be crying.

"What it is, Mom? What's going on?"

"Oh God, Margo. I hate to bother you at school and everything, but I don't know who else to talk to."

Margo's throat closed up. "What's happened?"

There was a silence. Then, "It's your father. He's drinking again."

Oh, God. Margo's stomach churned. She asked, "Is it the same as before?"

"Pretty much," her mom sounded defeated. "He's just not as strong as he used to be and I think, despite his condition, he feels some guilt, so I can stop him from hurting me as much. Which is good. You know, I never used to be able to stop him at all before."

"I know, Mom." Margo closed her eyes, remembering mornings when she found her mom on the living room couch with bruises on her face.

Her dad suffered blackouts when he was drunk. But one day, seven years ago, he remembered what had happened the night before. He remembered what he did. And he joined Alcoholics Anonymous. It was the beginning of a new era in their home. Her mom still listened with dread for his car to come home and, when he was late, feared the worst. But he wasn't stopping at the bar anymore. He was just working late. However, now, in his military retirement, he was striking out on one disastrous business venture after another and the stress was beating him up. Margo guessed he was seeking solace in an old companion. She wanted to be there to protect her mom. At the same time, she wanted to run so far away no one would ever be able to find her.

Her mom was crying. "Margo, I just don't know what to do. I wish your sister wasn't still at home to see this. But she's not afraid at all. She's such a tough little snit. I wish I could talk with her like I talk with you, but I can't. She just says I should divorce him. She says I shouldn't put up with it anymore. But I love him! I can't leave him! He needs me!" It was full-fledged sobbing now.

The lump in Margo's throat was choking her. "Mom, calm down. Mom, listen. You don't have to divorce him. This is probably just a relapse. I think what you need to do is call one of dad's AA buddies and tell them he's had a slip. What's that guy's name he's always talking about? Teddy or something."

"Freddy?"

"Yeah, Freddy. Do you have his number?"

"I think I can find it in your dad's address book."

"Good, call Freddy and tell him Dad's drinking again. If anyone can get him sober again it's the AA people. That's what they're there for after all, isn't it?"

Her mom was quieting down. "I guess so. That's a good idea. It's someplace to start anyway. He sure won't listen to me when he's like this. So maybe those people will know what to do."

"It's worth a try. Dad's not the first guy to have a slip. Call Freddy and let me know what happens."

"Thank you, Margo. It always helps to talk with you. You're the strong one. You always know what to do."

Margo felt herself falling into that familiar place where the roles of mother and daughter were in dangerous flux. She had to get off the phone.

"So you okay for now, Mom? Do you want me to try to come home?" Margo hoped not. It was a 45-mile drive and Margo didn't have a car. And, she didn't want to be there at all. Period. Maybe never again.

"No, no. You're busy. Aren't you in a play now? How's it going?"

"Terrific. Wonderful. It's going to be great."

"Good. Let us know when it is so we can come and see it."

"Okay." Margo needed to know one more thing. "So, is Dad there now?"

"No." Her mother's voice started to tremble again. "He went out to the hardware store three hours ago and he hasn't come back."

"That doesn't mean he's gone to a bar." Margo knew better.

"I know."

"Call Freddy right now. Maybe he can come over. Call him now."

"Okay. Okay I will. Thank you so much for listening. You have such great ideas."

"You're welcome, Mom. I love you."

"I love you too, sweetheart. Bye-bye."

The phone went dead and Margo replaced the receiver. Her head throbbed and her legs would not move. She fell back against the wall, slid to the floor, rested her arms on her knees and her head on her folded arms.

She felt tears welling up when someone put a hand on her shoulder and said:

"Margo? You okay?"

Margo lifted her head and jerked at the sight. It was her mother's face, covered with bruises, with a painful-looking shiner.

"Oh my God!" Margo gasped, her heart pounding. Then she stopped and looked more carefully. Something was off. It wasn't her mom. It was Jen. With renewed horror she sat up and grabbed Jen's arms. "Shit, Jen! What happened to you?"

Jen seemed surprised. "Me? Nothing. I'm fine. But you're just sitting here all bummed out."

"But your face! You've been beaten up!"

"Oh shit, I forgot!" She pulled a compact from her purse. "It's just make-up. Whoa, I do look like hell."

Margo exhaled with relief. "You really scared the crap outta me. What, is it for some scene you're doing?"

"No. Well, kinda." She sat next to Margo on the brown linoleum floor. "Did you see the notice on the casting board a couple of weeks ago about the Crim. Department wanting an actress?"

"No."

"Well, they were seeking an actress willing to play a rape victim for a 'Rape Investigation Practicum.'"

"And you signed up?"

"Yep." Her eyes sparkled. "And it's so great. They're doing a fantastic job – treating me gently as a 'victim,' asking questions, setting me up for a medical exam, stuff like that. Then I'll testify in a mock trial next week."

"That's amazing. And creepy. What made you want to do this?"

"Well," Jen paused for only a second before saying, "Three years ago, I was raped."

"Oh my God, you never told me."

"No. I don't really talk about it."

"Okay. But. Can you tell me a little now?"

Jen smiled. "Yeah. I can. It was the summer after I graduated from high school. My sister was living in Boston and I went to stay with her for the summer, doing temp jobs in offices and saving money for college. One weekend, my sister went to the Cape with a friend. It was hot and humid and the apartment didn't have air conditioning. So I was sleeping with the window open and the guy just came into my bedroom in the middle of the night and raped me. At knifepoint. It was so frightening to wake up with a strange man right there, standing by the bed. I was so scared. I just, you know, gave in. I didn't scream or fight or anything. I was afraid he would kill me. I mean, he hit me and wrestled me and overpowered me. But I did just give in. When he was done, he just took off out the window. He told me not to call the police, or he would come back and kill me. So I actually sat there and cried for about an hour. Then I did call the police and I was shaking, man. He never did come back, of course. And they never did catch him."

"Shit."

"I know. So this is my chance to get the bastard, sort of. And it's kinda healing." She smiled.

"I'm impressed."

"So what're you all bummed out about?"

"Nothing like what you've been through." After hearing Jen's story, she decided not to tell her about her mom. "Just shit with my parents."

"Okay. You gonna be okay?"

"Yes. Thanks." She got up. "And thanks for telling me about the rape. You're very brave."

She extended her arm to help Jen up.

Using the chrome on the pay phone like a mirror, Jen examined her bruises again.

"Pretty realistic make-up, huh?"

"Scared the crap outta me."

"I hate men who use their power – physical or otherwise – to abuse other people. I hate 'em, Margo. I mean it, I really hate 'em."

Margo believed her.

CHAPTER NINE

The next day was Sunday and an opportunity for another long rehearsal, this one devoted to dance.

"Ugh," Margo groaned as she squeezed into a leotard and sweat pants. "I do not like dance."

The glow of the previous day's rehearsal was gone in the wake of her mom's phone call and Jen's ugly revelation. As Margo dragged herself across the leafy campus to the theatre building, she was dreading the "greeting ritual."

"Shit," she talked to herself as she walked and studied the sideway. "I could just be honest and tell people I'm not into this lovey-dovey stuff today. But they're all so hippy-happy. I don't want to be a downer. I do not want to talk about what's really going on. I just hate being 'forced' to be affectionate. Oh hell. Just shut up and be there."

She put on a frozen smile as she entered the Black Box and thought, *Let's get this over with.*

She hugged around the room choosing to chat about her dance anxieties in her sharing: "Dance scares me. Whenever I take a dance class I feel like the biggest clod in the room. I get all off balance and can't remember which foot I'm supposed to be on. I can't remember the combinations. And I hate revealing dance clothes; my stomach pooches out no matter how much I try to suck it in. Yep, I'm really looking forward to this rehearsal." Her self-deprecation passed for honest sharing.

Until she encountered Doug.

When Doug came up to her he threw his arms around her, picked her up and spun her around saying, "You look wonderful today!" It was as if all of her problems had vanished. Before her feet were back on the ground, Margo was hooting breathlessly, surprised, embarrassed and secretly delighted. Doug looked wonderful himself and she felt a shiver run through her body as she gazed into his turquoise eyes. She was sure he wore tinted contacts, but she didn't care. At that moment, his eyes were the most penetrating, the most beautiful eyes she had ever seen. His stubbly beard was also more than attractive and the smile that was radiating from the center of it was a beacon of goodwill and festivity.

He massaged the tops of her arms and said with a knowing expression: "I've been watching you greet people today and you seem just too serious and worried. Like you were yesterday about your singing . . . and look what happened! Let go and trust yourself, baby. What have you got to worry about anyway?"

She didn't know how to answer such a direct question. So she chose her semi-lie of the day, "I hate to dance. I'm not real good at it and I'm scared I'll look like a jerk at this rehearsal."

"Oh, what's the worst thing that could happen?" Doug teased her. "That you'll fall flat on your ass and everyone will laugh at you?"

"That I'll fall flat on my ass and everyone will know I'm a fake."

"So what?"

"Then everyone will hate me," she said laughing, to hide the fact that the statement felt so fatalistic.

"That's bullshit," Doug said, "Why would anyone hate you for not being a great dancer? If anything, they'd be relieved because you seem to be able to do everything else so perfect. At least there's one thing you're not an expert at."

Margo was stunned into silence.

"And, just so you know, you don't have to be perfect with me! In fact, I'd prefer it if you fucked up now and then. You're awfully intimidating when you're so perfect."

Margo had her mouth open as she struggled to respond.

Doug was apparently amused by her inability to talk. "You gotta let 'er rip, Margo! Just let 'er rip!"

Harry called the Tribe back to attention, ending the greeting ritual.

Doug squeezed her hand and said one more thing, "By the way, I have a gift for you. For the ritual. Later." He grinned at her and Margo wanted to squeal a little. She stared at the floor instead.

Choreographer Zoe was in charge of this rehearsal, but she called Brandy to the front of the room to lead stretches. Margo obediently sat on the floor, spread her legs into a V and struggled to bend sideways, while her inner thighs screamed. She was trying to mirror Brandy, who was bending gracefully, confidently leading the Tribe. She easily touched her nose to her knee. *Shit.* Margo glanced over at Doug. He was bending over in a half-assed way and winked at her. She forgot about Brandy.

The dance portion of the rehearsal was awkward because the Black Box rehearsal space was smaller than the mainstage, where the play would be performed, and there was only a collection of wooden boxes to simulate platforms and risers and ramps. The outlines of the major pieces of the set had been marked on the floor with masking tape by the stage manager and the actors learned their moves and positions while imagining themselves on three-dimensional platforms. They were reminded by Zoe that the actual stage would be raked and, if they lost their balance, they might roll right into the orchestra pit.

"Just be aware of that as we're blocking movement," she said nonchalantly.

Just 'be aware' of that? Margo thought. *I'm no dancer. What the hell does she mean?* Dancing was hard enough on a horizontal surface; what would it feel like to dance on an incline?

Zoe was the grande dame of the Dance Department, well known for the daring recitals she choreographed and sometimes danced in, á là Martha Graham. She was still an active dancer and, despite being forty-something, she could hold her own with the younger crowd. She wore tight Danskin pants which slightly flared at the ankle and a tank-top leotard with a sweater tied around her waist. Margo suspected this was to hide a protruding tummy, a horrible thing for a dancer and simply a sign of her age. Zoe's hair was held in place by a floral scarf, though little wisps of brownish gray escaped to frame her face and she wore large gold hoop earrings. She resembled a slender dancing pirate, thought Margo, as her long ballet-shoed legs lunged out to demonstrate a step and her articulate hands expressed wonder or joy or rage or power. Margo marveled at this woman's ability to communicate through her body.

Eight of the actors had been cast largely for their dance and gymnastic abilities, and while they had floundered like fish out of water at yesterday's vocal rehearsal, this rehearsal was their opportunity to show off. The choreography was exciting and acrobatic. Several of the more athletic men would be throwing ropes over the edge of the balcony and shimmying into the laps of audience members at the top of the show. Margo admired the agility and grace of the real dancers in their midst; she didn't know and hadn't anticipated the physical prowess of her castmates. She was wowed by Greg Manning who could do a backward no-handed flip and Marissa Blake who could raise one of her long legs into a split while standing on the other one and then go over in a graceful back-bend walk-over.

It turned out that Doug was quite an athletic mover himself. Though not really a dancer, he was unafraid of daring doings. For his introductory number, "Donna," Zoe told him to go wild to feel his "sexual prowess" and see what he could come up with. He did not let her down. At one point he took a running leap, grabbed onto one of the ropes that was tied to the ceiling and swung way out over the audience area, knocking down a couple of folding chairs. He let go of the rope and landed in a squat, singing all the while. The Tribe howled. Watching his long blond hair fly out behind him as he swung on the rope reminded Margo of a graceful orangutan and she laughed in admiration.

As he skipped past her, still immersed in his song, he swatted her on the butt and smiled his big devilish smile, mouthing, "Let 'er rip!"

Margo stuck her tongue out at him.

Even though she was scared to dance, Doug's enthusiasm was contagious and Margo wanted to prove to him and to herself that she could throw herself into movement too and even fail in front of others. However, she wasn't given the chance. Her songs didn't lend themselves to any wild monkey business and, in the group numbers, Zoe kept placing her away from the main action. While the bulk of the cast was writhing about the stage and dancing around each other and having a damn good time, Margo frequently found herself above the action, on a platform or higher upstage than the rest of the Tribe, watching the fun below.

Zoe, after consultation with Harry, told Margo to observe the Tribe, encourage the Tribe, enjoy the childlike playfulness of the Tribe. While she was permitted to join in occasionally (like in a representation of a birth canal, which Margo found slightly distasteful), she was mostly detached from the rest of the cast. It began to frustrate her.

At a break, Harry came over to her. He hugged her too tightly.

"You're doing marvelously," he purred, as Margo felt her face get lost between his fleshy man-boobs.

He pulled away, held Margo by her shoulders and looked into her eyes, asking, "Are you comfortable with your blocking?"

His breath smelled garlicky and Margo tried not to grimace. "Well . . ." She felt uncomfortable that Harry had seen her frustration. "I admit I'm confused about being separate from most of the action. It feels like I'm just an observer, not really involved."

Harry cocked his head and one of his I'm-about-to-share-some-wisdom smiles curled his lips. She felt like the Kung Fu Master was about to stun her lowliness with the obvious.

"It's deliberate," he said. "Sheila is a 'mother' to the Tribe. She wouldn't be as involved in the dancing as everyone else. You overlook the action, making sure everyone is okay, making the Tribe feel comfortable and free to 'play' because you're watching over them."

Margo felt a door open in her mind.

Harry continued, "Your watchful protection also allows Berger to cut loose on his wild songs. You are the serious member of the Tribe. The student protester, the wise woman." He grinned at her, "You're the intellectual of the Tribe." Margo swallowed.

"We'll work on this more in improv," Harry finished. "But it was necessary to begin the choreography today." He patted her on the back, patronizingly, like he hoped she understood.

"Oh sure," Margo said as her face became warm. "What you said makes perfect sense. It's just that I should have known it." She was sure her cheeks were bright red.

Harry had had to explain her character to her and she felt ashamed. She was caught off guard and she wasn't as prepared as she liked to be. She should have known this stuff about her character if she was any kind of actress. She was getting too caught up in her fears of singing and dancing, and her dread of improvs, and she'd neglected the basic work of an actor – character analysis. She had been caught without having done her homework. She had anticipated failing at dance; she hadn't expected to fail at acting.

Harry smiled his ostrich smile, but it could have been Doug talking: "Don't be so hard on yourself, Margo. You're doing a wonderful job. You don't have to be perfect right now. In fact, I prefer it if my actors are not locked into anything before we explore through improv. You never know what's going to come up and we want to be free to experience and use whatever reveals itself." Then as if reading her mind he said, "The only way you can fail in one of my plays is to conceal yourself."

Margo nodded numbly and Harry waddled away to talk with Zoe. The only way you can fail in one of my plays is to conceal yourself. *Conceal myself?*

Why, oh why, is this play already so difficult for me? She moaned inside. *Everyone else is having a ball, but I feel all uptight and everyone keeps telling me to relax. This is infuriating! For once in my life I just want to have fun. Why can't I just have fun?*

As the rehearsal continued she tried to feel herself as Sheila, observing the Tribe as it danced, protecting the Tribe members from whatever she could imagine might intrude from the outside to harm them – the police? conservative politicians? their parents? Her blood went cold. Their parents. Of course, lots of the hippies were runaways. They were running away from their parents, possibly from abuse. Like violence in the home? Margo felt sick. She didn't have to act Sheila. She was Sheila. Damn. She slapped her head. She was the oldest sister looking out for her younger siblings. They were allowed to play and have fun, but she had to be serious. She had to be on watch in case danger was around the corner. She had to listen for that car weaving its way home late at night so she could make a quick get-away with the ones in her care. She had to get straight A's so it would appear like her family was normal.

This was her function in her family. Now this was her function in the Tribe. Is this why Harry cast her? Was it a coincidence? Or was Harry this intentional in his casting? She caught his eye once as these thoughts whirled around in her head and he nodded as he looked at her. The skin on the back of her skull tingled. Is he psychic too?

The dance rehearsal finished and everyone reached for bottles of water and towels. The Tribe was thirsty, sweaty and happy. The dancing would be fun for them. Even though to the audience the movement would seem sexual, provocative, daring, even disgusting, it was precisely choreographed and endowed with huge doses of humor. *Hair*, despite its serious reputation, was really a very funny show and Zoe had caught the joyous spirit of this musical romp.

Everyone cooled down in a large circle on the floor. People stretched legs, lay flat on their backs, changed out of dripping T-shirts and chatted happily. A couple of them also retrieved small paper bags from edges of the room and checked the contents, making sure the gifts they would be giving were still there.

Harry congratulated them on an excellent dance rehearsal. The Tribe hooted and exchanged high fives. Margo thought, *Look at everyone — it's important to everyone that Harry is pleased.* Zoe also congratulated them but couldn't resist telling them that there was a lot more of the show to get through and she expected them all to remember what they'd learned today and to be warmed up and ready to go *on time* for the next dance rehearsal. The Tribe nodded solemnly and applauded her work. She hugged Harry and left.

The Tribe's heart rate and respiration were returning to normal as Harry asked who would be giving gifts that afternoon. Three people raised their hands; Doug was one of them and Margo's heart skipped a beat when she saw his hand go up. Harry nodded, inviting them to begin.

The very first gift-giver of the Tribe was Mr. Big Hair himself, Tony Zampino.

Tony, the New York Italian, was a very funny man. He was always cracking people up with his good-natured sense of humor and could poke fun at others without insulting them.

He announced, "I'd like to begin by informing the blacks in the Tribe that the Afro was actually invented by Italians and should be called the Italiano." He stroked his mighty head of black curls and the Tribe laughed heartily.

He continued, reaching into his bag. "I have a gift for Jeremy." Jeremy was playing Claude, the "hero" of *Hair*, who refuses to burn his draft card and goes to Vietnam where he is killed. "Jeremy, you've got to have the greatest voice I've ever heard and I'm really glad you decided to take time off from your opera studies to get down and dirty with some rock 'n roll."

"My voice teacher will kill me," laughed Jeremy, a voice major.

"Well, anyway. My brother went to Vietnam and came home with a bunch of medals, but without an arm." The Tribe got real quiet as Tony got serious. "He's a great guy, an idol to me, and he wanted to go to college and play football and stuff but never got to because of his arm. He's okay now. He got married and works for an insurance company.

Well, he gave me his medals and I want you to have one of them. Here."

Tony walked over to Jeremy and pinned a medal onto his shirt.

Jeremy protested, "Hey, man, I can't take this! It's too personal, too important to you."

Tony was insistent. "Nope. I want you to have it. Now shut up and say thank you."

Jeremy got up and smiled at him. "Thank you," he said, as they hugged tightly. Several Tribe members dabbed at their eyes.

The tone for the gift-giving ritual had been established.

Brandy stood up next with a white paper bag. Margo kicked herself for not planning a gift at this first opportunity. Brandy's cheeks were flushed from the dance work-out and she had undone her ponytail. She tossed her head a little, swinging her silky hair over to one side of her head as she opened the bag. Margo looked around and every face in the room appeared spellbound. *How does she do that?*

The angel spoke, "I made a batch of *krumkake*. It's a Norwegian cookie that my grandmother taught me to make." She passed the bag around and everyone took one and passed the bag on. "I apologize for being so traditional and non-feminist, but I enjoy baking and wanted to share my love with all of you."

Margo took a bite of a *krumkake*. It was light and fragile and melted in her mouth.

"Plus," Brandy added in a very sweet way, "I want to 'nourish' the Tribe so that we all have the energy we need to do this play right. I love you all very much."

The Tribe mumbled "We love you too" and "Thank you" through cookie-filled mouths. Brandy sat down and managed to flip her hair again as she did so.

Okay, that takes the krumkake, Margo thought as she licked powdered sugar from her lips.

Finally, Doug stood up. He reached into his backpack and took out a sling-shot.

"This is for Hud," he said, referring to the character being played by Jackson, the handsome and humorous black actor whose rendition of "Colored Spade" elicited cheers and belly laughs from the Tribe during the music rehearsal the day before. "This is so you can bring down the Goliaths of prejudice and fear in our culture." Doug walked over and handed the sling-shot to Jackson who got up, aimed it at Doug's chest and said, "And you're the first to go, White Boy!"

The Tribe cracked up as Doug fell backwards onto the floor and begged mercy. Jackson bent over him and said, "Damn. This thing is good." Then he reached down for Doug's hand and pulled him up, saying, "Thanks, man." They hugged.

The Tribe applauded. Then Doug reached into his bag again and grinned sideways at Margo.

"And this is for my Sheila." He pulled out a little stuffed tiger, got down on one knee and handed it to Margo, like Prince Charming handing the glass slipper to Cinderella. Margo smiled and bit her lower lip. "This is Tigger, my stuffed tiger that I've had since I was a kid. I always liked it because it's a tiger, y'know, with claws and sharp teeth and stuff, but it's also cuddly and soft inside, which is how I think of you."

The Tribe said, "Ahhh" in unison.

Margo felt ashamed of her jealousy of Brandy. She looked down at the tiger and said, "Thanks Doug, I mean Berger. Being Sheila is teaching me so much about myself." Doug hugged her and gave her an extra squeeze. Margo smiled at him. The Tribe let out a big collective sigh.

The gift-giving ritual was over. The Tribe became individuals again. They gathered jackets, backpacks and water bottles and shuffled out, talking animatedly with one another as they left the theatre building and squinted into the bright light of that late afternoon spring day, like moles emerging from underground dens. Tulips were blooming, birds were singing. While almost everyone in New England had spent that Sunday outdoors, the Tribe of *Hair*, had been happy to spend the day in a small dark room, dancing and moving and sharing, and glowing more brightly than the springtime sun.

CHAPTER TEN

"So, dish, girl, dish. I want to hear *everything*." Jen was watching Margo go through a rack of tops at *The Way We Were* Thrift Shop, just off campus. Margo would stop occasionally, pull a blouse out and hold it up to herself, then either hand it to Jen or put it back on the rack. Jen had about four blouses over one arm and was tapping Margo on the shoulder with the other.

"There's really nothing to tell." This was the first chance Margo'd had to chat with Jen since she'd heard about her being raped. But Jen was bruise-free and her old rowdy self again and Margo was surprisingly disappointed that she had nothing really outrageous to report to her.

Jen shook her head. "Oh, no! It's happening! You're becoming one of them. You're a Harry Zombie. I can see it in your eyes. You don't want to tell me what's happened because you've all bonded and taken blood oaths or something never to tell. I knew it!" She placed the blouses over the rack, took a straw hat that was perched on a mannequin, stuck it on her head, and began to wave her arms around Margo's face. "I must do the anti-voodoo dance to ward off the evil spirits and snap you out of your trance. Harry-Spirit, go away! Ugh! Harry-Spirit, go away! Ugh!"

"Be quiet," Margo whispered, afraid people would be watching them. "You are sick!" She laughed at Jen who continued to wave her arms silently.

"There, you're free of the spell. Now tell me, tell me, tell me. I have to know. I'm obsessed with this. I can't sleep thinking about you locked up in that Black Box with horny Harry and his naked boys."

Margo picked up the blouses and placed them back on Jen's arm. "Jen, it's not like that at all. Okay. Well, for one thing, there *will* be nudity in the play."

Jen whistled. "What will your parents say?"

"Not me," Margo clarified, "just the men." She spun around and skipped toward a rack of old blue jeans.

Jen paused, then chased after her, "Just the men?" she asked matter-of-factly.

"Yep, just the men." Margo bent down so that she couldn't be seen over the rack. Jen bent down with her. "Get this, in the scene where they're getting a physical before being inducted into the army, the doctor tells them to drop their pants. When they do they will have their backs to the audience and they'll only be wearing . . . G-strings."

"I KNEW IT!" Jen practically shouted as she stood up with her fist in the air.

"Shhhh!" Margo pulled her back down.

"Didn't I tell you? G-strings, I love it!"

"So from the audience it will look like they're completely naked."

"Excellent! Bare butted boys. Harry must be in pig heaven. Oh man!" Jen stood up with her hand on her hips. "He's going to rehearse that scene over and over." She ducked back down. "What else?"

"Nothing else. Really. So far, it's been a normal rehearsal period," Margo got up and started to go through the blue jeans on the rack, feigning nonchalance. "You know, learning the parts in the songs, learning the choreography, feeling each other's genitalia, nothing unusual."

"What!" Jen squealed.

"I'm kidding."

"Damn."

"The only thing that makes this different from other plays I've done is that there's a lot of hugging and Harry is really working on making us trust and really know each another with these exercises he calls 'rituals.' Here, take these." She handed Jen a couple of pairs of blue jeans. "I'm gonna try these on."

"Sure." Jen followed her to the dressing room. "Well, you know, it doesn't sound like anything really. We've been doing trust exercises since Acting 101. You know, 'You're a big bowling pin rolling into the arms of your classmates; trust them not to drop you.' Shit like that."

"I know, but it's deeper than that. It's like a big 60s encounter group and Harry's our beloved guru." She got into a dressing room, took the clothes from Jen, and shut and latched the door.

Through the door Jen asked conspiratorially, "What does your gut say?"

"Well," Margo hesitated, "My gut is scared. Part of my gut thinks I'm not right for this play, that I'm too uptight a person to be in *Hair*, especially Harry's *Hair*."

"That's the stupid part of your gut. What does the smart part of your gut say?"

"The smart part of my gut says that Harry is very clever. In the first rehearsal he made it clear that whatever goes on in rehearsal is secret. He made us vow not to talk to anyone about what goes on." Margo opened the door and showed Jen the first outfit.

"Not bad." Jen nodded and pointed to a full-length mirror. "So you're breaking your vow, aren't you?"

Margo grimaced. "I guess so. Some Tribe member, huh?" She studied herself in the mirror and shrugged.

"And how does that feel?" Jen asked.

Margo groaned, "Oh God, it feels like betrayal." She went back into the dressing room.

Through the door again, Jen whispered. "Shit, you're hooked. Harry's got you. I'd better do my voodoo dance again." She banged on the door softly with a jungle rhythm, then stopped. "So? What do you think's gonna happen?"

"I don't know. I've gotta wait and see, I guess." Margo emerged in outfit number two.

"Better." Jen nodded.

Margo stood in front of the full-length mirror again and turned side to side, checking herself out. "Next Saturday on the rehearsal schedule it just says, 'IMPROV.' Now that has me spooked."

"Understandably." Jen reached for a couple of brown bead necklaces on the jewelry display in front of her. As she put them over Margo's head, she said, "Listen. Just stay true to yourself. Don't let him get to you. You could play Sheila with one arm tied behind your back. Improvs are bullshit, for the most part."

Margo wasn't sure she believed that, but she was listening to Jen. Jen took her by the shoulders and shook her a little.

"Whatever happens, don't get sucked in. It's a college play, for Chrissakes, not a spiritual mission. Don't get upset. Have fun and trust your gut. Your smart gut. Stay safe. And be sure to tell me everything."

"Betrayal of the Tribe," Margo said with mock importance, and looked back into the mirror, admiring the necklaces.

"Shut up. Now tell me about Doug."

Margo inhaled and choked on her own saliva. Jen laughed.

"Ha! So, the leading lady is interested in her leading man, huh?"

"No, c'mon, it's Doug Mulloy, gimme a break." Margo tried to sound annoyed. She went over to the jewelry display and started going through the necklaces.

"Uh huh, just as I thought. Now we have come to the real reason you feel uncomfortable. You are having feelings for the tin soldier."

Margo and Jen had dissected every actor in the Department and had code words for most of them. They had agreed that Doug was a nice enough guy, but a fairly wooden actor. They disagreed on the amount of sex appeal he exuded. A couple of weeks ago Margo had thought none; Jen thought a smidge-and-a-half.

"Okay, I am beginning to see him differently. You see, we have to be believable as lovers on stage, so it's in the interest of the play that I find positive things about him." She found a sweet silver heart pendant and held it up for Jen.

"Uh huh. Nice. Are you going to sleep with him? For the interest of the play, I mean." Jen smiled broadly.

"God, shut up." Margo put the necklace back. She thought back to the *Much Ado* cast party and shuddered. She felt like the oldest living virgin in America.

Jen took the heart pendant, turned Margo toward her and put it over her head where it joined the beads. "So the tin soldier is becoming a hot blooded hunk, huh? Goody."

"And I think he'll look damn good in a G-string." Margo pushed her away. But she didn't take off the heart.

"Excellent. God, I can't wait to see this play. Go for it, Margo!"

They laughed together.

"So, what do you think?" Margo asked posing in her outfit. She made a peace sign and sang the intro to Sheila from the play, *"Sheila Franklin /*

"Perfect," declared Jen. "Now get out of the clothes, buy 'em, and let's go get coffee. I have something to tell you." She gave Margo a raised eyebrow. Margo suddenly got the chills and wondered what the heck Jen was up to now.

Just before getting to the checkout, Margo spied a display with knickknacks and trinkets on it. Hanging there was a keychain with a grinning orangutan on it. She thought it was probably the orangutan king from Disney's "The Jungle Book," the one who wants to be like "You-oo-oo-oo-oo." She pulled it off the rack and added it to her pile of clothes.

The Brewed Awakening was just a block away. They ordered coffee and muffins and went to a small table in the back. Jen grabbed an ashtray and planted it in the middle of the table. She lit a cigarette as they settled in. Margo reached into her bag and pulled out the receipt.

"Not bad for an entire outfit," she exclaimed. "I've gotta shop in thrift stores more often."

"All right, are you ready to listen? I have some news." Jen took a swig of her coffee as if to add to the drama of the moment.

"Okay, I'm listening," said Margo. "What?"

"I did some more digging and I found that guy, Mike Matthews."

"Who's Mike Matthews?" Margo couldn't remember.

"Some Private Eye you'd make. Mike Matthews. He was in *Death of a Salesman* with the kid who killed himself."

"You found him?"

Jen sat up proudly. "I found him," she slumped, "But I lost him. He graduated in May of 1970, and moved to New York where he was an actor for a couple of years. After that, I don't know anything."

"How did you find that out?" Margo was amazed.

"I called Actors' Equity in New York and told them that I was a producer casting an off-Broadway play and needed to find an actor named Mike Matthews. They had his name on file, R. Michael Matthews. He became a member in '73, worked a little in Equity summer stock, then went on hiatus or something in '75. They gave me the number for his answering service, but when I called it, he was no longer signed up with them, and there was no forwarding number or address."

"You're good. You're really good." Margo said.

"Why, thank you, ma'am," Jen said with a Texas accent, blowing on the top of a mimed gun and putting it away in a mimed holster at her hip. "All in a day's work."

"I can't believe you called Equity." Margo shook her head. Margo was in awe of the concept of being in the union for professional stage actors someday and wouldn't have even dreamed that you could just call them up and talk with them. Something else was bothering her. After the other night, she wasn't sure this "investigation" was such a good idea for Jen. Was Jen just trying to "get the bastard" like she said? Margo hesitated, then had to ask, "Jen, why are you investigating this? I mean, it's tragic. And the kid was in Harry's play. But, it was supposedly just a suicide of a kid who was on drugs."

"You don't believe that, do you?" Jen seemed hurt.

"Well, geez, I mean, Harry just doesn't seem that bad. I mean, I just don't see how anything we're doing could lead to someone jumping out of a window." She held onto her coffee and let the cup warm her hands. She wasn't entirely convinced that Harry was harmless.

"Not yet," said Jen, staring at Margo. Margo was silent and stared into her coffee. "Well, shit," Jen spat as she flicked ash off of her cigarette, "I just feel like there's something seriously rotten in the State of Denmark. It's *my* gut, or intuition or something."

"Okay, don't get mad!" Margo winced at her. "My intuition tells me there's something more to all of this also. And I admit I'm scared about the big Improv day coming up." She paused. "So, what're you going to do next? Are you going to keep searching for him?"

"I think so. I just haven't figured out the next step yet."

They ate their muffins silently for a moment.

Jen smiled at Margo and spoke sincerely, "Hey, thanks for breaking your Tribal vow." She leaned in with another intense expression, "And promise you'll tell me everything that goes on."

Margo leaned in and acted equally intense, "Promise."

Jen sat back and announced, "Ah, what the hell good are your promises anyway? You've already betrayed the Tribe!"

"Oh, fuck you." Margo laughed, balled up her napkin and chucked it at her.

CHAPTER ELEVEN

Monday. A day off from rehearsals and Margo had papers calling to her from three of her classes. She was also concerned about her mother. She wondered what had happened and thought about calling her, but decided to wait until her mom called her. She didn't even consider calling her dad. She felt guilty, but didn't want to relive the old stuff again.

She also hadn't had a chance to do much analysis of Sheila and she wanted to take some time to dig a little and get more of a handle on her character. There was so little to go from in the script, no wonder she was floundering at rehearsals. Having Harry explain her character to her at the dance rehearsal embarrassed her. That was *her* work. She wasn't the kind of actress that directors had to spoon feed.

Rather than do a formal character analysis: Date of Birth, Background of Parents, Where the Character Grew Up, etc. – Margo opted for a stream-of-consciousness journal-type entry-thing. She had already decorated the front of a spiral notebook with the word HAIR and some pseudo-60s line art. She opened the notebook, took out a green felt-tip pen, mustered up all her training in Harry's Anthropological Approach to Acting and took a deep breath:

ABOUT BERGER AND ME . . .
I love Berger. I am his.
Berger loves me. He is not mine.
I mean, he is mine, but he's not mine.

The Tribe.
We are the Tribe.
He is the Tribe.
Berger is the Tribe.
The Tribe comes first.
The Tribe must come first.
I accept this.
I do not like this
But I accept it.
I must.
Or the Tribe would not be.
We would not be.
I love Berger. I am his. And his alone.
I don't fuck around.
There is only one Berger.
There is only one Sheila.
There is only one Berger.
He is the One. The only One. The main One.
He is the Leader.
There can only be one — and he is it.
It is because he is the One that he is mine.
That I love him.
I can't have anyone less than the Best.
Berger is the best
Therefore
I love Berger.
No one else is worthy of my affection.
I love everyone.
But I love Berger. And I am his.
Since Berger is the One, it stands to reason that everyone loves him — and that he
loves everyone.
They do. And he does.
It is up to him to keep the Tribe alive.
So I must share him with the Tribe.
He moves the men.
He loves the women.
He has to.
I love Berger. I wish he were all mine.
I know he can't be — but I can't help my feelings.
I am not a hypocrite — but there is conflict between my heart and my head.
And it's killing me.
I don't come first.
The Tribe comes first.

But I want to come first.
And when I do "come" first – that is my ecstasy.

Margo smiled at this last line and reread what she'd written. What a lot of garbage, she thought. This is what gives college theatre a bad name. But, actually, the writing helped. It helped clarify why the hell Sheila sings the break-your-heart ballad "Easy to be Hard" after Berger rips up a shirt she's given him as a gift. Sheila is jealous of his devotion to the Tribe and, of course, to the other women of the Tribe.

Margo felt a little jealous too. She remembered how the Tribe, especially the women of the Tribe, enjoyed watching Doug dance and appreciated his meaningful hugs in the greeting ritual. Even Andrea had called him a fine specimen of a white male. Hmm.

She started writing again:

Berger is the Leader of the Tribe. It is for the survival of the Tribe that he is Leader. How does a male get to be Leader among other males? He earns it by proving himself, fighting with the other males, maybe killing some of them in the battle. Once he's established as Leader, the other males demonstrate their allegiance to him and bond with him, work with him to protect the Tribe, until one of them challenges him as Leader and they fight, etc. The Leader can mate with all of the females in his Tribe. The reward of leadership is being able to father as many offspring as possible. The Leader gets to spread his seed around.

This is so-o-o sexist, Margo thought.

One day, in one of his classes, Harry was asked by an angry actress, "What about women?" Harry calmly explained that the Anthropological Approach to Acting states that because a woman can bear a child and because she knows when she gives birth that the child is hers, women are secure in their "immortality" through their children. Because a man can never really be absolutely, completely certain that a child is his, he is not absolutely secure in his immortality. Men have found it necessary, therefore, to bond together to build societies and cities and dynasties and empires – naming buildings and monuments and books and inventions after themselves – securing their immortality this way. It follows, then, that the whole reason that society is so male-dominated is because men can't have babies. All the wars and football games are about men making their mark on the world. They are male cats spraying on the tree trunks of life.

Margo remembered feeling somewhat smug in her anthropological "superiority" at the time. But now, the image of a sultan with his harem came to mind, and Margo suddenly saw Sheila as Wife Number One. The maternal care-taker of the offspring and the other wives. She wasn't enjoying this vision of the Tribe or her position in the Tribe.

She thought about Doug. She was really beginning to like Doug, but she didn't think of him as a leader, let alone Leader of the Tribe, and she didn't think the other cast members did either. Hell, they could pull off a decent rendering of *Hair* by singing the songs, dancing the dances, acting wild on stage and baring their butts, but she suspected this wasn't enough for Harry. She could kinda see why Harry might use improvisation to induce the Tribe to recognize and embrace Doug as the Leader, the One, the only One – deserving of their admiration, their love, their loyalty. To convert them to the Church of Berger.

She figured Harry would also use improvisation to help Doug "become" Berger. Doug, it seemed to Margo now, was a sweet, sincere guy who was devoted to acting and wanted desperately to do a good job. He wanted to be the best Berger possible and Margo believed that he trusted Harry completely as a director and mentor.

If Andrea was right, it was the men who would be needing protection. Women are never in trouble in Harry's plays. In the Anthropological Approach to Acting, it was men who jousted and struggled and bonded. Women were on the sidelines of the real action. The women would be fine.

She smirked. Harry was good. He was using the greeting and gift-giving rituals to mesmerize everyone into adoring and trusting him. It was working. The Tribe was eating out of his hand. It wouldn't take much to convince them to . . . what? She didn't know. But she did suspect that Doug was in some kind of danger. Sweet Doug. Doug who would be Leader of the Tribe. Who wanted to be the best actor he could be in this part and trusted Harry to get him there. She shuddered as she remembered the kid from fifteen years ago who jumped from his dorm window. Could that possibly have been because of a Harry improv? She shook her head as if it could get the thought out.

Knowing Harry as she did now and seeing how rehearsals were going, she wondered how (or if) he was going to turn things around. So far he'd been nothing but a fatherly teddy bear, delighted in his Tribe's rituals. She chastised herself for being as morbid and melodramatic as Jen and turned her thoughts to meaningful gifts she could bestow. The orangutan keychain was sitting on her desk smiling at her.

CHAPTER TWELVE

The second week of rehearsals became almost rhythmic in its structure. The greeting ritual happened organically as people arrived, then it wound down comfortably, moving into the physical warm-up which was led by Brandy. Then, depending on the rehearsal schedule, people would break up into large or small groups and work on specific scenes, dance sections or songs, sometimes going off into different classrooms or even venturing onto the mainstage as it became ready to receive actors. At the end of each rehearsal, everyone reconvened in the Black Box for the gift-giving ritual.

Every evening, Margo came home exhausted but with some new piece of information about someone in the cast (this one had been adopted and was instituting a search to find her birth mother; that one's brother had some kind of severe cerebral palsy and was living in a home), and some new gift (a thingy for her hair, a book of poetry, a button with the masks of comedy and tragedy). She would walk to and from her classes humming the infectious songs of *Hair*. It was all coming together bit by bit, and touching every part of Margo's life. Things were flowing and growing. Other classes were a temporary distraction from the elaborate process of weaving the living tapestry that was *Hair*. It was like building a big, bold, beautiful, breathing house from the foundation up and, as it took shape, it took on personality and life. *Hair* had a lot of life.

Margo was losing track of the days. She felt present; and just when she was feeling comfortable with the rehearsal ritual, the Tribe, her role and her director, Harry introduced a new element to the rehearsal process. After a sweaty movement rehearsal, while everyone was gathering their gifts and water bottles and getting settled into a circle on the floor, Harry stood and smiled with his fleshy hands folded across his belly.

"Okay! Great rehearsal!" he chirped and clapped, quieting them down. "Great rehearsal!"

The Tribe settled and gazed at their guru.

"I've posted a piece of paper where you can sign up for for a private meeting with me – as a couple."

The Tribe looked around quizzically. Margo felt her scalp prickle.

Harry continued, "Basically, everyone in this play partners up with one or more other people. As we continue to block and stage the movements and dances, couples will find one another, dance together, sprawl sexually, comfort one another when Claude dies, and so on. It's up to you, as a couple to decide on your relationships – lovers, spouses, friends. And not all couples will be one male and one female!" There was a murmur among Tribe members. Harry paced a little, "So, each couple will have an opportunity to meet with me and discuss their relationship with each other and their relationship with the Tribe. While a dance piece is being worked out with Zoe or a song is being shaped by Jimmy, I'll be in my office meeting with each of the couples. Privately."

Margo glanced over at Doug and was embarrassed that he was staring at her. And he was grinning. Margo quickly looked away and to the floor. She felt her ears getting red.

"The sign-up sheet for the meetings is on my door. Sign up after rehearsal. Okay, let's give gifts!"

Margo heard a few coughs and glanced around at the slow-moving group as they got ready to give gifts. She doubted that many members of the Tribe were particularly anxious to sit in Harry's office with a randomly picked "mate" and "explore their relationship" in his presence. But she knew that after the rehearsal, couples would dutifully sign up on the sheet on Harry's office door. She and Doug would be among them.

She reached into her pocket, thought, *Here goes!* and stood up. She turned to face Doug and cocked her head at him. He still wore his goofy grin and she had trouble maintaining eye contact.

"Berger!" she announced.

"Yes ma'am!" He stood and saluted.

She took the keychain from her pocket and held it high. "This is for you." She showed it to the Tribe, "It's an orangutan!" Doug crouched like an ape and scratched under his arms, coming at her like a monkey and reaching up for the keychain. He made "ooh, ooh, ooh" sounds. The Tribe laughed

Margo held the keychain high, away from Doug's playful grabs at it. "It reminds me of you!" Doug stopped reaching and cocked his head with a monkey grunt. Margo explained, "You're playful and full of monkey business!" Doug squealed and did a backward roll. "But this is the King of the Monkeys and you are the head of the Tribe. So, you're playful, but you're also a leader." Doug stood up as straight as an orangutan can and pounded his chest. The Tribe was howling. "And," Margo finished, "You're cute and huggable too!"

Doug yelped a big "Whoop!" then ran at Margo like an ape, with his arms high over his head. Margo was alarmed by his animal approach and was shocked when he took hold of her, lifted her up, and threw her over his shoulder. Then he ran around the room holding her with one arm while pounding his chest with the other. Margo held onto his waist for dear life.

When he finally put her down, she lost her footing and almost fell. He caught her and saved her from tipping over. Suddenly, he was a man again and gazed piercingly into her eyes. Margo was paralyzed in his arms. Then he bent over and kissed her passionately. The Tribe cheered and the men made encouraging hoots of their own. When their lips parted, Margo swayed a little again and held up the keychain. Doug took it, clipped it onto his belt loop and swaggered away, accepting high-fives from the men in the room. Margo watched him go, sat cross-legged back on the floor and buried her head in her hands, laughing with mortification and deliberately hiding how thrilled she felt.

* * *

During the following rehearsal, the private meetings began. Four individual couples entered Harry's lair two by two, and emerged intact. After the rehearsal, Margo and a few others stopped one of the couples and grilled them about the meeting. They shrugged, saying it was okay, no big deal, and that they really couldn't discuss details about what happened because they had promised each other and Harry that what went on was confidential. Then they went off smiling a funny smile.

Or so Margo thought. She cornered Jackson and Andrea after their private meeting and Jackson walked off in a huff about Margo presuming to ask him what had happened. Andrea rolled her eyes at him and turned to Margo.

"Oh, hon, this one was nothin' to worry about. Since Jackson and I are the big black couple in the play, Harry wanted us to talk about how we feel as blacks and all that. He had me sit on Jackson's lap and kinda hug him as we talked. The only weird thing was him asking me how it was with a white guy. I was all shocked until I realized that this was like one of them improvs you told me about – you know, he was calling us by our character names and all, not our real names – and so he was askin' my *character* what it was like with a white guy since I sing the song 'White Boys' and all. Once I got what he was doin', it was cool. And Jackson really got into it – you know, pretendin' to be all mad and shit because I was with some white guy once. It was cool. It was okay."

Margo felt better now that she knew something about what was going on. She was a little nervous about having to sit on Doug's lap while they discussed their relationship. She felt confident about her grasp of Sheila and felt she could express her character's ideas openly and easily. But what about her character's feelings?

The offices of the Drama Department professors were in the basement of the theatre building, directly behind the stage of the theatre itself, along the dark narrow hallway that led to the Black Box. When Doug and Margo met at Harry's office door for their private meeting they made eye contact and grinned stupidly. They couldn't hear much of what was going on with the previous couple still in there, but it sounded like an argument and like someone was maybe crying or moaning or something. Doug and Margo shared an I-don't-know look. Then they looked away from each other, each examining some significant piece of brick on the opposite side of the hallway. Margo started to hum along with "Aquarius" which was being rehearsed down the hall in the Black Box.

Harry's door finally opened to reveal the gymnast/dancer Greg Manning and his partner, Brandy. They came out of his office appearing flushed and happy. Brandy had tears brimming in her eyes, but they must have been happy tears because she and Greg waltzed off down the hall arm in arm, chatting excitedly. They blatantly ignored Doug and Margo, who watched their animated exit. Margo realized her mouth was open a little.

She turned back to Doug, who put his arm out, indicating she should go in first – the perfect gentleman, or a piece of chicken shit who wanted her to go into the lion's den first.

Harry was sitting behind his ancient wooden desk which was piled with old papers and office supplies. There were no windows and the room had a musty, dusty smell, combined with a hint of rotting french fries. Margo had never spent any time in Harry's office and was surprised at the extensive mask collection that covered its walls. There were masks from Africa, China, Greece, and from the American Northwest Coast Indians. Propped on the desk were two Indonesian shadow puppets which were intricately carved. Strangely enough, directly above his desk, was a painting of a snake-handling revivalist.

"Cool masks, Harry," said Doug in awe.

"Thank you. I love masks. I collect them wherever I go. I have many more at home." Harry glanced up at the faces on his walls. "Shut the door. Have a seat and relax."

Margo turned around and saw that the back wall of his office was covered with posters from plays he had directed. As she shut the door, she saw on the wall behind where the door had been, a poster that was tattered around the edges and partially covered by another poster. The title of the play, however, was readable. It was *Death of a Salesman*, and the dates were from October of 1969. Margo froze only for a second, then reached out to touch the gray and brown poster. It hadn't occurred to her that they would have gone on to do the play after all, after one of the lead actors had died. Or that Harry would have wanted to put the poster on his wall. She turned around quickly so that the men wouldn't notice her lingering and muttered, "Great posters."

"Oh yes," said Harry. "Those go way back to when I was a graduate student here in the early 60s."

"Cool," said Doug respectfully.

There were two seats opposite Harry's desk. Margo was relieved she didn't have to park on Doug's lap right off the bat. She and Doug took their seats, but Margo couldn't relax. She couldn't take her eyes off of a fairly sinister mask over Harry's head that she believed was Hawaiian. Finally Harry's words released her from the mask's spell.

"Well, I finally get to spend some time with my Berger and Sheila," he said as he lit a candle on his desk. He said to Doug, "Turn out the light, will you, please?" Doug did. Margo inhaled. She glanced at the masks again and the many eyes looked ominous in the flickering candlelight. Her heart skipped a beat. Harry asked them, "How are you two doing? How are rehearsals going for you?"

"I think they're great, Harry! They're really working for me." Doug was enthusiastic. "I love the rituals and how everyone is really working together. Zoe is great. The songs sound fantastic. I think the play is going to be great."

"Everything is going okay for me too," said Margo. "I can't say I'm as comfortable with everything as Doug seems to be, but I'm . . ."

"Doug? Who's Doug?" Harry interrupted her.

Margo stopped, "Oh, uh, I mean Berger," she said haltingly. *Okay*, she thought, *no transition. We're already into some kind of improv right off the bat. We're already Berger and Sheila.*

Harry was smiling, "Oh, yes, *Berger.*" He nodded. "You were saying, Sheila – you're not comfortable with what's happening?"

Margo hesitated, "Uh, well, what I meant is that I'm not as comfortable as, uh, Berger seems to be. You know, I'm more aloof than he is and I think I analyze too much."

Harry seemed concerned, "Give me an example."

Margo (Sheila?) was regretting having admitted that she was uncomfortable. "Oh, like the greeting ritual. I don't feel I'm as open as everyone else. Everyone else seems to be really getting into the thing and I feel like I'm sort of holding back, maybe not trusting as much as everyone else. But now I'm more into it. I feel okay now. I do. I really do." *The lady doth protest too much, methinks*, quoted Margo silently, and she felt her head start to ache.

Harry nodded, "I'm sensing some hesitation on your part, so before we go on, I want you both to understand that everything we say in here is completely confidential, just as our rehearsals are. I want you to feel safe to say whatever you're feeling. We have to trust one another. And you two, especially, have to trust each other." He studied them both. "Is that understood? Nothing goes outside these walls?"

"Oh yes," said Doug.

"Of course," said Margo.

"Berger," Harry addressed Doug, "Sheila is not feeling as comfortable as you are in the Tribe. How does this make you feel?"

Doug was immediately into the improv. "Oh, man, I knew she was worrying too much and I guess I tease her a little about it, but I had no idea she was feeling so uncomfortable. Basically, I'm doing my job, you know – learning my parts and my dances and songs and stuff and relating to the Tribe. I guess I'm not spending enough time with her, helping her feel comfortable and all."

"You gave me a cute little stuffed tiger," Margo offered. "And you were pretty, um, demonstrative when I gave you the orangutan keychain."

"Yep," Doug agreed with a shit-eatin' grin.

"And how did that make you feel, Sheila?" Harry asked.

"Um, stunned and embarrassed, I guess." She glanced at Doug and he seemed a little hurt. She added, "But I was pleased too. Okay, I was delighted." Doug actually giggled.

Margo was striving to be entirely honest. To herself and to Doug. Skeptical as she was about what was going on, she wanted to do her best to get at the character of Sheila, and Harry was known for getting the most out of his actors. She just felt so uncomfortable talking about herself this way. The room was so small and everyone was staring at her in the flickering candlelight – Doug, Harry, the masks.

"Is it hard for you to talk about your feelings?" Harry asked with apparent concern.

Was he reading her mind? "A little. Yes. Yes, I guess it is. I'm not really sure why this is necessary. Isn't it enough that I'm doing good work?"

Harry put his elbows on his desk and propped his chin on his hands. "Yes, you are indeed a good worker. You've been a good worker your whole life. You're a motivated, independent, intelligent woman, Sheila. These are your strengths. But they are also your weaknesses because they separate you from other people. From the love of other people."

"I know what you mean," Doug said softly, turning to face Margo. "Sometimes I feel awkward around you – like you have more important things to do than talk with me."

"Are you listening, Sheila?" Harry asked.

Margo nodded. She felt the blood draining out of her face.

"Sheila, are you lonely sometimes?" Doug asked the question with such compassion that Margo felt tears well up in her eyes.

Harry saw it. "Sheila, what are you feeling right now?"

Margo was losing it. "I don't know. I feel a little like crying. This is stupid."

"It's not stupid." Doug reached out to take her hand. "Your feelings are important to me."

Margo struggled to stay calm. What the hell was going on? Shit. It was probably the stuff with her parents coming up, or with Jen, but these guys are thinking it was because she felt vulnerable or something. She was mad at herself, but she didn't think she could stop the gusher that was coming.

"Thank you," she said to Doug, patting his hand and pulling away.

"Sheila," Harry said, "You seem to have some resistance to Berger's need to comfort you."

Oh shit, Margo thought. *I'm resisting the improv. Or something.* "No, not really. Why do you say that?"

"Don't you want to get closer to him? Don't you want him to hold you?" Harry asked.

Doug was sympathetic, "Yes, Sheila, come here, let me hold you."

Margo wasn't sure what to do. She knew *she* did not want to be held by Doug, not in Harry's office anyway. But she guessed Sheila *did* want to be held by Berger. She decided to do the improv and see what happened. *This is what improv is about,* she thought, *breaking through the ole inhibitions. Okay, here I go.* And she got up and moved onto Doug's lap. *Okay, shit, I'm sitting on Doug's lap. How the hell did this happen?*

Doug put his arms around her and held her to his chest. Then he took one of his large hands and cradled the side of her face, pulling her head into the crook of his neck beneath his chin in an act of almost fatherly affection.

Margo had never been held so tenderly and sweetly by a man. Doug/Berger really was comforting her and she let herself feel how warm and wonderful it felt. She also felt how much this affection and warmth was missing from her life. Her driven, work-obsessed life was devoid of relationships with men. She relaxed into his embrace and began to cry in earnest. She cried for her mother's pain, for what Jen went through, for all abused women. She cried for her own lonely life. She sobbed for the 8-year-old who only saw the ugly things that can go on between a man and a woman. She mourned a childhood spent achieving things in order to prove to the outside world that her family was normal.

"Sheila, Sheila," Doug cooed, "I had no idea you hurt so much."

"I'm sorry."

"Don't be sorry. It's okay. I like when you're like this."

Harry interjected, "Sheila, you're always so strong – for the Tribe, for the women. Berger is the one person you can be weak with. He's the one you come to when *you* need help and comforting."

Margo pulled back and wiped at her eyes. "And I'm the person he can come to when *he* needs help and comforting."

"That's right," Harry acknowledged, "You protect and help each other. You give so much to the Tribe, you lead them, protect them. And it is in the privacy of this relationship that you can reveal your own vulnerabilities, and get the strength to go back out into the world."

Margo heard that. That's what she hoped a real relationship would be like someday. Two strong people leading their own lives, blazing trails through the jungles, then coming home to comfort and love and support each other so that they could go back out into the jungle the next day, and the next. She was enjoying this feeling of letting a man comfort her. Her life was so hard sometimes. So much work, so many responsibilities – classes, the play, graduation, her future life, her family . . . so much she had to do all by herself. It felt so good to stop and have someone hold her. She relaxed into Doug's embrace.

Doug felt the change in her. "Sheila," he said tenderly, "You are a wonderful woman and I love that we can be honest with each other and support each other."

Margo played with the collar on Doug's shirt. "Well, you are a wonderful person too. You're strong and alive and tender all at the same time. I think the whole Tribe respects and cares about you. It's an honor to be your partner. Please let me be a support to you too."

"Of course," he said. He took her hand from his collar up to his lips and kissed it. It was the most sincerely gallant thing a man had ever done to Margo. She could feel herself trembling and she wondered if Doug could tell. She had no idea what to say or do next.

But Harry had ideas. He said softly, "Berger, what do you want to do right now?"

Doug lifted Margo's chin so that he could gaze into her eyes and said, "Sheila, I want to kiss you."

Margo felt herself slip out of her body. She called this her "third eye" – her ability to see herself as she did things, like she was hovering over herself in an out-of-body experience. She'd read somewhere that lots of actors do this. She believed that is what enabled her to be an objective (and sometimes harsh) critic of her own performance. As though she were simultaneously actor and audience.

The observer part of Margo split out of her, got up off of Doug's lap and started talking to the masks on the wall. *"Okay, here we go! Ladies and gentlemen, step right up. Don't be shy! You won't believe your eyes! Yes, watch as the vestal virgin gets laid for her art! And with an audience too! Hey, Harry, you wanna join in? We can have a lovely ménage à trois right here on top of the McDonald's wrappers falling out of your trash can!"*

The solid, visible part of Margo sat trembling on Doug's lap and simply nodded her head. Their lips came together and they shared a sweet kiss. Margo pulled back and gazed into Doug's startlingly turquoise eyes. He seemed intently serious and they came together again in another kiss, this one more passionate than their first.

While this long kiss progressed, explored and was enjoyed, the observer Margo was going nuts. *"All right! Nice kiss! Nice lo-o-o-ng kiss. And what's this? Why it's Doug's hand moving ever so slowly toward the bottom of the blouse. How far will they go, folks?"*

Doug was indeed pulling Margo's blouse up from where it was tucked into her pants and was moving his fingers to touch the bare skin of her waist. Margo felt a tingle and continued to kiss Doug, whose hand moved to her back where he pulled her closer, his palm on her bare skin.

From outside the office and down the hall, the song had changed. "Aquarius" was now over and the song "Sodomy" was wafting down the hall. Solid Margo had trouble not laughing. Observer Margo was yucking it up.

"It only gets better! Can you believe it?" She sang along with the lyrics, *"Sodomy, fellatio, cunnilingus, pederasty. / Father, why do these words sound so nasty?"*

Doug's hand was moving up to her bra and beneath it. Margo shuddered and the observer got serious.

"Okay, how far are we going to let this go? It feels good. Doug's a lovely kisser, and if we were in some private place, I wouldn't mind at all. But WE'RE IN HARRY'S OFFICE AND HARRY IS WATCHING US! This is ridiculous! How far is Doug going to go? Will I have to stop it? How?"

Doug's hand had moved forward and was now stroking the bottom of her breast. Margo loved how it felt but couldn't fully enjoy it with Harry watching. She could even hear his wheezy breathing across the room from them and she thought she heard him smack his lips! Doug's hand reached up and stroked her nipple. She felt a tingle shoot through her body and felt herself getting wet.

"It sure don't take much when you've been without for so long," her observer noted. Then she got an idea. *"I will only be able to stop this thing as Sheila and Sheila would be more involved than Margo is. I need to take control until I can think of something. Okay. Here goes Sheila!"*

She seized Doug's wandering hands and pulled them away from her, then she took hold of Doug's shirt and yanked it off of him, over his head. Doug was startled and she thought she detected Harry tilting forward.

"Very nice chest," observer Margo thought. *"I especially like the blond curly chest hairs."*

She started running her fingers through the hairs and blew on them to watch them move with her breath. She leaned forward and kissed Doug again on the lips, then moved down to his neck and to his chest. When she came to one of his nipples she sucked on it and moved her tongue over it in fast little flicks. She had only read about this and was surprised at the effect it had. Doug sighed heavily and moaned a little. Her elbow brushed against Doug's crotch and she felt him getting hard. She was a little embarrassed, but was also proud of herself.

Doug reached down and took her head in his hands. Pulling her face up to his he kissed her violently, his tongue hard in her mouth. Well, Sheila's efforts were having an effect – but Margo was getting really scared. It was time to end this. *But how?*

Doug grabbed Margo's blouse and began unbuttoning it wildly. Margo protested a little, but knew that Sheila would not be protesting and was confused about how to stop what was going on without it seeming like it was Margo who was stopping it.

Doug had managed to fully unbutton Margo's blouse and he opened it up, admiring her breasts. He put his hands on her waist and moved them up to beneath her bra.

Observer Margo was getting frantic. *"Stupid stupid Sheila! You get him excited – what do we do now? And why isn't Harry stopping this? Shit, you know why Harry isn't stopping it. So how can Sheila stop it? What would make her stop . . . ?"*

Just as Doug's mouth was nearing Margo's breasts, a scream emanated from down the hall. It was the high-pitched scream of a woman and it sounded like it was coming from the Black Box where the strains of "Sodomy" had diminished.

Margo jumped off Doug's lap and quickly buttoned up her blouse. Doug hurriedly put his shirt back on – inside-out – and they were both down the hall in an instant, with Harry stumbling after them.

In the Black Box, one of the dancers was on the floor holding her ankle and rocking in pain. Zoe was squatting next to her, checking on the injury. She saw Harry and got up to report that the dancer had slipped on a slick spot on the floor and had apparently only sprained her ankle. Someone was getting ice and they were going to take her to the infirmary to have it X-rayed.

Margo and Doug hung back at the door to the Black Box, tucking in their shirts. Andrea was across the room and caught Margo's eye, giving her a girl-we-have-to-talk glare. Margo blushed and looked at her feet.

Once it was determined that everything was under control, Harry came over to Margo and Doug, put his arms around their shoulders and walked them back to his office like they were lodge buddies.

Back in the dark, musty room that smelled of sweaty humans, Harry turned on the light and blew out the candle.

He leaned back in his chair and congratulated his actors. "Excellent work, you two. Too bad we got interrupted, but there's no sense in trying to go back to where we were. I think you both got something out of that. Tell me what you're feeling. Doug?"

So it was Doug and Margo again, not Berger and Sheila, thought Margo.

"Whew. Well. I felt really turned on and it was helpful because Berger and Sheila are supposed to be really hot for each other, you know. And right now, um, right now I feel really close to you, Margo. It feels, you know, good."

"Good, Doug. So some intimacy was gained by this experience?"

"Oh definitely," Doug said enthusiastically. "Definitely. It was an excellent exercise."

"Margo?" asked Harry.

Margo hesitated. "Uh. For me too. It helped me feel more intimate with Doug. And I think it'll help our relationship as Sheila and Berger. Yes. Definitely." She coughed.

"Good. Any questions?"

Margo and Doug glanced at each other and shrugged.

"Can't think of any," said Margo.

"Me neither," said Doug.

"Well, perhaps we can do this again before we get further along in the rehearsal process. Since we got interrupted, it might be helpful to finish what we started. But right now, the next couple should be here in a minute." Harry got up and moved around his desk. "I want to congratulate you on the good work you did today. I'm pleased your trust levels are so high and that you can feel so free to explore. You're both doing very good work and I believe your work in this play will be remarkable. And this ability to trust will definitely help you as you grow as actors."

Margo and Doug stood up and Harry hugged each of them. When he hugged Margo he whispered in her ear, "Good job. You really let go today."

Observer Margo said in Margo's head, *"Yep, and that's about as far as she goes, Bub. Don't get any ideas."*

Back out in the hallway outside of Harry's office, Margo and Doug were suddenly shy with each other. They walked silently to the end of the hall, and stood outside the Black Box, hesitating to go in and rejoin the rehearsal which had begun again after the injured dancer had been removed. Strains of "Hare Krishna" could be heard through the door and Margo knew the "Be-In" was in full swing. She wasn't sure she was ready to jump right into the frenzy.

Finally, Doug said, "That was pretty powerful."

Margo agreed, "Yes. It was. And it was pretty weird with Harry being right there too."

Doug cleared his throat. "You wanna have dinner after rehearsal and talk about it?"

Margo stopped breathing for a second, then blurted. "Sure. Why not?"

"Okay." Doug smiled. "Shall we?" And he opened the door to the writhing and shrieking Tribe.

CHAPTER THIRTEEN

"Uh huh. Shirt hanging out, faced all flushed. And what went on with you two in Harry's office?" Andrea was behind Margo, about an hour later, whispering in her ear as they sat cross-legged on the sidelines watching Jeremy/Claude sing "I Got Life."

Jeremy, the opera singer who was exploring his rock voice, was not much of a dancer or mover and Zoe was getting frustrated in her attempts to get him to loosen up and get hip. The rest of the cast took a break and watched while Zoe tried to funk up Jeremy who was singing self-consciously about his body parts.

"Well, things got pretty hot and heavy in there." Margo tried to keep her voice low.

"Uh huh." Andrea said. "You mean they got sexual?"

"Well, yeah. But not much."

"What's 'not much?'"

"Well, you know, Berger and Sheila are supposed to be hot and heavy lovers and our improv got us exploring that. It got us being more intimate."

"How intimate?" Andrea was nothing if not persistent.

"We had our shirts off and were, uh, petting each other, I guess," Margo admitted. "But I still had my bra on," she added hastily.

"Uh huh. And that's when Harry stopped y'all?"

"Well, no. We would have probably kept going if Ruth hadn't screamed and we hadn't run in here to see what had happened."

"Hmm. How far would it have gone? I mean, you wouldn't have done 'it' right there in Harry's office, would you?" Andrea was practically hissing at her.

"Of course not! If Ruth hadn't have screamed, I would have found a way to stop it at about that time anyway. I was already feeling uncomfortable about what was going on and there was no way I was going to go any further with Harry watching!"

"Uh huh."

"I would have!"

"I believe you." Andrea assured her. Jeremy was singing "I got my ass!" while struggling to cradle his butt cheeks in the triumphant way Zoe was demonstrating. Andrea winced at Jeremy, then went on, "So, you think this is the worst of it? You think this is as bad as it gets?"

Margo thought for a minute. "Maybe. I don't know. Somehow I don't think so. I'm so conflicted. I mean, I did get something out of it . . ."

"I'm sure you did." Andrea teased her.

"Shut up. I mean, we did break a barrier into some intimacy. But it had gone far enough and I would have found a way to stop it. I would have. The thing is, I don't think Doug would have stopped it. I don't think he wanted to stop it. I don't think he even cared that Harry was in the room. He enjoyed what we were doing. Either he's just a guy who will take sex on any terms, or he truly believes this kind of thing will make him a better actor, a better Berger. I do believe it's the latter."

Andrea nodded. "It's men. They're willing to do all kinds of shit for a leader. How else do they get them to fight wars and stuff?"

"It's actors too. You're right. We are willing to do all kinds of shit for our 'art.' Plus, we're afraid that if we don't do it, we'll get kicked out of the play, black balled in the Department so we won't get to do another play, and, worst of all, it will mean we're not meant to be actors in the first place. I mean, while I was sitting there on Doug's lap and getting felt up with Harry watching, I was thinking that I should be doing this because it will help my character. And I think it did help my character, and my relationship with Doug or Berger. Shit. I am confused." Margo shook her head.

"I can see that," Andrea said, "But I'm not sure you couldn't get to intimacy or whatever some other way. I mean, if you were playing, you know, a murderer, would you have to murder someone to know how to play it?"

Margo laughed. "Touché!"

"What I want to know is," Andrea's voice got lower, "did Harry enjoy it?"

Margo thought about it. "Hard to say. I couldn't see him because it was dark in there and I was, uh, involved. But I could hear him breathing and I could tell that he was, you know, watching. Once we got going he really didn't say anything." She paused. "If I had to give you an answer, I'd have to say, yes, he enjoyed it."

Andrea watched Jeremy gyrate for a bit. "If there's going to be a weak part in this play, this dude is it." Jeremy's attempts at hipness were resulting in some jerky elbow activity combined with a twitchy legginess that made Margo think of Ichabod Crane at a disco.

"Unless Harry can loosen him up in improv." Margo teased.

Andrea got serious. "Don't laugh. Did you notice that the big IMPROV day is now divided into two parts? On the rehearsal schedule, the morning part says 'MEN' and the afternoon part says 'WOMEN.'"

"So he's going to have the men by themselves for a couple of hours, huh?"

"Seems like."

Andrea started to say something else when Zoe addressed the Tribe. It seemed she had had enough. She told Jeremy to take a break as she got the rest of the cast on their feet. She was going to get everyone else dancing *around* Jeremy and simply have him stand in the center and sing his heart out. She began to choreograph the Tribe around the hopelessly ungraceful body of the opera singer. Jeremy, who was sweating profusely, smiled as he watched her arrange the Tribe around him. When they ran through the number with the new choreography, he stood stock still and sang out in a voice that would make an angel swoon. When he finished with "I got life, life, life, life, LIFE" he raised his left arm. And an opera star became a rock star.

CHAPTER FOURTEEN

Margo got back to her dorm room with barely fifteen minutes to change clothes for her dinner with Doug. She told herself that this was simply a dinner between two actors in a play, but the butterflies in her heart fluttered with the truth.

There was a note on her message board. "Call your mother." Margo's mood slumped and she decided not to call her back. There wasn't time. She wanted to know what was happening with her dad, but she sure didn't want to get into it with her mom before dinner with Doug.

As she opened the door to her dorm room, she noticed a note that had been slid under her door. It was from Jen: "Need to talk. More info on '69 incident. I'll be up late. - Jen" Damn. *This* she wanted to find out about. She thought about knocking on Jen's door to get a briefing and then going to her dinner, but she didn't want to tell Jen she was dining with Doug. Not yet. She shoved the note in her pocket and kept walking.

Once inside her room she saw her desk piled with books and the beginnings of the three papers she still had to do. Her typewriter was sitting there with a blank page sticking out of it. She had been neglecting her class work for this play and she thought she saw the blank page wave to her from across the room. She really shouldn't be having dinner out; she had so much work to do. But she always had work to do and she hardly ever had a dinner date. For once she was going to have a good time and let her studies slide. They wouldn't slide far, she knew.

She opened her closet and sighed in despair at the pitiful collection of clothes hanging there. Several Danskin skirts and leotards for dance and mime classes, auditions and the occasional embarrassing "experimental theatre" piece; a couple of nasty polyester blouses purchased for her by her mother in the late 70s; and a gray wool man's cardigan sweater that she wore almost constantly in the winter. She grunted at the selection and went to her bureau where she pulled out an emerald green turtleneck. At least it shows off my tits, she thought, adding her new silver heart pendant to the ensemble, and smiling. A quick brush through her hair, a dab at her make-up and she was off.

Before shutting her door, she went back in her room and grabbed her *Hair* notebook. She could at least pretend that this was a meeting of actors in a play.

Margo had been to Crib Notes several times for an after-the-play ice cream sundae. This was the first time she has going to dinner at the popular college hang out. She liked how it was decorated with baby things and got a kick out of the stories of the annual "Diaper Dinner" that the fraternities threw for charity where everyone wore diapers and sucked beer from baby bottles. The next day the local papers would always carry some outrageous photo of mustachioed frat brothers decked out in baby bonnets with beer bellies flopping over their diapers. It was always a big hit.

When she arrived, Doug was waiting for her at a table, already cradling a bottle of imported beer. He was dressed in the clothes he had worn at rehearsal and looked as if he had come straight from there. Margo was embarrassed at having changed. It looked like she cared about this dinner.

When Doug saw her he got up and waved. He smiled when she reached the table and kissed her – on the mouth. This was new, Margo noted, and she sat down. Doug waited until she was seated before he sat. Margo smiled down at the table as he took his seat, the perfect gentleman.

A college-age waitress came to their table wearing a baby-doll kind of dress. On her chest was a diaper pin with a baby rattle tied to it.

"You wanna beer?" Doug asked. The image of chivalry faded from her shiny knight. Despite four years at a state university, Margo had not gotten used to the amount of beer consumed by college students. At least she was beyond her freshman fears that every beer drinker would become a violent lunatic like her father. But she still disapproved of drinking and didn't drink at all herself. Another reason her social life was far from active.

"No thanks," she said, "I think I'll have a Diet Coke. With lemon, please." The waitress pursed her lips and nodded as she walked away, carefully writing down the order.

"This place has great pizza." Doug picked up his menu. "We could share if you want." Margo noticed that he couldn't decide whether or not to look her in the eye. He would look at her, then look away, then look at her again, then study the menu. It was kinda cute, Margo decided.

"Sure. That would be fine. I like pepperoni."

"Me too!" Doug seemed astonished at their similar taste in pizza, as though it was divine proof that they were star-crossed lovers.

The waitress came back with Margo's drink, minus the lemon. Margo decided to let it go, but Doug noticed.

"Excuse me, she ordered lemon with her drink."

The waitress studied her note pad. "Oh yeah. Sorry." Just as Margo was reaching for the drink, the waitress took it and disappeared.

Doug laughed. "Sorry. I just think a person should get what a person orders."

"Thank you." Margo was impressed that he noticed her lack of lemon, let alone corrected the mistake.

"Well, I figure I'm going to be making my living as a waiter before I get my big break. Might as well pay attention to the business now!" He laughed again and his turquoise eyes twinkled. His laugh was infectious and Margo laughed with him.

The waitress returned with Margo's drink, complete with lemon, and took their pizza order. She walked off slowly, concentrating on writing down the order, as if misspelling "pepperoni" would result in the end of the human race.

Margo picked up her drink and proposed a toast, "To our careers waiting tables! May they be brief and less stressful than hers!" They clinked glasses and sipped their drinks.

Doug put his drink down and gazed at her with admiration. "You won't be waiting tables long. You're going to go to New York and take Broadway by storm."

"From your mouth to God's ears." Margo said, raising her glass and taking another sip. She set the glass down and sighed. "I wish I believed in myself that much."

"I wish you did too." Doug put his elbows on the table and leaned forward. "Because you are incredible."

Margo lowered her eyes. "Thank you. You are too."

They were silent. Margo admired at the centerpiece of tiny flowers stuck in a baby food jar. Doug took another gulp of his beer.

Finally Doug said, "I enjoyed our improv today."

Margo felt the tops of her ears blush. She hated when that happened. She looked up so that Doug would have more to see than the tops of her ears.

Doug's magnificent eyes were searching hers and he smiled his boyish smile through his dark blond beard.

Margo nodded. "It was a good exercise."

"I really felt us getting close. More intimate, you know?"

"Oh yeah. I definitely felt like we were getting more intimate." *Duh,* said Margo's inner observer.

Doug hesitated. "And, uh, it felt really comfortable. You know. Like it wasn't awkward or anything."

"Uh huh." *Were we in the same room?* Margo thought. *It was comfortable sucking face while Harry watched?!?* She took a deep breath. "But didn't you think it was a bit weird having Harry there watching us and all?"

"Well, sure, a little. But that's what acting is all about, you know. Being able to do anything with an audience watching."

"Anything?"

"Shit, just about. Been to any movies lately? They do all kinds of sex shit and you know there's a camera guy right there, with all kinds of crew all around watching. You gotta be able to do that if you're an actor. Might as well get used to it now."

"I guess so." Margo thought about this. She wasn't sure she was willing to do "anything" for her craft. The thought of doing a nude love scene gave her the willies. "Do you think you could do that? I mean, make love on screen – with your butt hanging out and all that moaning and groaning?"

"Sure! I'd love to!" Doug was using grand gestures. "Give me a gorgeous leading lady and let me at it!" He laughed at himself. "I don't know. It would be weird, but I guess I could do it. I figure I'd just get into it and sort of forget the other people are there."

"Is that what you did today?"

"Sort of. I mean," his voice got quieter, "When you pulled my shirt off and sucked on my nipple, whew, I forgot where we were and what we were supposed to be doing. I was into it. I didn't want it to stop. I was real bummed when that scream stopped us. How 'bout you? Didn't you get into it?"

"Sure, pretty much. But I never totally let go. And I never forgot that Harry was in the room."

Doug seemed disappointed. Margo guessed that he'd wanted her to have been oblivious to everything except the ecstasy she felt in his embrace.

"That's what makes you such a good actress." He sighed. "I really thought you were totally into it. Man. Do you ever let go? I mean, totally?"

"Not really," she admitted.

"C'mon. What about when you're drunk?"

"I've never been drunk."

Doug's mouth dropped open. "You've never been drunk?! Everybody's been drunk!"

Margo had had this conversation before. Doug's glow was wearing off. "Not me." She decided to tell him. "I don't drink."

Doug gaped like he'd seen an alien. *Playboy* had once done an article on the 20 biggest party campuses in the U.S. Their hallowed educational institution had come in fourth in the nation. Margo figured Doug pulled his weight in activities that had earned the college its impressive reputation.

"Unbelievable." Doug shook his head and finished his beer. "Don't you have any fun?"

Margo was getting angry. This line of questioning always pissed her off. Why was it that so many people equated drinking with fun? And if you didn't drink you were a bore? Drinking to her was dangerous and horrible; she couldn't shake her early encounters with a drinking man. But could she have fun? Did she have fun?

"Of course I have fun. I act. I love to act. Acting is my fun. It is my passion. It fills me with joy and fulfillment. I don't think anything could come close to the joy I feel when I'm on stage and I'm clicking in a role and the audience is right there with me. Nothing feels that good."

"Not even sex?" Doug asked her, raising his eyebrows like Groucho.

Before Margo had a chance to say anything, the waitress mercifully arrived with the pizza.

Doug ordered another beer. Then stopped himself. "Do you mind?" he asked, suddenly aware that his dinner mate might be offended by his drinking.

"Of course not! Just because I don't drink doesn't mean I think you shouldn't." She lied. She wished nobody drank and she was feeling like she wanted to leave. But she was touched that he asked.

Doug took a plate, put a slice of pizza on it and handed it to her. He was still being a gentleman, Margo thought. Might as well eat the pizza.

"So acting is your fun, huh?"

Margo wanted to change the subject. "Yes. And I enjoy my work."

"Your schoolwork?!" Doug gawked at her like she was insane. "I have never met anyone like you. If it wasn't for theatre, we never woulda met." The waitress returned with his drink and he thanked her, swallowing a hunk of pizza. "So, is that enough for you? I mean your acting, and your schoolwork."

"I guess I'm kinda driven." Margo talked through a mass of mozzarella. "This *is* good pizza!"

"Told ya." His smile returned. "What about guys? I never see you with any guys. Are you seeing anybody? Or don't you date either?"

"No. I'm not seeing anyone right now. I haven't really dated much. I'm too busy, I guess. I don't make time for it."

Doug nodded at her and chewed his pizza. He swallowed. "What about us? Could you make time for us?"

Margo almost choked on her Diet Coke. She thought for sure that once she revealed her lack of experience and her temperate ways, Doug would be one of those guys who sped away fast enough to leave skid marks.

She collected herself and used her acting skill to appear nonchalant. Doug's smile told her that he was not fooled.

"Hmm. I'm not sure. I admit I'm interested and wouldn't mind taking up where we left off this afternoon . . . without Harry watching. But I'm really busy right now, what with the play and everything. I've got three papers waiting for me back in my room."

Doug seemed to enjoy her squirming.

She finished up. "I guess what I'm saying is that I really like you and would maybe like to pursue something, but I'm not sure I have time right now. I mean, I don't think I'm ready right now. Does that make sense?"

"You're scared."

"I'm scared."

"Fair enough." There was that smile again.

Margo put her head in her hands and groaned, "I'm sorry."

"Don't be. I like your honesty. And I'm willing to wait." Margo almost gasped when she heard that.

"Tell you what," he continued. "Let's see how it goes with the play. We'll be lovers on stage and see where it takes us after that."

Margo was so relieved. "That sounds great."

Doug reached out and took her hand. "But I'd like to be the one to help you let go and really enjoy yourself. You're holding so much in, Margo. And you're too beautiful a woman not to enjoy all that life has to offer."

Margo could hardly breathe. She certainly couldn't eat another bite of pizza.

Doug finished the pizza with easy huge mouthfuls and their dinner conversation turned to their stories. Or rather, Doug's story. Doug spoke easily and expansively about his past and his dreams, and Margo was content to listen and ask meaningful questions. And stare at this man who was becoming more and more attractive the more she knew him.

He was born in Mississippi and had moved to the Northeast when his dad transferred jobs. He had moved long enough ago that he had lost all but a hint of a southern accent, though he said his mom was still a "mush mouth."

Margo chuckled. "What about your dad?"

"Oh, I lost him when I was thirteen. Car accident."

Margo stopped chuckling and bit her lip. "Oh, I'm sorry."

"Yeah, it was hard. And my mom had to go to work full time. My brothers and I got by the best we could. It was never the same."

He was silent for a second, then went on. He was the youngest of three boys and felt kinda lost. His oldest brother got straight As and had worked part-time after school at a warehouse. He was in graduate school now. The middle brother was a superstar jock and his mom's favorite. Doug didn't know who he was. Until he found theatre.

Like Margo, he was bitten by the bug in high school. Unlike Margo, his family had ties to show biz. A second cousin, once-removed, was actually a fairly big star in Hollywood. Doug had his career all figured out. He would move to New York and get some notoriety, experience and credits as a stage actor, then move to L.A. and call on his cousin to open some doors for him.

He seemed much more confident about his career and eventual success than Margo was, and he seemed patient and methodical on his planned path. He knew he wasn't the brightest kid on the block and acting didn't come effortlessly to him. He knew he needed to study and enrolled in the best program his family could afford – the drama department at the local state university. He planned on taking lots of classes when he got to New York and knew he would be waiting on tables for years perhaps. But he knew, he knew deep down inside, that he would eventually "make it." He was committed to his chosen field, singled minded in his pursuit, and would do anything if he thought it would make him a better actor or get him in some door he needed to get through.

That's why getting cast in *Hair* was such a coup for him. "This is my big break, Margo! It's my first lead here and it's in a Harry play!" Harry's actors got noticed. They were electric on stage. They were sexy. That is what Doug wanted. That and a good party. Doug figured he only needed three things in life to be happy – a good woman, a cold beer and an Oscar – and not necessarily in that order.

When the check arrived, Doug scooped it up and paid, leaving a decent tip. Margo was stunned. Again, Doug just grinned. And shrugged, "I ate most of the pizza."

Because Doug had said it a couple of times, Margo wanted to know what doing "anything" for acting meant. On their walk back to Margo's dorm, she asked, "Are you at all nervous about Harry's improvs?"

"Not so far." Doug poked her in the ribs with an elbow.

Margo snorted. "What about the big one coming up this Saturday?"

"I don't know. A little, I guess, because all improv is kinda scary. But I trust Harry. He really knows what he's doing."

Margo kicked a rock. "Have you heard any rumors about his improvs?"

"Sure I heard rumors. So what? So far I haven't seen anything that bad. People just like to talk. You know what Anderson said?" Paul Anderson had been the lead in Harry's *Oedipus* the year before. Margo shook her head. "He said, 'Don't worry about Harry's improvs. You'll get great reviews!'" Doug grinned his 1,000-watt grin.

They walked along in silence for a bit as Margo recalled having heard the same refrain from Rob McCall a month earlier.

Doug picked up a piece of litter, balled it up and tossed it into a garbage can. "I mean, look at our improv today. Some people would be mortified if they knew what happened, but those people just don't understand. It really got us closer together and it really helped our characters, and that's the important thing."

"But what if you're in an improv and you have to do something you really don't want to do?" Margo protested.

"That's probably because you have something you have to break through and you have to get past your fear and experience it. That's why they call it a 'breakthrough!'" He laughed at his own cleverness and made a face that said, "Duh!"

Margo wrinkled her nose at him. "No matter what?"

"No matter what. I mean, Harry wouldn't make us do anything that would really hurt us, you know. It's all for our acting. We have to trust him."

Doug jumped up onto a small brick wall and tight-rope walked along the top of it. Margo watched him and smiled. *Harry wouldn't make us do anything that would really hurt us. We have to trust him,* she repeated to herself. *Okay, Doug's right. It's all okay. And I wouldn't be here right now with this sweet man if it weren't for Harry's improv. Okay, I'm a believer.*

Enough speculation about Harry's improvs. She had more important things to speculate – like whether Doug was going to kiss her.

"This is my dorm. Thanks for dinner." Margo stopped and scuffed her foot on the ground.

"My pleasure." He jumped down like a Shakespearean hero and bowed. *He sure enjoys the gallant act,* Margo thought, *must be the southern upbringing.* Doug stood up and grinned at her. "It was great talking with you. I really feel like I can talk with you, you know." He paused and leaned up against a brick dividing wall, as if waiting for something. "You're not going to invite me in, are you?"

Margo bit her lip and shook her head. "Not yet. After *Hair.*"

"Okay. After *Hair* then. But this doesn't have to wait until after *Hair.*" He put his hand on her shoulder and kissed her sweetly. Margo reached up and stroked his cheek. They kissed again, a little more passionately. Margo turned and ran up the steps to her building. Once inside the door she stopped and then peeked at Doug from behind the sheer curtain in a window. He was gazing up at the door, then smiled and walked away shaking his head. Margo silently prayed that Harry's improvs *were* basically harmless. She would hate to have this sweet man hurt in any way.

CHAPTER FIFTEEN

Margo danced around the corner to her hallway and almost ran straight into Jen, who was sitting cross-legged in front of her door. She was knocking ashes from her cigarette into an ashtray with one hand, holding a can of Diet Coke in the other, and in her lap was a textbook. When Margo almost stepped on her she peered up from her little camp and chastised her friend:

"Hey, watch it! Some of us are studying here!"

Margo giggled. "Geez, sorry. I didn't see you."

"Uh huh. And what have you been up to, Missy? Rehearsal could not have gone this late. Don't tell me you got that silly grin from studying in the library."

Margo huffed and decided to remain aloof, "I don't have to tell you everything. You're not my mother."

Jen struggled to get to her feet with a measure of élan and said, "Oh, by the way, I spoke with your mother. She didn't sound good."

"Shit." Margo muttered as she unlocked her door. "I should call her."

"Is she sick or something?"

"Or something. My dad's the one who's sick. He's drinking again." Margo had confided in Jen some of the horror of growing up in her family.

"Oh fuck."

"Yeah. And I feel guilty, but I just don't want to hear about it. I don't want to be the big protector this time. Or my father's parole officer." She threw her notebook down on her bed. "I'm having such a good time doing

Hair. For once in my life I just want to have fun. I'm sick of being the responsible oldest child."

"Yeah," said Jen, dragging heavily on her cigarette as she sat at Margo's desk and set up camp all over Margo's work. "And I'm sick of being the outrageous youngest kid who's always getting into trouble. It's such a lot of work."

Margo plopped onto her bed and lay back. "Of course I'll call her and deal with it. But not tonight. So tell me – what's the new info on," she sat up and pulled Jen's note out of her pocket, "the '69 incident?"

"Oh, nice change of subject. But we haven't finished with our first subject. Where were you tonight? You seemed a little distracted out there in the hall." She switched to a French accent, "Could zer be a bit of – how you say? – 'Amour' in zee air?"

Margo exhaled heavily. "Okay. Yes, sort of. I had dinner with Doug tonight."

"Yessir! An affair with her leading man. How do you do it?!"

"It's not an affair. It's just an interest. And we have a lot to discuss about the play so it was mostly a working dinner." She coughed.

"Sure. I believe you." Jen said. Then she pretended to cry, dabbing her eyes with a pretend hanky. "Don't tell your best friend. That's okay. I don't need to know. Just because I confide everything in you. Don't feel you have to do me the same honor." She pretended to blow her nose loudly.

"Okay, okay." Margo spoke quickly, "You see, we had this improv today where we got hot and heavy in Harry's office . . ."

"What?" Jen sat up at attention. "Do tell!"

Margo smirked. "Well, we did, uh, a lot of, uh, exploring and it was sort of uncomfortable, so we went to dinner to talk about it and we did talk a little about having a relationship but we agreed to wait till after the play is over and it was very nice and he kissed me on the mouth, uh, three times tonight. There. You satisfied?"

Jen seemed stunned. "Hold on. Go back. Hot and heavy? What the hell? So, you're fucking each other in improvs, kissing each other on your own time, and it's all hunky-dory."

"Exactly."

"Wonderful. More."

Margo put her hands on her head, leaned back against the cinderblock wall and moaned. It was all so special and new. She didn't want Jen to tarnish things quite yet. She decided to buy some time.

"You know what? I'm not quite ready to talk about it all. Give me a minute to process things, okay? And tell me your news."

Jen seemed grumpy. "Damn! But okay." She scooted her chair closer to Margo's bed and looked around as if she was afraid to be overheard. "Mike Matthews, the actor who . . ."

" . . . who was in the improv with the guy who killed himself," Margo finished, "I remember."

"Good. Well get this – Mike Matthews is a subscriber!" Jen was excited.

"He's a what?"

"A subscriber!"

"A subscriber to what?"

"National Geographic. What do you think, dummy? He subscribes to the University Stage play season! . . . He comes to all of the plays!"

Margo was stunned. "I thought he lived in New York."

"He used to live in New York. Now I guess he lives back here. Or else he lives in New York and flies back for all of the plays. What do I know? All I know is that he's a subscriber and we may be able to contact him!" Jen raised her fist in victory.

"How did you find out that he was a subscriber?"

This time Jen spoke with a German accent, "Ve haf our vays!"

"Oh c'mon!" Margo pleaded.

Jen was back to her version of normal. "Okay, since you begged – I slept with Alan Rubenstein and he is now putty in my hands."

"Excuse me?"

Alan Rubenstein was a happily confident gay man who loved his job in and around the theatre. He was the Theatre Administrator, in charge of the box office, publicity and subscriptions to the student plays of the University Stage. He was a sweet enough guy, a bit soft around the edges, who sported an exquisitely dapper wardrobe and an impressive head of well-styled hair, and he reveled in schmoozing. He especially adored opening nights when he would hold a pre-show seminar for high rolling donors and a post-play cocktail party for subscribers and any press that showed up. He was also known to be meticulous and tight-lipped in all of his dealings, including his beloved donor and subscriber lists. The fact that Jen got any information from him was a feather in her detective cap.

Jen took a drag on her cigarette and laughed like Lauren Bacall. "He couldn't resist my feminine wiles."

"Give me a break. How did you get the information? What even made you think of it in the first place?"

Jen dropped all of her dramatics. "I honestly don't know. I was thinking of ways to find out where Mike Matthews could be and I wondered if maybe he was a subscriber."

"But how did you get at Rubenstein's list? Remember when we took Theatre Admin? His list is sacred to him. He doesn't want people bugging his subscribers and donors or sending them junk mail, so only he and his employees see the list."

"Right." Jen smiled like the cat who caught the canary.

Margo caught on. "Are you working for him now?"

"I just started. I'm working part-time in the box office and today someone was showing me how to print out mailing labels and I got to see the list. And there was the name of R. Michael Matthews! Unfortunately, my trainer was breathing over my shoulder the whole time so I couldn't stop to write down the address and I don't remember it because it went by too fast. But next time . . ."

"You took this job just to see if Mike Matthews was a subscriber?"

"Yep."

"You're wacko."

"Perhaps. But I'm going to crack this case, chickadee."

"Impressive."

"Now here's what I need from you. I'm getting a key to the box office so I can go in on Saturday and do some clean-up work. I want you to come with me and help me get into the computer because I'm helpless around machinery. Then, get this, I found out that there's a file cabinet somewhere with publicity photos from all of the plays, I thought we could see if we could find a picture of Mr. Matthews . . ."

Margo was lying back on her bed, playing with the little stuffed tiger that Doug had given her. Jen stopped her plotting.

"Margo. Are you listening?"

"Yes. Mostly." She sat up again. "Jen. I'm not so sure I want to get into the spy thing with you."

"What're you, chicken?" Jen teased.

"A little. But mostly I'm not so sure Harry is so dangerous after all. I don't feel comfortable digging up evidence or whatever," she squished up her face, anticipating Jen's reaction, "to try to somehow implicate him in something that happened over fifteen years ago."

"Hey, hey, hey! I thought you were into this. I thought you wanted to know what Harry was capable of to protect yourself and other actors from his sicko improvs!"

"That's just it. I'm not so sure they're sicko after all."

Jen almost dropped her cigarette from her open mouth. "*Now* you're telling me this? Why the sudden change of heart? As if I didn't know. What happened in Harry's office today?"

"I really shouldn't tell. We promised to keep it confidential."

Jen stood up violently, almost knocking over her chair. "What! Now you're pulling that crap with me?! Are you a Harry zombie after all? I don't fuckin' believe you."

Margo winced. She had agreed to tell Jen everything, and now she was letting her down.

"Look," Jen sat back down and crossed her arms. "Whether you want to believe it or not, this man is doing something seriously wrong. A boy killed himself over one of his improvs."

"We don't know that for sure."

"Maybe not, but we will once I track down Mike Matthews. And I will track down Mike Matthews, whether you help me or not." Jen was gesticulating dramatically. "I don't know how Harry seduced you into becoming one of his drones, but . . ."

"Okay, hold it!" Margo held out her arms as if stopping an orchestra. "Harry didn't seduce me into anything and I'm not one of his 'drones.' I'm still concerned about his improvs, but after the one I did today, I can see how people could take them the wrong way."

"How could people take them the wrong way?"

"Well," Margo hesitated and stared at her hands, "because it was sexual. I mean, Harry talked about how our characters needed to trust and love each other and needed to gain more intimacy. Which we do! And intimacy for Berger and Sheila involves sex. This is *Hair* after all! So Doug and I kinda made out as a way of exploring our intimacy."

"Kinda made out? Uh huh. And how far did you explore your intimacy under the tutorial eye of the helpful professor?"

"See, you make it sound horrible. And I admit, I was nervous while it was going on because I didn't know how far it would go. But, it didn't go too far. And, despite the weirdness of it, Doug and I are feeling more intimate with each other and I have no doubt that our characters on stage will be more electric and realistic than if we had approached this strictly intellectually."

Jen's arms were folded. She appraised Margo and nodded. "So Miss Analysis is becoming a fan of improv after all."

"Jen, look. The fact is, now that it's over, I mostly get what went on in our improv today. Honestly, it really did break down barriers and help me feel more like Sheila. You know what a prude I am." Jen grunted. Margo smiled. "Okay, I enjoyed it. And I'm really loving *Hair*. I guess I'm tired of always having to do the right thing and for once I just want to let go and have fun." Margo put her head in her hands.

Jen came over, sat on the bed beside her and put her arm around her. "So have fun. Fall in love, make love, whatever. But be careful too. I don't believe Harry's improvs are harmless and I don't want to see you hurt."

Margo smiled at her friend. "Thanks. I'm sorry I'm being such a jerk."

"Shit, you don't even know what being a jerk is. You're just a little confused. That's what happens when Cupid strings up his bow." She got up and started to pack up her camp. "Look, I'm going over to the box office around 3:00 on Saturday to do my sleuthing. Come along if you want. Or don't. I don't care."

"Saturday is the big Improv day. We should be finishing up around then. I'll see how I'm feeling. Okay?"

"Okay." Jen lit one more cigarette before leaving. "And since you asked, I think you and Doug make a darling couple."

Margo groaned and rolled over on her bed. "Leave me alone in my bliss!"

"Good night sweetie!" Jen blew Margo a kiss and left.

Margo stretched and got up, walked over to her desk and sat down, determined to get some homework done, despite the nagging feeling right behind her eyes.

CHAPTER SIXTEEN

*"**G**ood morning Starshine! The earth says hello! / You twinkle above us. We twinkle below."* Probably the silliest song in *Hair*, Margo couldn't get it out of her head as she showered in the morning. *"Good morning Starshine! You lead us along / my love and me as we sing our early morning singing song."*

Here it was, the day she'd been dreading since rehearsals began, the day of the big Improv, and all she could do was sing, *"Gliddee glop gloobie, nibby nobby noobie, la la la lo lo."* Dumbest lyrics in history.

But she felt like the lyrics, giddily stupidly in love. Or at least in "like." Margo was cautious about the word "love." In fact, she was pretty sure that what she was feeling was infatuation. Whatever it was, it felt great. She sang to the stuffed tiger Doug had given her, *"Toobie oobie walla, noobie abba nabba, early morning singing song."* She laughed at herself as she combed out her hair.

She knew that at that very moment, Doug and the men were deep into their big ugly Improv, but she couldn't worry about it. If Doug wasn't worried, why should she be? Doug was looking forward to it. He was into Harry's method. He was looking forward to whatever breakthroughs were awaiting him in the Black Box with the men of his Tribe. And Margo was looking forward to seeing him when she arrived for the women's part of the Improv in a couple of hours.

The past six days since their intimacy improv had been happy ones for Margo. She felt like the New England spring that was blossoming all around her. All daffodils and tulips and budding trees and tweeting birdies. Seeing Doug at rehearsals, working on their relationship in the play, doing their scenes together and catching each others' eyes when they weren't in a scene together . . . it all made the rehearsals thrilling. Their greeting ritual was something to look forward to, and during the gift-giving ritual they sat together, frequently with Margo resting on Doug's knee or chest while he put his arm around her.

Putting a restriction on their relationship until after the play made their time together at rehearsals all the more fun and enticing. Like the old precept about not having sex until marriage, it made them yearn for each other all the more.

Aside from the infatuation thing, Margo felt that the rehearsals had been going great. The Tribe was coming together like a big happy school of dolphins, and the group numbers were dynamic, especially the "up" songs like "Aquarius," "I Got Life" and the "Be-In." The Tribe was getting good at celebrating and being wildly happy with each other.

One of the most electric songs so far was the title song, "Hair." Doug's natural mischievousness poked at stiff old Jeremy's opera-singer demeanor and together they managed to create a hilarious atmosphere in which Jeremy actually seemed able to be funky and terribly funny. It got so that every time Jeremy launched into: *"She asks me why I'm just a hairy guy,"* the Tribe would crack up laughing at his delivery. His magnificently trained voice combined with Doug's gutsy one for a thrilling vocal duet. The Tribe fell naturally into the spirit of the song with those two at the helm and the piece worked. Even tight-mouthed Zoe cheered the last time they ran through it.

Harry, however, was not satisfied. As Friday evening's rehearsal ended, he said: "I feel things are moving along well in our rehearsal process. You all have a dynamism and energy level that is contagious. However, there are emotional aspects of the play that are missing. We haven't touched heavily on the darker elements of the play yet. Tomorrow's Improv will help elicit these emotions."

Margo momentarily wondered what darker elements were on the way. Then Doug squeezed her knee.

She spent the morning studying, polishing off a pile of homework that had been stacking up on her desk. Just as she was putting on her make-up and preparing to walk to the theatre building, Jen knocked on her door.

"Hi, good luck today." Jen offered.

"Thanks." Hearing Jen wish her luck made her skin prickle. Suddenly she was afraid.

"Look," said Jen, "Like I said, I'll be in the box office around 3:00. It would be great if you could come by."

"Okay. I'll see how I feel."

"Okay." Jen rearranged some books she was carrying. "Well, I'm off to the library. See ya."

Margo watched her friend go, thinking about the day ahead, then returned to her make-up and her mirror. "Good Morning Starshine" was no longer playing in her head.

The phone in the hallway rang. Margo hoped someone else would pick it up, but it seemed no one else on the hall was in. After six rings she ran out into the hall and answered.

"Oh, thank God, it's you," her mom's voice was trembling.

Margo slumped. This was the last thing she wanted to deal with at this moment.

"Geez, Mom. I'm sorry I haven't called you back . . ."

"It's just that you're always so good at calling back. Have you been sick?"

"No, not sick." Though Margo was beginning to feel sick because her mom sounded so needy and pitiful. "Just busy." *And in love.* But she wasn't about to share that with her mom. Not yet. "What's been happening?"

"Well. You know your dad has been drinking again and it hasn't been good. It hasn't been good." She started to cry.

Margo rolled her eyes. She glanced at her watch. She could spare her mom four minutes.

"Is he hurting you, Mom?"

"Yes. But not as much as before." She sighed.

"Did you call Freddy?"

"Not yet. I didn't want to bother him."

Margo almost threw the phone on the floor. "Why didn't you call him? It's not bothering him! It's what AA people do for other AA people. Please call him."

"I think I can handle this by myself. I don't want to involve other people. This is about our family. You know what your father always says,

'Nothing goes outside these walls.'"

Margo tried to remember where she had heard that sentence recently. "Yeah, he says that so no one will see that his shiny fucking armor is tarnished."

"Do you have to use words like that? Ever since you went into drama you started using words like that."

Margo's finger was poised over the hang-up switch. "You know, Mom. I have to be at rehearsal in ten minutes, can I call you later?"

"Oh, I don't want to make you late for rehearsal. I'm sorry. It's just that you're the only one I can talk to sometimes. But I know you're busy and I shouldn't bother you."

Margo felt the guilt arrows being slung. But she wasn't going to let them get to her. "That's right. You shouldn't bother me. You should bother Freddy. He's an expert. And he lives right around the corner. Call Freddy."

There was a silence on the other end of the phone. Margo had rarely been short with her mother. "Okay. Maybe I will." There was another pause. "Margo?"

"Yes Mom."

"Do you think you could come home any time soon? Maybe for an overnight or a weekend? It would be so nice to talk with you in person. I'll make turkey tetrazzini." This was Margo's favorite meal. The one her mom always made for her birthday.

"Mom," Margo struggled to keep her voice calm, "I'm going to be really busy for the next few weeks until *Hair* is over. I've got classes all day and rehearsals almost every evening and on weekends. I just can't get away right now."

"I understand. I didn't mean to burden you."

"You're not burdening me . . . But I have to go. I'll call you later, okay?"

"Okay."

"Call Freddy."

"I'll think about it . . . Margo?"

"Yes Mom?"

"Break a leg!"

"Thanks Mom." She smiled ruefully as she hung up.

CHAPTER SEVENTEEN

Margo arrived for rehearsal a couple of minutes late, panting from running across campus. It didn't matter because when she turned the corner to the hallway that led to the Black Box, she saw the Tribe's women sitting on the floor or leaning against the wall. The door to the Black Box was closed. The women greeted her with whispers.

"It's been closed since I got here and I was fifteen minutes early."

"We haven't heard a thing from inside. I wonder if they're even in there."

"Maybe they took a break for lunch."

"Do you think we should knock?"

"Let's wait a few more minutes," suggested Margo. "Harry knows we're supposed to be here now. They're probably just finishing up."

She stood up against the wall and struggled to hear something from behind the closed door.

Andrea made her way over to Margo and whispered to her: "I was here pretty early too and I thought I heard one of the guys crying in there."

Margo had never heard Andrea so serious. All of her funky black girl persona was gone. She asked with foreboding, "Real crying or acting crying?"

"It's a Harry improv, what do you think?"

Bumps rose up on Margo's skin. She thought of young Scott Warren who had thrown himself from a high-rise window after one of Harry's improvs. She wanted to run to the box office and meet Jen there and find the information on Mike Matthews and call him and find out, find out what had happened, find out if . . .

The door suddenly swung open and the women jumped.

"Shit!" Andrea whispered in her alarm as she took Margo's arm.

Harry emerged from the room and closed the door behind him. The women looked up at him with wide eyes. He was bedraggled. His shirt was damp and his face was flushed, as if he had a fever. The little tuft of hair on his head was more unruly than usual and he seemed to be having trouble breathing.

He scanned the women and smiled.

"Welcome to the Improv, women of the Tribe. Before you go in, I must tell you a little about what's been going on with the men so that you may enter in the proper frame of mind."

Andrea, who still had hold of Margo's arm, squeezed it and shot a look at her.

Harry went on, "The men have been through an ordeal this morning. They have bravely faced their own dark sides and have uncovered some frightening but truthful things about themselves."

"What the hell does that mean?" Andrea mumbled into Margo's ear.

"Shhh," Margo hissed at her without turning her head.

Harry was now walking up and down the hall among the women like an army sergeant. "The men have done well. They've proven themselves to be worthy – worthy of the Tribe, and worthy of you, their women. Your first duty as you enter the room will be to find your man and comfort him. Hold him. Nurture him. Tell him that you are proud of him for being your man. Give him the love and support he needs right now."

The women were staring at him and each other with confused and concerned expressions.

Harry made his way back to the door. "I'm going to open the door now. Slowly, quietly, come in, find your man and comfort him."

Margo and Andrea shared an expression of "Yikes!" Margo took a deep breath and exhaled. She felt her stomach shudder.

Harry opened the door and stood aside. One by one the women filed into the Black Box, hesitantly, slowly, carefully.

It took Margo's eyes a few seconds to adjust to the candle-lit darkness of the Black Box. As she tip-toed into the room she almost gagged at the sudden clamminess. It was as if she was entering a dark warm locker room where sweaty players had dumped their soiled uniforms on the floor. The Black Box smelled of men's activity.

Women were finding their men and couples were hugging and stroking. But Margo couldn't find Doug. She walked warily into the crowded humid gloom, careful to avoid touching anyone. She fought a feeling of dread that threatened to choke her. She finally saw him. He stood dead center in the room. He was facing away. Not moving. The back of his hair was stringy and mashed – like he had just gotten out of bed and hadn't had a chance to comb it after lying on it all night. His shirt was untucked and uneven, like it was buttoned a button off. He was barefoot. He stood straight, head held high, and he was absolutely motionless, as though he were fixated on a point directly ahead of him. Margo thought he resembled a tall, proud zombie. She was afraid to see his face.

Margo swallowed, then reached out and touched his shoulder. As though hit by a shock wave, Doug spun around and glared at her. His turquoise eyes were red and wrathful and Margo's knees felt suddenly wobbly. It was the face of her drunken father. Those wild eyes that conveyed the desire to seize a lover by the face and throw her across the room. Margo let out a little involuntary whimper and felt herself brace for whatever storm was about to break.

Like a sudden change of weather, Doug's face softened and his stare relaxed. He pulled Margo to his chest and hugged her tightly, tightly, tightly, swaying back and forth as he held her, burying his face in her hair. He didn't make a sound. He just hugged and swayed and hugged.

Margo's arms were around him and she held on tightly, swaying with him. She wanted to ask him a dozen questions, but no one in the Black Box was talking and it didn't seem like Doug was capable of responding verbally anyway. So she hugged him and stroked his back.

She nestled her head into the space beneath his chin and moved her cheek along his neck. Some of Doug's curly blond chest hairs were peeking out from the top of his button-down shirt. As Margo's cheek rubbed against them, they scratched her skin. She put the bottom of her cheek on them and moved slightly, feeling the chest hairs with her lower jaw. The hairs felt hard and scratchy, as though they had been sprayed with a stiff hairspray.

Margo pulled her right arm out from under Doug's hug and moved her hand to the top of Doug's shirt. She unbuttoned the top two buttons and stroked the top of Doug's chest as though being affectionate. His chest hairs were all hard and matted. The skin on his neck felt sticky.

Margo moved her face up to kiss Doug sweetly on the cheek. She kissed him with little delicate kisses that moved from his cheek, down his chin to the side of his neck. When she got there she pushed her tongue out between her lips and licked Doug, ever so softly. Sweet. He tasted sweet. Like sugar. Not salty like sweat.

She licked him again to make sure. Definitely sweet. Like candy.

She raised her mouth to his ear. "What the hell went on in here?"

Doug exhaled and held her even more tightly. His whispered voice cracked, "I'll tell you later."

Margo fondled the top of Doug's chest to feel again the hard and matted chest hairs.

"Ow!" Doug winced. "That hurts."

She must have pulled on the hairs without meaning too. She drew back an inch. They continued to hug each other just less passionately, waiting for whatever was going to happen next.

Margo glanced at the other couples over Doug's shoulder. It was dark in the room. Harry's damn one little candle was all that lit the space. All she could see were hugging couples who seemed to be having private conversations. She couldn't hear anything more than whispers. She peered into the darkness searching for Andrea who would be hugging Jackson. She needed an anchor in her confusion and hoped to share a meaningful glance with her friend. No luck. She was alone with Doug who trembled in her embrace. Or was she the one trembling?

She sensed some movement from the audience side of the room. Harry? She was suddenly terrified. What would he have them do next?

CHAPTER EIGHTEEN

Harry spoke: "Welcome women of the Tribe. Welcome to our bonding ritual." *So that's what's been going on in here. Some kind of male bonding. What a bunch of shit.*

He continued: "Yes, comfort your men. They have been through an ordeal. An ordeal that has brought them closer together and more determined to help and protect you, their women." Doug seemed to gain energy from Harry's words and he pulled back to look at Margo with a noble I'm-going-to-protect-you kind of expression. He then resumed hugging her. Margo rolled her eyes. *I'm definitely not into this Improv,* she thought.

Harry's voice got quieter, more intimate. Everyone seemed to stop breathing in order to hear him:

"Women of the Tribe, you should know that the leader of the Tribe has been firmly established." Then louder he asked, "Who is he, Men?"

"BERGER!" the men barked together suddenly. Startled women gasped as their men pulled away and shouted the name of their leader.

Harry repeated his question more loudly, "Men, who is your leader?"

The men shouted, "BERGER!"

It was militaristic. Or post-hypnotic. The long-haired hippy boys who yesterday had been sprawling on the floor making peace signs and decorating themselves with love beads were suddenly standing at attention and bellowing the name of their general. In the middle of it was Berger himself, Doug, who had separated himself from Margo and was now standing stock still, staring straight ahead, like Patton about to address his troops.

"Women of the Tribe," Harry said with significance, "Who is your leader?"

The women did not answer as confidently as the men. It came out sort of like a question, "Berger?"

"Are you not sure, Women of the Tribe?" Harry chastised them. "Who is your leader?"

The women were ready this time. They still weren't as bombastic as the men, but when they answered, "Berger!" it sounded confident and more in unison.

Margo wasn't feeling like declaring Berger as her leader, and she wondered how many of the women felt the same. But like them, she opted to state her loyalty as clearly as she could. At least they all still had their clothes on.

"Men," Harry ordered, "Present your leader."

With emotionless faces, the men approached Berger/Doug. Berger threw his arms out in a Christ-like pose and two of the men took hold of his arms and lifted him up. Another bowed beneath him and put his head between Berger's legs. When he stood up, Berger was sitting on his shoulders and the men who had lifted up his arms were holding onto to his hands to steady him.

In a sort of parade, the men marched Berger around the room. The women moved back to make space for their pageant. Margo watched the procession and wondered if the men had spent all morning choreographing this little spectacle. She couldn't believe that they were really into it. Surely they were humoring Harry. But their eyes told her differently.

"Women!" Harry yelled proudly, "Cheer for your leader! Your hero! Make music! Congratulate him! Show him your appreciation!"

Now, there were women in the Tribe who were, for lack of a better word, idiots. They just didn't think. They drove Margo crazy. But they had an edge over Margo in a context like this. They could throw themselves into anything because their brains weren't involved. They were the instant lovers in the greeting ritual, the most sensitive givers and criers in the gift-giving ritual, and here, they were the immediately appreciative throng. With a hearty, "Ooooooh!" they swooped upon Berger and stroked his legs, overpowering his carrier who had to put him down and back away in the midst of the women's ardor.

The rest of the women became involved at their own speed. Around the edges of the Black Box, some of them discovered percussion instruments. There were little hand-held drums, tambourines and wooden blocks to hit together. Some of the more rhythmically inclined picked up the instruments and initiated a rhythm. The movers in the group, including Brandy, gyrated and sashayed around their leader. Someone got a chair for Berger and he sat there while the small band of adoring females stroked his arms, gave him a shoulder massage, rubbed his feet and occasionally venerated his face with little kisses. Brandy danced around him in an Indian goddess kind of way – with flexed bare feet and hands bent at the wrist in an "a-okay" kind of shape.

Margo felt detached as she watched the adoration. Suddenly, over her shoulder, she heard Harry's voice whisper to her, "Sheila, the women love your man. How does this make you feel?"

From her toes to the top of her head she felt cold grip her. How had Harry managed to sneak up on her like that? She took a deep breath to calm her nerves and give herself time to come up with a Sheila-like answer. Finally, not moving her eyes from Berger and the women, she said, with as much confidence as she could fake:

"Proud. Proud that he is my partner. I deserve no less."

"Excellent Sheila." She would have bet that Harry was smiling. He handed her a bongo drum from behind. "Help the rhythm."

She took the drum reluctantly. Then she sat on the floor cross-legged, put the drum between her legs, and started to beat on it, keeping her eyes on the activity around Doug. The women were dancing around their Berger, touching and stroking him. One of them sat on his lap, unbuttoned his shirt, pulled it open, tucked her arms around him, and planted a huge kiss on his lips. Berger returned her embrace and the two of them sucked face for a good while. Margo said, "Wow, look at the *acting!*" but it was inaudible above the noise in the room. There was Doug doing "anything" for his art. *Fuck this*, she thought. She did not enjoy watching her maybe-future boyfriend make this kind of acting breakthrough.

"Join in, Sheila," Harry said from behind her. She could feel his breath on the back of her neck. It reeked. Margo felt like retching.

She stopped drumming, swallowed and got a grip on herself.

"You forget," she announced, with more confidence than she felt, "I'm

Sheila. It wouldn't be proper for me to join the other women."

A few women turned to watch her and fell silent at her refusal to kowtow. Then they giggled and went back to the otherwise-engaged Berger.

"Very good, Sheila," Harry murmured. Margo felt him back away and she shuddered. She was struggling with how to stop the nonsense when an "Oooh!" came from the Tribe surrounding Doug/Berger.

"What the hell . . .?" Margo spat as Andrea entered the circle of love nymphs who were stroking Berger. Andrea stood before Berger and the other women backed away. Then she created an adulation ceremony all her own. First she closed her eyes and seemed to be feeling the rhythm of the drums. Then she began to dance and sway before him. She took off the silky vest she was wearing and used it like Salome would have used one of her veils. One of the men whistled. Berger smiled and nodded with approval.

"Berger Baby!" She swooned, prostrated herself before him and crawled toward Berger's feet.

The Tribe chanted "Berger Baby! Berger Baby! . . ."

"Oh please." Margo muttered. It was like a crazy dream. Andrea, Doug, flailing idiot women, the chanting. "What the hell is going on?"

In one of the most sensual and startling gestures Margo had ever seen, Andrea took one of Berger's big toes into her mouth and sucked on it. The chanting became more frenzied. Berger reached down, took Andrea by her upper arms and pulled her up until she was straddling his lap, facing him. Andrea paused for a second, then put her hands on his thighs and moved them down, between his legs and toward his crotch. Berger groaned.

Margo put her drum down and, without taking her eyes off of Doug and Andrea, she stood up. She was dizzy. She put her hand on the wall for support and felt her eyes brimming with tears. Her friend was seducing her man while she watched. After they had agreed to protect one another.

How can I stop this? She felt panicked and paralyzed. *Should I shout? Should I slap her? Or him?*

Margo made a move toward the panting couple when she saw Andrea, who seemed to be intensely involved in her seduction, turn her focus away from Berger to scan the room for a split second. *She isn't into it at all!* Margo realized. *She is "acting."* Margo followed her gaze and saw that she was looking at Harry, who turned abruptly and walked to the back of the room.

When Margo glanced back at Andrea, she had resumed her role as seductress. Margo searched for Harry again just in time to see him pass behind Jackson. Harry whispered something to Jackson. Jackson's eyes frightened her. They flashed pure unholy rage. *Is this an acting exercise? Or is something else going on?* When she tried to find Harry again, he was lost in the gloom.

Andrea let out a yelp and Margo saw that Berger had pulled her to his chest, holding her aggressively. The men hooted and whistled. Women drummed and danced and reached out to caress Berger, as though helping Andrea arouse him. To Margo, it seemed like Andrea was fighting Berger's embrace.

The drumming, the hooting, the dancing and the seduction crescendoed with bodies, hands, sounds and smells creating a delirium of eroticism. Berger seemed to become an animal. He grunted as he tore Andrea's shirt up over her head. She wasn't wearing a bra and the sight of her beautiful brown breasts standing erect before their leader threw the Tribe into a frenzy – except for three of them: Margo, who was feeling nauseous over what she was witnessing; Andrea, who was struggling to extricate herself from a display that had gotten out of control; and Jackson, who looked like he wanted to murder somebody.

Andrea locked eyes with Margo. Her face was contorted with terror and as Berger buried his face in her breasts, she mouthed, "Help me!" Then she shrieked and pushed at his forehead.

Behind Andrea's scream came a roar of fury that sounded like, "Fuckin' white asshole bastard! Think you can have anything you want?!" and Jackson charged into Berger's love circle. He pushed writhing women out of the way, before any of the other men could react, and pushed Andrea off Berger's lap. He seized Berger by the sides of his shirt and pulled him up from his throne. Berger's knees weren't ready to bear weight and he wobbled in a way that landed both of the men on the floor.

The men wrestled, creating a sweaty slick spot on the black-painted concrete floor. Women hustled to the edges of the room. Margo snapped out of her paralysis and ran over to Andrea who was struggling to put her blouse back on.

In the dark chaos, a gong sounded. Once, twice, three times a loud gong boomed from behind the black curtain at the back of the room. It gonged until the room was practically vibrating and everyone in the room froze.

Even Berger and Jackson stopped wrestling and scrambled to their hands and knees, breathing heavily, eyes wide.

From behind the curtain, Harry emerged, carrying what appeared to be a shrouded human body. He walked with slow dignity and people scrambled to make way for him, removing Berger's chair and backing away. When he reached the center of the room, he said, "Assist me." Two men jumped forward and helped him lower the body to the floor, arranging the shroud neatly over its form. The two men then backed away and Harry knelt beside the body.

No one spoke. The single candle sputtered and Margo saw confused and panicked faces in the dim flicker. Harry reached for the shroud at the head of the body and pulled it down, revealing the face. There were gasps around the room and a couple of women began to whimper. In the eeriness, the face appeared to be dead. It was the face of Jeremy — the unfunky opera singer who was growing as a performer and was becoming everyone's beloved friend.

Harry stood up and addressed the Tribe. "Behold our friend. Behold Claude. Claude did his duty. Claude obeyed his country's leaders. Claude left the Tribe. And Claude gave his life on the banks of the Mekong. On the banks of the Mekong he fell. Grieve for our friend. Grieve for our brother. Grieve for Claude."

Until that moment, Margo hadn't noticed that Jeremy had not been among the men in the room and hadn't been involved in the Berger love fest. She peered at him through the gloom and wondered if he really was dead. People were reacting as if he was and panic gripped her stomach again. Then she saw a twitch below Jeremy's nose and, concentrating on his chest, she saw that he was breathing. Okay. This is still an improv.

All around her, grieving was going on. In the midst of the moaning, Margo checked on Andrea.

"Are you okay?" she whispered.

"Yeah, I guess. I just feel stupid."

"What the hell were you doing?"

Andrea tucked in her blouse. "What Harry told me to do . . . fuck, I'll tell you later. Let's do this grieving shit and get this thing over with."

Margo was about to say something else when she glanced across the room and saw Harry glaring at her. He made a gesture that seemed to say, "Get back into the Improv!" Margo gritted her teeth. Maybe Sheila was okay with the free love thing, but Margo was furious. She wanted this travesty to end but didn't know how to manage it. Until she could think of what to do, she decided to grieve for Claude.

She moved to where Claude lay and knelt beside his head. She kissed his forehead, then lifted up his head and gently placed it in her lap. She felt the Tribe watching her. Summoning up her years of training, she became the Pieta. She stroked the face of the boy killed in Vietnam and a tear spilled down her cheek. A moan welled up inside of her and she became Medea, mourning for her dead children. "Claaaaaaude," she wailed and her body began to sway. Back and forth, back and forth, she swayed over the fallen soldier, moaning and crying, "Claude. My Claude. Oh God. Oh Claude." The rhyme surprised her and she fought the urge to snicker. She noticed Jeremy's dead lips struggling not to smile and she had to turn her head away in order to remain composed.

She took a breath and was back into it. Strangely, her tears did not feel phony. She was grieving. Grieving for the death of the fun-filled frolic she'd been enjoying for less than two weeks. She'd been having such a good time letting the world be safe and carefree and full of love. Now the world was sick and dangerous again. The same crazy man who had created the lovely happy universe she'd been experiencing had turned the world topsy-turvy and she blamed herself for letting down her guard. She had begun to trust. She had begun to love. She sobbed over the body of Claude, the sweet young kid who believed he was doing the right thing and had gotten killed.

Large hands gently placed themselves on Margo's shoulders and a shiver ran through her body. The hands became arms which embraced her from behind and she felt the body of a man pressing against her back. He held her and swayed with her for a moment, then in her ear she heard Doug's voice, "Shhh. It's okay. He's gone but we will never forget him."

"Get off of me!" she howled as she forced her arms out to push his embrace away. "Leave me alone!" She collapsed over the body of Claude.

Berger was stricken. "Sheila!" he said helplessly.

"What?" shrieked Sheila. "What do you want from me? He's dead because of you! You couldn't save him! He trusted you and now look." She stood up and faced him. "He trusted you!" She gestured to the Tribe which was standing around them silently watching. "We trusted you!"

The Tribe murmured assent in its unified grief.

Sheila went on. "You are supposed to be our leader. Where were you when Claude died? Making love with another woman? Bastard!"

She turned around because she couldn't stomach his confused expression. Harry was right there and she gasped with surprise. He handed her a big rubber ball. Like a playground ball. But harder. He said, "Use the ball."

She was confused for a second, then spun around and shrieked, "Fuck you, Berger! You say you care about people. Fuck you!" She threw the ball with enough force that she nearly fell over.

Mickey Mantle, she wasn't. The ball glanced off Doug's arm and he swatted it away. But it had surprised him and he stood stock still. His face became stern.

The Tribe encircled Berger and Sheila to watch the amazing scene of their fight. Someone had dragged Claude off to the side, or maybe he moved himself, not wanting to really get hurt. At any rate, he was sort of propped up in a corner of the Black Box, watching the sparks fly through partly opened eyes, as though he still wanted to appear dead. Jackson caught the ball on the other side of the circle and held it with a menacing smirk.

Harry's voice rose from behind Sheila raising the hairs on her neck, "Berger has failed. He has failed as your leader. Claude is dead. Berger must take responsibility. He must suffer. He must either prove himself again as your leader, or fail and be replaced."

A great nasty smile appeared on Jackson's face. Unlike Margo, he was a crack shot and he raised his arm to throw the ball. Andrea shrieked, "No!" but it was too late. He hurled the ball at Berger with a guttural sound. Berger had just enough time to turn his back and it bounced off one of his shoulder blades, making a hideous "Thwack!" Everyone in the room winced and Berger grunted at the sting.

Tony, whose brother had lost an arm in Vietnam, picked up the ball on the other side and pitched it at Berger with a mighty force shouting, "This is for my brother!" It bounced off of Berger's upper arm and left a distinct red mark. Berger gritted his teeth but didn't say anything.

The ball made its way around the circle, back and forth, making violent contact with Berger in the middle. Men and women both took the ball when it came to them and heaved it at their leader while flinging insults at him:

"You are no leader!"

"Don't you have any feelings?"

"Asshole!"

"Who do you think you are?!"

"Hypocrite!"

At each blow of the ball, Berger looked more and more like an animal. He didn't say a word, he just took it and took it. But his eyes were wild and vicious. It scared Margo. *What was happening to Doug?* The big red rubber ball was a torpedo in the hands of the men and Doug was hurting. The women weren't playing any more. They had moved out of the circle. *This had gone on long enough.* The point was made. But Harry wasn't stopping it.

She searched for him and found him seated on a folding chair with his hands behind his head, like Caligula watching the gladiators.

This has to stop, she thought. She tried to get the ball, but it never came back to her. She contemplated running in and shouting "Stop!" but she wasn't sure that would do it, and she didn't want to get hurt.

Then she heard Harry's voice, "Berger, you must pass on your leadership!"

This incited the men of the Tribe and Berger took a particular hard hit to the side of his head as one of the men yelled, "It's me!"

"Berger," Harry continued, "Who will carry on after you?"

Berger seemed confused. He seemed to be trying to figure out the "right" answer, but the pummeling continued, which appeared to make him more confused. Finally he said, "Claude. Except he's dead."

Men were shouting and throwing the ball, claiming the leadership of the Tribe.

Harry repeated his question, "Berger, who will carry on after you?"

Berger tried again. "The strongest man!" he said with forced bravado.

The men cheered, but this wasn't the right answer either.

Harry asked one more time. "Berger, who will carry on after you?"

Berger seemed at his wit's end. He had no more answers. He fell to the floor in a crouch and buried his face in his hands.

CHAPTER NINETEEN

Margo was frozen. She knew she had to do something. She couldn't just pull the covers over her head and pray to fall asleep. She looked at Doug and the angry faces around him. Suddenly it hit her. Unbelievably, Harry was still being "anthropological." She realized what Harry was asking. She had to push herself into this violent and very male scene and declare herself.

Harry bellowed, "Who will carry on after you, Berger?"

There was no time to think about it. Margo shoved a couple of men aside and made her way into the circle. The ball ricocheted off of Berger's back and landed in her arms. She held it high in the air and declared, "His son!"

Berger looked up from the floor with rage in his eyes. He seemed embarrassed and disgusted that Sheila, a woman, had come to his aid. He also seemed confused.

"What?!" bellowed Harry, apparently also flustered that a woman had entered his male game.

Sheila did not falter, "His son! His son will carry on after him. Berger's son."

Harry was on his feet and walking toward her. "And where will this son come from?" he asked her.

"From me. I am carrying his son."

The Tribe was struck dumb by this piece of news and Harry seemed at a complete loss for words himself.

Sheila stood there staring into Harry's face, daring him to do anything else to hurt her or her Tribe, challenging him to give one more dramatic suggestion that would throw this panting and sweating group into one more emotional frenzy.

A strange knowing smile spread over his face. He nodded at her in silent acknowledgement of her victory and stepped back two steps. Then he spoke:

"Congratulations, Sheila! Congratulations to you and your son! Go to your man and comfort him. Invite the Tribe to do the same. He has proven himself strong. He has proven himself worthy. He has given us a son."

Margo smirked at him and sighed. *Good one, Harry.*

She walked over to Doug. Berger didn't seem to want her comfort. But she persisted and put her arms around him and he let go, collapsing into them. She used the bottom of her blouse to wipe the sweat off his face and she stroked his hair. This was not a lovers' embrace. It was more parental; it was tribal. She looked up and invited the Tribe to comfort their leader.

"Sheila!" she heard Harry say, "Stand apart from the Tribe." Berger sat up and she stood up and backed away, wondering what the hell could possibly be next.

"Sheila, you are a powerful woman." *Damn right,* she thought. "Sheila, stretch your arms to the sky. Feel your power. Take in the universe."

Self-conscious as she felt doing this, Margo did what Harry suggested. She stretched her arms high above her head. *Okay,* she thought, *My Rocky moment.*

"Sheila, you have achieved what few women have achieved. You are to be congratulated."

Despite herself, Margo felt elated. She had been able to stand up to Harry and the men of the Tribe and end the Improv. She felt powerful.

Then she saw Doug who was being caressed by two of the idiot women. He looked small and beaten. He glanced up at her and she saw only bitterness there.

She turned her head and there was Harry, nodding at her. He waddled over to her and enveloped her in one of his famous bear hugs. She hugged him back and felt like Brutus. *If only I had a knife,* she thought.

The Improv wound down in a customary way for any improv. Harry told everyone to lie on the floor and breathe and relax and visualize what had happened in the Improv, to remember the feelings they'd felt, how they'd behaved, and so on. While they lay there in the dark he congratulated them.

"Bravo to you. Bravo to our Tribe. You've done good work today. You've seen your dark sides and come through to the light. You've fought and struggled and bonded together. I'm looking forward to seeing how you translate this experience to your work on the stage."

He paused. Margo could hear the Tribe breathing almost in unison. Harry's voice changed. It was less declaratory, more intimate. "I am convinced that this is the most creative, the most open cast I've ever worked with. I believe *Hair* is going to be the finest experience of my directing career."

Margo started to feel warmth spread through her chest. She was basking in Harry's compliments. Then she gasped and felt the cold chill again. *Fucking Harry! What a manipulator! I'm believing him!* And two questions banged in her skull:

What had gone on with the men that morning? and

Has Jen found out anything about Mike Matthews?

There was a third question she tried to ignore: *How will things be between Doug and me?* She was afraid she knew the answer.

Harry had the Tribe sit in a big circle for one more concluding rite, the vow. "I want to reiterate my beliefs about improvs. They are private and for the eyes and ears of the performers alone. You must be able to trust each other when exploring like you did today. We must promise each other that we will keep confidential what has gone on in the Improv. If we speak about it, it will dilute the experience. I urge you not to talk with each other about it either. Do you promise?" The Tribe members mumbled, "I promise. I do. Yes. . . ." Margo literally crossed her fingers behind her back. She felt like a third grader but she did it anyway.

Once set free from the Black Box, the Tribe barely spoke with one another. The men, in particular, were exhausted and as much as Margo wanted to snare Doug and grill him about the morning, she knew this wasn't the time. She walked a few paces behind him, thinking he might turn around and look for her. When he didn't, she stopped and waited for Andrea to catch up.

Before she could say anything, Andrea said, "Okay, Margo, can I talk with you later? I need to be alone for a little bit. I'm not feeling very well."

Margo nodded and slowed her pace so that Andrea could make her getaway.

Fine. Margo knew what she wanted to do. She made an about-face and headed for the stage door.

The carpenters, painters and electricians were hard at work getting the mainstage ready for the cast who would be fully rehearsing on the finished set starting Monday. Margo knew half the crew from her days of wielding hammers and paint brushes and she paused for a second to say hello and compliment this one's craftsmanship or that one's design.

Tim Delaney, the set designer and her former Stagecraft professor, yelled at her from across the stage, "Hey Margo, how do you like the jungle gym?"

She stopped before the gigantic tangle of bars, ramps and ropes and was amazed by the structure. "It's fantastic!"

"Only the best for our leading lady." He got up from his pneumatic nail gun, wiped his hands on his coveralls and lumbered over to her. "So how's it going? Are you happy?"

Margo was surprised by the question. Then she realized he meant the play.

"Oh, it's going great. It's going to be a big hit."

"Harry's amazing." Tim shook his head in admiration.

"Oh yes, he certainly is." Margo didn't think Tim caught her double meaning.

"So what are you going to do when you graduate?"

It was clear that the gregarious Mr. Delaney wanted a break from his day's work of set building and was preparing to dig in for a lengthy chat. As much as she enjoyed chewing the fat with the easy-going Tim Delaney, it was almost 3:30 and she wanted to find Jen and see what she'd found.

"I'm moving to New York. Who knows from there!" She laughed and poked him in the arm. "I'll send you my address so you can send me money!" She tip-toed downstage, to avoid pieces of lumber and metal, and reached the steps down to the audience level, talking all the while, "Keep up the good work. And make it strong. The guys in this cast are a bunch of apes. Hey, is it safe to go through the house?" She looked up at the "trapeze artists" who were hanging and aiming lighting instruments at a dizzying height above the red velvet seats of the audience.

"Sure," Tim assured her. "Just don't knock down any of the ladders."

"Ha ha," someone yelled from the ceiling.

"Thanks!" Margo yelled over her shoulder as she made her way to the back of the house.

Tim kept talking, "You going to the box office? 'Cause I don't think there's anyone back there."

"My friend is. I'm helping her. See ya!" Margo shouted from the back of the house then made her exit into the lobby.

The lobby was dark; only a few high windows barely illuminated it with the late afternoon sun. Margo suppressed an anxiety attack. "Dark rooms are beginning to freak me out," she whispered to no one as she stopped to breathe. She felt reassured when she heard the thunk-thunk of Tim Delaney's pneumatic nail gun from the stage. Then from a stairway to her left she heard a voice say, "Shit!" It was Jen. She found her way to the stairs that led to the Theatre Administration Office and picked her way down the dark staircase.

Jen's back was to her. She was hunched over a computer screen. Margo walked over to her and said, "How's it going?"

Jen jumped straight up out of her chair and screamed a husky scream. "Fuck! Oh fuck, it's you! You scared the crap outta me. I thought it was Rubenstein. Shit."

"Sorry."

"God, you almost gave me heart failure." Jen walked around in a circle holding her chest and breathing hard. "Okay. Okay, I feel my pulse returning to normal."

"You gotta quit smoking."

"You gotta quit sneakin' up on people." She coughed and sat back down, pulling a chair up for Margo. "Okay. I'm fine now. Hey, good to see you! You're alive."

Margo sat down beside her and nodded. "Barely."

"Oh shit. I just realized, if you're here, things must've been horrible."

"You could say that." And before Margo could get another word out, she started to cry. She hadn't realized that she even needed to cry, but once she started, she couldn't stop. She had felt so scared, so sickened, so angry, and felt so betrayed and so alone in that room that all she could do was weep.

Jen let her cry. She put an arm around her friend and stroked her shoulder. After Margo calmed down a bit Jen began to ask questions, "Did he hurt you?"

Margo shook her head from side to side.

"Did he make you do things you didn't want to do?"

"Sort of." Margo didn't know how to explain. She put her hands on her mouth.

"You wanna get Harry, don't you?" Jen asked with hopeful eyes.

Margo met her eyes and paused for a moment. "Yes. Yes I do," she said quietly.

"YES!" Jen shouted and high-fived Margo's hand. "He's a perverted shit! I knew it! I'm so excited." She got suddenly quiet. "Okay, can you tell me what happened?"

As briefly as possible, Margo related to Jen the highlights of the women's part of the Improv. She included her concern about the men and the unusual condition of Doug's chest hairs.

Jen winced at that information. "His chest hairs were hard and matted?"

"Yeah. And when I touched them he said it hurt."

"Ick." Jen made a face. "What else?"

"This will sound weird, but when I licked him, he tasted sweet."

Jen grimaced. "When you licked him?"

Margo cocked her head. "His skin felt sticky, so I made like I was kissing him, but I stuck my tongue out and licked him. He tasted sweet."

"Sweet. Like sugar?"

"Yeah, like candy, or syrup. Watered down maybe. Like he had bathed in sugar water or something."

"Maybe it was his cologne?"

"No, I don't think so. Who wears candy-flavored cologne? Besides, I think the same stuff that was on Doug's neck is what made his chest hairs stiff."

"Did you lick his chest hairs too?" Jen winced again.

"No, of course not." Margo sneered at her. "And it wasn't just the chest hairs and the sweet taste, Doug's whole demeanor was different."

"Like how?"

"Like he had been on a holy mission and had returned . . ." Margo spoke with mock importance, ". . . never to be the same again."

"Okay," Jen let out a long breath. "You've gotta ask him what happened. Do you think he'll tell you?"

"He said he'll tell me later. I hope so. I've got to find out what went on in the men's Improv." She paced back and forth. "At the end of the Improv, Harry made us promise not to tell anyone what went on . . ."

"And here you are breaking your vow again," Jen teased.

"I had my fingers crossed," Margo said like a snotty teenager.

"Oh good," said Jen with mock seriousness, "Now it's okay."

"Well, not only did most of us promise not to tell outsiders what went on," Margo continued, "But, Harry made us promise not to talk with our fellow Tribe members about what happened either. He said it would dilute our experience." Margo paused for a second. "I honestly don't know if Doug will go against Harry's will and talk with me."

"Uh huh." Jen said through squinty eyes. "He doesn't want anyone sharing their experience. There might be power in numbers to shut him down."

"I guess. The way it is now, no one is strong enough or sure enough to bring him down single-handedly."

"So you think he needs bringing down?"

"I'm not sure. There wasn't anything in the women's part of the Improv that was that bad really. Strange, but not really harmful."

"What about Andrea's shirt coming off?"

"No one could prove that Harry forced that to happen."

"So we really need to find out what happened with the men in the morning."

"Yes." Margo examined the computer screen. "And what happened with the men fifteen years ago. Have you found anything?"

"Oh." Jen spun around to face the computer. "I think I found the correct data base. Give me a second." Her fingers started hitting keys inexpertly and the computer whirred as screens blinked. While waiting for something to load, Jen asked, "Do you think any of the other men will talk?"

"I don't know. I'll have to sound them each out separately."

Jen nodded her head, staring at the screen. "See, this is the right one, I think." The screen froze. "Shit! That's what happened last time." She began banging on the keyboard.

"Let me try," Margo urged.

Margo and Jen switched places and the scientist in Margo took over. She hadn't actually worked much with computers, but her analytical mind was able to penetrate the logic of the database. After several wrong turns, she finally came to the list of subscribers. She scrolled down through the alphabetical list and landed on R. Michael Matthews. The name blinked inside its amber highlight.

"There it is," whispered Jen. "How do you get to his address?"

"I think I just press ENTER now." She did. The hard drive whirred and even squeaked a little, then his name appeared on the screen again, with an address. The phone number said "Unlisted."

"Oh my God. You did it. You did it! There he is." Jen squeezed her shoulders from behind. She reached across Margo to the pen and paper on the desk and scribbled down the information. "God, he only lives about an hour away."

Margo stared at the screen. She noticed a prompt at the bottom of the page. FOR MORE, HIT ENTER. She hit ENTER.

The hard drive did its gymnastics again and another page appeared on the screen. It said:

INFO: FORMER STUDENT, THEATRE, CLASS OF '70
DON: ANNUAL COMMITMENT
TKT: H101, LAST SAT

Jen squinted at the screen. "What's all that?"

"Well," Margo thought about it. "The first line is easy. In the second line I would guess that 'DON' means 'donation' or 'donor' and that Mr. Matthews gives annually."

"Uh huh." Jen nodded. "What about 'TKT: H101, LAST SAT?'"

They were both silent for a second. Then Margo got it.

"It's his seat number! 'TKT' means 'ticket' and 'H101' is his seat for all the shows!"

"Of course." Jen said excitedly. "Then 'LAST SAT' must mean he comes to the last Saturday performance of every show."

They looked at each other and said simultaneously,

"Closing night!"

"So Mike Matthews will be at closing night of *Hair*. H101 is right on the aisle in the middle section."

"He's got a good seat." Margo conceded. "And only one. I guess he's not married or anything."

"Hey, back away for a sec, will you?" She practically pushed Margo out of the seat in front of the computer.

Jen began typing awkwardly, but the screens were moving under her touch. Eventually she reached a prompt which said, "HOUSE DIAGRAM?" She pushed "Y" and up came a graphical representation of the audience section of the theatre. Some of the seats were a bright amber box, others were outlined boxes.

"Wow, *Hair* is really selling well." Jen said hitting the PAGE DOWN button over and over again as the days of *Hair*'s run flipped by. Finally, the diagrams stopped shifting and a little bell rang five times. "Voila," said Jen, "closing night."

Margo and Jen leaned forward to see the tiny seats better. Jen was able to enlarge a small section of the audience.

"Look," said Margo, "H101 is all lit up."

"Yep," Jen agreed, "someone is sitting there. And most of the seats around H101 are taken too. Now watch this."

Jen pointed to K5, a seat across the aisle and up a few rows from H101, which was just an outline. Jen pushed a button and K5 suddenly became solid glowing amber.

"And now," Jen said proudly, "someone will be sitting in K5 too."

"You?"

"Of course. I'll pick up my ticket later." She leaned back in her chair with her hands clasped behind hear head. "It pays to have friends in high places."

Suddenly, Margo felt a chill. She had to get out of the theatre building. "Okay. We're done. Let's go."

"Wait, we're not done. We've still got to look for a photo."

Margo couldn't concentrate. "A photo?"

"Yes. Of Mike Matthews in *Death of a Salesman*. I need to know what he looks like." She walked to a bank of file cabinets on the wall behind them. "Here are the archives."

Alan Rubenstein was nothing if not efficient. The file cabinets were neatly marked and the first two, which contained financial information and lists of the subscribers and donors, were locked. The last three cabinets, which held publicity material from as far back as 1960, were not locked.

"Hot dog!" Jen exclaimed as she opened one of the drawers.

Margo's fears dissipated as she opened a drawer of her own and began to thumb through photographs and programs from plays gone by. The earliest photos were in black and white. Otherwise, they could have been photos from last week. College actors in Shakespearean dress or as characters from *Our Town* or *Oklahoma* look pretty much the same no matter what the decade. Only the "modern" plays dated a file and it was great to see the kids of the mid-60s looking very "real" in *Bus Stop, Who's Afraid of Virginia Woolf?* or *A Thousand Clowns.* Margo knew she was searching for something specific, but she couldn't resist thumbing through this history of her college's theatre.

Jen remained focused on her detective work and she located 1969.

"What a season." she said. "In 1969, they did *Harvey, Death of a Salesman*, as we know, *The Tempest* and *A Funny Thing Happened on the Way to the Forum.*"

Margo craned her neck to see into the file drawer that Jen had pulled out. "Let me see. Where's *Death*?"

"Right here," Jen said quietly as she pulled out a manila envelope. They opened it carefully and pulled out a dozen or so photos. Some of them were black and white and some of them were color.

"Okay," said Margo pointing. "So that would be Biff, right, and that guy there is Happy?"

"I think so." Jen turned the photo over. "Here, it's written on the back. Yeah, 'Robert Armstrong as Biff and Mike Matthews as Happy in *Death of a Salesman.*'"

The two of them studied the face of the man they were trying to locate.

Jen said, "I wonder how different he looks today."

Margo rooted through the file. "Hey, here's the *Utterance* article on Scott Warren."

Jen looked at it. "Wow, the photo is much better here than in the microfilm thing I had."

They studied his face. "God, he looks a little like Doug," Margo said, feeling cold.

Jen pulled the article closer, "Shit, he really does."

Margo shook her head. "How could they have gone on and done the play anyway after he died? It must've been so weird."

"Yeah," Jen agreed. "I mean, if someone from *Hair* committed suicide tonight, would you want to go on and do the play?"

Margo scowled at her friend. "I don't think I'm going to answer that."

"Sorry."

In silence, they examined the rest of the photos in the file, then carefully put them back in the envelope and returned them to the drawer.

Just as Jen was shutting the drawer, they heard a noise from behind them. Jen slammed the drawer shut and she and Margo turned around as though they were jewel thieves caught in a heist.

"Mr. Rubenstein?" Jen asked haltingly.

"Who's in here?" a high-pitched male voice asked.

Margo recognized the eunuch voice before the man rounded the corner. She looked for some place to hide. It was too late. Harry came into view and approached the two women.

"Margo? Is that you?"

"Yes, Dr. Adler." What the hell made her call him "Dr. Adler" she just didn't know.

"What are you doing here?" He sounded suspicious and ominous and blaming. Or so Margo thought.

Jen got perky. "Oh, hi Harry! I work for Alan Rubenstein in the box office and he asked me to do a little housekeeping this weekend."

"And, uh, I'm just here to keep her company, then we're going to walk home together." Margo wasn't sure she was sounding sincere, so she added, "We live in the same dorm."

"Oh." Harry seemed less ominous. "Is Alan here?"

"No," said Jen. "Just me. He gave me the key." She held it up to show him.

"I see." He waved his hand. "Never mind. I just wanted to talk with him about some comps I need for my wife and kid."

Jen walked over to him. "You can tell me and I'll leave him a note."

"I think I'll just talk with him on Monday. Thank you anyway." He turned to go, then turned around again. "Margo, excellent work today."

"Thank you, Harry," Margo said, her heart still pounding.

They waited in silence until they were sure he was gone. Then Margo whispered:

"What were we saying just before he walked in?"

"I don't know." Jen scrunched up her face. "I don't think it was anything bad."

"Let's get the hell outta here." Margo ran to the desk and gathered up her things.

"I'm with you." Jen turned off the computer, gathered her stuff and ran after Margo.

CHAPTER TWENTY

After the big freaky Improv, rehearsals for *Hair* continued almost as if it had never happened. No one spoke of it. Songs and scenes were solidified. The cast moved to the mainstage and worked and reworked the play there until it flowed. In the tech rehearsals, the lights, slides and special effects were all added and made to work. The orchestra joined the process the final week before opening. Finally, hippy costumes, jewelry, wigs and make-up were added. The play finished its gestation and became ready for birth before its first audience.

Margo stared at her face in the make-up mirror. It was opening night of *Hair*, and she was feeling all the conflicting emotions actors feel before a first curtain. Am I ready? I'm so excited! Will I be good enough? I'm gonna be fabulous! Will the audience like the play? The play rocks! Will they like me? I'm a star!

The wreath of break-a-leg cards she had taped around the edge of her mirror was full of good wishes and heartfelt kudos from Tribe members who had "so enjoyed working with such an accomplished actress . . ." But they told only part of the story of what she was feeling on this opening night.

As Margo applied her eyeliner, she wished that she was simply feeling opening night jitters. Her jitters were far beyond the scope of *Hair* and she was beginning to wonder if she would be able to abide by the instructions of the great Russian acting teacher, Stanislavski, to "Never come into the theatre with mud on your feet." She knew she needed to clear her mind and leave her confusions and problems "outside" in order to perform well. She had tried to silence the noise in her brain while she did her physical and vocal warm-ups before arriving at the theatre. But sitting here now, examining her face in the make-up mirror, she thought, *I don't look like the confident Sheila at all. C'mon face, get it together.*

She could not shake the big question – what to do about Harry? None of the men had confessed to Margo what had gone on in the men's Improv. It was over two weeks ago now. Were they being true to their vow of confidentiality? Were they too embarrassed to talk about what had gone on? Neither had Jen heard from Mike Matthews after writing him two letters, the second with Margo's input. Margo was due to graduate in one month. She could just leave this school and never think about Harry again.

In fact, based on what she herself had experienced in her part of Harry's *Hair* improvs, there was nothing really to warrant bringing up any grievance against him. Okay, it was freaky and creepy and intense, but no one had really been hurt, had they? The worst thing she had seen was Andrea's blouse being pulled off. When she and Andrea finally talked about it, Andrea seemed all right.

"Shit, girl. When Harry said, 'There's your White Boy. Go get him!' in the Improv, I don't know where it came from, but I thought, *Okay Fat Man – Watch this! I am an actor. I can do this.* And I threw myself into it. And part of me wanted to be as ridiculous as could be – so I sucked Doug's toe – for pity's sake! But when he pulled me up and seemed to be turned on for real? – I kinda freaked out. I mean, I was still playing along, y'know?, while trying like hell to figure out a way out of my situation. Then Doug pulled my shirt off. Then Jackson got into it. And the rest is history. But now, shit, now that it's over – it doesn't seem so bad. Believe it or not, the Improv actually kinda worked for me. I mean, now, when I sing 'White Boys,' I feel more real somehow. I feel sorta proud that I could turn that white guy on like I did. Am I totally messed up – or what? I mean, I can see what improvs can do."

Margo had nodded. It's what everyone always says once it's over. But Andrea was different. She was freer, more confident and more of a tease in her song since the Improv. She was still playful, but she had a dash of rage and black pride that added depth and heat to her performance. Because of the Improv.

So, it could be argued that the Improv had helped the play. The show had a new intensity and an edge that hadn't existed among the happy hippies of the Tribe before the Improv. Characters were fleshed out. *Hair* was working. It was the dynamic, forceful kind of play that Harry was known for, and the Tribe members were talking among themselves about how they suspected that the audiences would be blown away.

If everything was so peachy keen, why was Margo feeling so bad? "Ah shit!" she swore as she blinked and sent a big black blob of mascara onto her cheek. She grabbed a Q-tip to swab it off and started over in that spot. Events of the past two weeks played over in her head as she re-applied her base make-up.

First there was the "coming out" of the Italian Stallion, Tony "Big-Hair" Zampino. At the first gift-giving ritual after the Improv, Tony stood up with tears in his eyes and gave a "gift" of thanksgiving to the whole Tribe for enabling him to confess something he wasn't sure he had wanted to, but knew he did now. And he told them that he was gay. A shocked surprise registered among the Tribe members, then people fell over one another to congratulate him, hug him and thank him for his honesty and courage. Harry too, looking just like a proud papa.

After that, it was suddenly cool to be openly gay. Jeremy/Claude, who up to that point had neither hidden his homosexuality nor "pushed it," became something of a beacon for the other gay men (or "gay wannabes?" she wondered). They became a clique and took on almost stereotypical gay behavior – calling each other "Hon" and "Girl" and irritating some of the more macho men. Especially Doug, it seemed to Margo.

She found it somewhat disturbing, especially since the change in attitude came right on the heels of the big Improv. But she was also impressed with the dynamics that the now fearlessly gay men added to the diversity of the play. Gay actor Robert Lipscomb, who played Woof, gave "Sodomy" a whole new depth thanks to the new openness in the cast. And when Steve Milburn sang about how *"longer hair and other flamboyant affectations of appearance are nothing more than the male's emergence from his drab camouflage into the gaudy plumage which is the birthright of his sex,"* the Tribe was thrown into hysterics at his un-self-consciously drag impersonation of anthropologist Margaret Mead.

Jeremy himself was stronger in all aspects of his performance. Being respected for being gay seemed to buoy his confidence. And the experience of "dying" in the Improv seemed to have affected him deeply. When he sang *"Where do I go? Follow my heartbeat. Where do I go? Follow my hand. Where will they lead me? And will I ever discover why I live and die?"* – Margo loved to close her eyes and feel her chest burn with compassion for this man in this moment. It was a thrill joining in on the chorus part and connecting with the powerful intensity he created with the simple lyrics, his beautiful voice and his loving spirit.

Where earlier in rehearsals the Tribe had melted into one big happy family-soup, the post-Improv Tribe was splitting off into factions exerting their group identities. The gay group was one example; the black group was another.

Jackson, in particular, had developed an angry edge to his performance. It was as though he had an awakened personal stake in civil rights. His songs, "Colored Spade" and "Abie Baby" were full of spit and venom, some of it leveled directly at Berger/Doug, Margo noticed. He was reading a book about the Black Panthers and had taped pictures of Malcolm X to his make-up mirror. His newfound black anger made his character, Hud, darker and scarier. It added a militant racial edge the play needed.

On a different note, Jackson completely surprised Margo with an act of *Hair*-appropriate defiance. A couple of rehearsals after the Improv, during the song "Black Boys," the black men in the show were strutting their stuff in front of the three crooning white women when Jackson broke rank and climbed up to the platform where Margo was doing a little boogie. He held her and danced rather sexually with her, eventually dipping her like a tango master and kissing her quite passionately. When he released her, Margo was dizzy as she watched him jump off the platform to the hoots of the Tribe. It may have been some kind of display for the benefit of Doug and Andrea, but its effect had been more than momentary. Jackson "apologized" later with a big beautiful smile and a wink, and a friendship began to develop. Once, while walking across campus, Margo found herself singing and giggling: *"Black boys are delicious, chocolate flavored love . . . I have such a sweet tooth when it comes to love!"*

Jackson walked into the co-ed make-up room at that moment and caught Margo's eye in her mirror. He gave her a thumbs up, flashed her one of his contagious smiles and mouthed "Break a leg" across the room. Margo smiled back and nodded, then quickly moved to touch up the mascara that didn't need touching up at that point.

Right behind Jackson, Doug arrived in the make-up room. He seemed hyped up and energized, as though he could have climbed straight up the wall like Spiderman. He came over to Margo and bent over her, saying "Break a leg" as he placed a single red rose in a bud vase in front of her mirror. Margo got up and hugged him, saying "Break a leg to you too" into his ear. They held each other for a good moment, speaking encouragements. Doug: "I want you to know how great it has been working with you and I'm really looking forward to tonight." Margo: "I've enjoyed working with you too and the play is gonna be wonderful." They pulled apart and smiled at each other. They'd shared a lot during rehearsals and tonight was the moment of truth. She noticed he only mentioned the play.

Doug squeezed her hands and said, "I'd better get ready. Knock 'em dead, my Sheila." And he gave her a quick kiss on the mouth.

"Kick ass yourself, Berger," said Margo and she swatted his butt. She watched him straddle his seat at his mirror and open the first in the small pile of break-a-leg cards waiting for him. Her heart was pounding with what? – lust? fear? pride? sympathy? jealousy? Argh! Indecision!

Since the Improv, there had been a change in Doug's character as well. Berger was still full of energy and enthusiasm and wacky good fun. But there was an added dimension. An intensity that hadn't been there before. He was a more angry war protester, a more violent draft dodger, a less passive hippy. He was more of a leader to be sure. The character was fleshed out.

The Improv seemed to have worked for Margo's Sheila too. Sheila was more at ease with Berger and exhibited a more fiery desire for him. She also found it simple now to sing the Berger/Sheila betrayal song, "Easy to be Hard." All Margo had to do was conjure up images of Doug groaning as he was being slobbered on by other women and the words came out easily: *"How can people have no feelings? You know I'm hung up on you! . . . Easy to be hard. Easy to be cold."*

Yes, the Improv had been good for Berger and Sheila.

But had it been good for Doug and Margo?

For Margo, the last two weeks with Doug had been a strain. Something had changed in him since the Improv. He wasn't the happy-go-lucky sweet southern gentleman he had been before with her. Berger's newfound on-stage intensity remained with Doug off-stage and he became somehow distant. His fabulous smile and twinkling eyes made their appearance less frequently. He became something Margo hadn't seen before. Moody. Like there was something disturbing or distracting him.

Margo tried several times to ask him what had gone on in the men's part of the Improv and his answer was always the same, "I'll tell you later." At least he didn't say that he would never tell her. She just didn't know when "later" was.

She did know one thing. There would not be a relationship with Doug after the play. That was clear. The little spark of affection they had shared had been snuffed out. Doug no longer teased her about "after the play" and Margo felt her school girl crush break into tiny pieces and blow away. Bringing her an opening night rose was a lovely gesture, but it was performed perfunctorily.

Looking back in the mirror, Margo drew a little peace sign in blue make-up on her left cheek. She impulsively drew a little blue tear below her eye, but then she quickly wiped it off.

There was a bustle of activity at the door to the make-up room and Margo was startled out of her concentration by the arrival of an ostentatious arrangement of flowers that was placed next to her. Several Tribe members came over to see who they had come from. Margo opened the little florist card and read, "Break a leg in your last college show! We love you. Mom and Dad." The Tribe said, "Ahhhh!" in unison and returned to their make-up. Margo moved the flowers next to Doug's rosebud.

Her parents and sister were supposed to be in the audience this evening. They always came to her opening nights. Her mother would be as excited as could be for Margo; her dad would be looking forward to Alan Rubenstein's post-play cocktail party; her sister would be itching to go home. Margo didn't want to have to deal with them.

She hadn't seen them since Christmas and she knew her dad was still drinking and her mom hadn't done anything about it except occasionally cry to Margo on the phone. She didn't want them becoming a part of *Hair*. This play was not for them. Yet there they would be.

Opening night was always a strange phenomenon, Margo had come to learn. Up to that point, the play belonged to the cast and crew. No outsiders were allowed to visit and observe and be a part of it. It was a precious, fragile ornament that was reserved for the performers. With the arrival of the audience on opening night, the play became public.

She knew that a play wasn't a play until it was placed before an audience. But she couldn't help feeling like she was being served up to a hungry throng. It was even called "public consumption" for heaven's sake. The paradox of the artist. The work is private and personal and delicate; yet it must be viewed and consumed and critiqued by the public. A delicious yet horrible thing.

She exhaled and tried to shake these thoughts from her mind. This was opening night! She would normally be excited and thrilled and full of joyous anticipation. She loved opening nights. She loved displaying her wares before an audience. What was this morose crap?

She inhaled deeply and filled her lungs with the smell of the greasepaint. She closed her eyes and listened to the animated chatter of her fellow Tribe members. Through her closed eyelids she could see the filtered light from the bright bulbs of the make-up mirror. She brought her focus to the center of her gut. She felt the butterflies. Her career Air Force dad loved to impart words of wisdom, and once he had said to her, "Butterflies in the stomach are good, if you make them fly in formation." She inhaled deeply again – visualized her butterflies as fighter pilots, said to herself, *Tonight is about the play. Let the other shit go for now. Right now, I'm Sheila.* She opened her eyes and there she was – the hippy leader, the student protester, the powerful confident woman. Sheila.

She went into the dressing room and joined the other women of the Tribe who were taking off their 80s-wear to don patched-up bell bottoms and halter tops. The talk was pure excitement – who would be in the audience, how many newspaper reviewers would be there, how sick to her stomach someone felt. Margo put on Sheila's costume, beads, the heart pendant, and completed her transformation. Her voice was warmed up, her muscles were primed, her clothes, make-up and hair were groovy. She was ready.

At fifteen minutes to curtain, her anxieties had vanished and she was consumed with the kind of thrill that only opening nights in the theatre can produce. She emerged from the dressing room and hoofed it to the green room, the room (not painted green) where the actors awaited their cues. Tribe members were saying "Break a leg!" to each other when Harry arrived for his opening night speech.

The Tribe held hands in a big circle and became quiet. With eyes closed, they listened to Harry remind them to trust one another, to give to one another and to the audience, and to remember that they were a tribe of individuals. Each individual contributes to the whole; the whole does not diminish the individual. They were not a melting pot. They were a tossed salad.

With that bit of silliness, the Tribe laughed, opened its eyes and gazed at Harry with adoration.

Finally, Harry told them he loved them.

CHAPTER TWENTY-ONE

When the Moon is in the Seventh House and Jupiter aligns with Mars,
Then peace will guide the planets and love will steer the stars!

The Age of Aquarius dawned gloriously in Hancock Theatre with a cast of Tribe members who were wholly, completely, absolutely and fabulously committed to delivering the clearest, funniest, funkiest and bravest performance of *Hair* ever produced in the history of the universe.

When Margo heard the music begin to pulse from the orchestra pit with the rockin' space music that was the beginning of "Aquarius," she felt giddy, light headed. Nothing, she believed, nothing else felt like this moment, standing in the wings waiting to go on stage, and hearing the first strains of the orchestra.

She peered out and saw Jeremy/Claude sitting cross-legged in the middle of the exposed stage. Then she watched the graceful Brandy ceremoniously place a large bowl in front of Claude, light a match and throw it into the bowl. A huge flame leapt out of the bowl, but Claude didn't budge. The rock vamp continued and Tribe members emerged from all parts of the set and from the back of the house to move through the audience toward the stage. At one point in the music, they froze. This was Margo's cue.

From opposite sides of the stage, Berger and Sheila entered and walked slowly to where Claude was sitting. Berger handed Sheila a pair of scissors. Sheila reached out for Claude's hair and cut off a lock, held it up high for all to see, and threw it into the fire which leapt again. Claude was thus established as the sacrifice, and the Tribe circled around him. From the middle of the circle, the golden throated Paul Rodriquez emerged, and to the delight of everyone in the theatre he crooned the lyrics that promise: *"Harmony and understanding / Sympathy and trust abounding / No more falsehoods or derisions / Golden living dreams of visions / Mystic crystal revelation / And the mind's true liberation / Aquarius."*

It had begun – everything from that moment on simply worked. The audience was electrically charged too. They seemed eager to embrace with open arms and hearts the hi-jinks of the high energy cast. For two and a half magical hours, the theatre was like a gigantic lung, breathing in and out with a unified breath. Together the cast and the audience romped and played and teased and fought and died together. The play achieved what theatre was supposed to achieve. It was catharsis. As one prosaic reviewer put it later, "There were cheers, there were tears." Basically, the audience seemed to be having a hell of a good time.

So did Margo and the Tribe. All the hard work, all the bonding, all the fun and fears they had shared, and all that youth and talent congealed in what every director dreams of – a perfect performance. They achieved that paradoxical balance between spontaneity and restraint. It was controlled mayhem, rehearsed impulsiveness, chaotic order. Most of all, it was truthful. The performance, for all of its lunacy and improbability and irreverence, never went off the deep end. Like serious children at play, no one was trying too hard or holding back from going full out.

The set was the perfect playground for the boisterous Tribe, who swung on ropes over astonished audience members, climbed like monkeys on a gigantic erector set, and became enveloped in fog which covered the stage at opportune times. The lighting was dramatic. Especially powerful was the blue wash that covered the actors as they were "Walking in Space," "tripped out" on drugs.

One of the last elements to be added to the production was the slide show. On a huge screen that was stretched behind and above the jungle gym set, the slides from the 60s appeared at powerful moments. During one evening rehearsal, the Tribe had been able to sit and watch all of the slides and it was a mind-blowing experience. The famous photo of the child putting a flower in a soldier's gun was there, as was the frightening image of the young woman screaming with her arms outstretched at Kent State, and the photo of the terrified Vietnamese girl running naked in abject fear, which Margo thought she remembered from *Life* magazine.

The photos which stunned the Tribe the most were the ones from their own campus. The National Guard marching on the great lawn in front of the Graduate Library; German Shepherd dogs baring their teeth at flower children; protesting students blocking the state highway on the edge of campus and being beaten by police; smoke bombs being launched at a campus gathering; an angry young man in the middle of a riot flashing his middle finger, his mouth forming an obvious "F" as he cursed at the photographer. To them, the present student body, this college was a safe and carefree place where apathetic students pursued degrees in accounting so they could get a good job. To see their own campus pitched to the edge of war shocked them, and shamed them because they themselves were not so motivated or politically active. It inspired the Tribe to make *Hair* all the more meaningful – their generation's contribution to the social good.

Finally, it was the music, those crazy, stupid, brilliant songs that carried the show. Some audience members couldn't help but sing along and dance in the aisles. It was a Be-In!

Each song hit its mark. From "Aquarius" to "Let the Sun Shine In," the singers took the stage, embraced their moment in the spotlight and flung five weeks' worth of practice and growth into their musical numbers. Jackson was especially brilliant and black members of the audience could be heard vocalizing their reactions to him, "Sing it, brother!" "You said it!"

Andrea was a hit, as Margo had expected. Her gutsy, hilarious rendition of "White Boys" was rewarded with huge applause.

Jeremy's Claude was right on. He still wasn't much of a mover, but an actor had been born in this opera singer and, from dreaming of being somebody else in "Manchester England" to returning from the dead to speak a warning in "The Flesh Failures," he embodied the confused young man of the day who wanted to do the right thing for a nation making grave mistakes. Margo wondered if there were any Vietnam vets in the audience.

Finally, Margo couldn't help but feel enormous pangs of affection for Doug as she watched him perform Berger. Whatever had made her think, way back at the beginning of rehearsals, that he wasn't right for the role? She was mesmerized as she watched him and felt him seduce the audience and the Tribe . . . and her. Sheila was madly in love with Berger, that was for sure, and "Easy to Be Hard" floated out of her on the same waves that Margo herself felt because she knew they wouldn't be a couple in real life.

The play was cathartic for her and by the time she was standing full front to the audience singing with all her might at play's end "Let the sun shine! Let the sun shine in!" she felt that totally filled, yet completely depleted feeling she always felt at the end of a play. Times ten.

Sweating and high on themselves, the Tribe stood at the front of the stage for their curtain call. The audience rewarded them with roaring approval and jumped to its unified feet in a full-throttle standing ovation.

Margo knew there would be few moments in her life that would match this one. She knew enough to savor it.

CHAPTER TWENTY-TWO

Fresh from a shower and feeling light and lovely in her opening night post-play finery, Margo walked with Andrea from the basement make-up room to the theatre lobby where the cocktail party was in full swing. This was not a cast party. That would come on closing night. Tonight was Theatre Administrator Alan Rubenstein's affair. He always invited the cast so that his subscribers could brush up against them and feel the special thrill of really "knowing" the actors and be more inclined to subscribe again next year. The cast came because there was free food and alcohol.

While she would rather have been at Crib Notes enjoying an ice cream sundae with a few of the cast members jawing about how the play had gone, Margo didn't really mind attending Rubenstein's little soirée. She'd been to several of them since she began getting leads in the Department. She mostly enjoyed being swooped down upon by the mostly-heavy-set, bedazzled, overly-perfumed theatre patrons who gave her a hug and a compliment and wanted some bit of wisdom about how she had achieved her stellar performance. Like the classic question, "How did you memorize all those lines?!" And she took pleasure in chatting with any reviewers who wanted a quote from her. She didn't even mind it when Alan Rubenstein squeezed her upper arm and said, "Marvelous job, my dear," while wrinkling his nose and giving her a knowing wink.

Tonight, she felt especially blissful because, twenty minutes earlier, in the heat of the spotlight as she stepped forward for her curtain call and felt applause and approval beaming at her from the audience, Margo had made a decision. She had decided to do nothing with regard to Harry. The end clearly justified the means. *Hair* was a hit. More than a hit, it was a triumph. She could find no fault in either the individual performances or the ensemble work. All of the levels were there, all perfectly orchestrated and felt, thanks to the genius of Dr. Harrison P. Adler. If only she had trusted him from the start, she could have enjoyed the process so much more. As it was, she didn't think she could have enjoyed opening night any more. Her college swan song was a joy. And she had Harry to thank for it.

She felt so buoyantly ecstatic, she was even looking forward to seeing her family.

She and Andrea heaped praises upon each another as they made their way to the theatre lobby.

"Girl, you were hot tonight! I could feel your guts when you sang to your man."

"Well, your 'White Boys' brought down the house, just like I thought."

"Shit. It felt great. It felt fuckin' great!"

"Does it make you want to become an actor?"

Andrea paused, then nodded her head. "I can't believe it, but yeah. Even after all the shit with Harry. Hell. It was worth it!"

Margo stopped her by touching her arm. "It was, wasn't it?"

Andrea smiled and shrugged. "I think it was."

They started walking again. "Do you think the men are feeling the same way?"

"What do *you* think?" Andrea said, pointing ahead to a colorful scene in the lobby just ahead. Doug was holding a drink and laughing very loudly as he tousled Harry's patchy hair for two subscribers. They could hear him saying, "How could a man with this hair direct *Hair?*" The delighted subscribers guffawed.

Andrea shook her head. "Let's get a drink."

As Margo headed for the bar to get a Diet Coke, she heard the familiar Mary-Tyler-Moore voice behind her, "Margo! There you are! Margo!"

She turned around. "Mom!" She was smartly put together, as usual, with a powder blue dress Margo remembered her wearing to Christmas mass, a gold necklace-and-earring set, and lipstick that looked freshly applied. It looked like she'd gotten her hair done that afternoon with the poofy perm she'd worn since the early 60s. Only the puffiness around her eyes betrayed the stress she was under. Margo held her arms out for the inevitable hug.

"You were so good. I can't believe you're my daughter! The play was really good. I didn't think I'd like *Hair*, but I did! Though I'm so glad you didn't have to go nude!"

Margo grabbed Andrea, who was trying to make an escape. "Mom, this is Andrea. Andrea, my mom."

She shook hands with Margo's mom and dropped her black chick lingo to say, "How do you do, Mrs. Laughton."

Margo's mom smiled graciously. "Nice to meet you, Andrea. You know, you blacks were very good in the show too."

Margo froze at her mother's attempt at racial civility. Andrea glanced at Margo with a "what can you do?" expression.

She said, "Thank you Mrs. Laughton. It was a great opportunity for us blacks."

Margo almost laughed out loud.

"Yes it was, Andrea. Yes it was. And I think it's high time there were more parts for black people. Because blacks are such talented performers. I just love Sammy Davis, Jr. And Sidney Poitier was just wonderful in *To Sir With Love*."

Margo couldn't take it anymore. "Where's Dad? And Bridget?"

Margo's mom scanned the room. "Oh, they're here somewhere." She started to sound worried. "Somewhere. It was nice meeting you, dear. Margo, help me find your father."

"Sure, Mom." Margo's mom had already rushed off and Margo turned to Andrea. "Can you carry on without me?"

"I'll muddle through somehow," said Andrea, patting her back.

Margo grimaced and said, "Tally ho!" as she went after her mom.

When she caught up, her mother said, "I don't understand. He was right behind me."

"There's Bridget." Margo pointed to a corner of the room where her lovely still-in-high-school sister was listening spellbound to the conversation of two handsome actors. Margo walked up to them.

"And here's my sweet little sister."

Bridget feigned a smile and gave her sister a hug. "Congratulations, you were wonderful!" Then quietly in Margo's ear, "Shut up with the 'little sister' stuff, will you?"

One of the attentive actors said, "I didn't know there was such beauty in your family, Margo."

Bridget was the jewel of the family. She was tall and slender with blond hair that was long and thick. She had a cover girl smile that made men's knees weak. Margo had gotten used to thinking of herself as the tomboy nerd and her sister as the feminine beauty. Even after losing her teenage gawkiness and getting a nose job, Margo still felt like the ugly duckling of the family. *Shit,* she thought, *Let it go!*

"Ha ha ha." Margo turned to Bridget. "Where's Dad?"

"He went outside for a smoke."

Margo pulled her away from the ears of the eager suitors. "Is he drinking?"

"Of course he's drinking. And Mom is just about holding it together. The ride home is going to be swell."

Despite her cocky outward appearance, Margo could tell that her sister was worn down by the tension between her parents. They weren't the best of friends, but Margo and Bridget were bonded by a childhood of shared stress.

"I'm sorry you've had to deal with all of this alone," Margo said sincerely.

"Yeah, yeah, yeah. I know you're busy being the Star." Her voice was venomous and Margo felt herself blush with shame.

"C'mon, Mom." Margo turned back to her mother who was digging anxiously in her purse. "I need a tranquilizer," her mother mumbled.

Margo took her mother's arm and led her out of the lobby and into the chilly spring evening. There on the steps to the theatre was her dad. He was holding a drink and a cigarette and staring off into the night sky. For all of his gregarious Irish charm and gift of the gab, Margo's dad was basically a loner who had no real friends except for his wife.

"Here you are!" her mother said, pulling free from Margo. "Why don't you come in where all the people are?" She took her husband's elbow and tried to pull him toward the door.

"Goddammit, lemme go!" He pulled his arm away from her and sloshed his drink down the front of his shirt and tie. "Shit. See what you made me do." He put his glass down on the brick handrail and, after some fumbling, managed to get a handkerchief out of his pocket and wipe at his chest.

"Please." Margo's mother was begging him in an embarrassing way.

Margo glanced back to make sure that no one was peeking through the doors to watch this scene. "Please, honey. Please come inside. This is Margo's night. Let's not disappoint her." She took her husband's arm again and tried to guide him to the door.

He yanked his arm away. "Lemme alone."

"Hey, Dad!" Margo came between them. "Thanks for coming to see the play."

Her dad straightened his shoulders, held his hand out and shook his daughter's hand. "You were very good tonight, uh, very good, indeed."

"Thanks Dad." Margo pulled her hand away and smiled at her mom. "Hey Mom, why don't we go back in? I'd like you to meet some more of my friends. Dad, you wanna just wait out here?"

"Hell no. I'll meet some of your friends too," her dad said in an executive sort of way, and he threw his cigarette on the ground and stomped his way back into the theatre lobby. Margo and her mom shared a worried moment and hurried after him.

Once inside, the first person they encountered was Jeremy along with a man she didn't recognize. Margo's dad had been in Personnel in the Air Force and had come home on more than one occasion boasting of having gotten another "homo" sniffed out and dishonorably discharged. Margo tried to steer her parents clear of the two of them, but her dad reached out for a handshake.

"Excellent job, young man. You're quite a singer."

"Why thank you, sir," said Jeremy, copying his deep, official-sounding voice and looking at Margo for an introduction.

"This is my dad, Don Laughton. Dad, this is Jeremy Stover. He's an opera singer who has lowered himself to sing rock for this play."

"And I adored every minute of it," Jeremy gushed.

"At least you went off to fight in Vietnam. Not like all the fags who burned their draft cards, goddamn them!" His deep, official-sounding voice was getting a little loud.

The man with Jeremy got red in the face and looked like he was about to forcibly inject himself into the conversation when Jeremy politely pulled him in and said, "Margo, have you met Phillip, my, uh, friend?"

"No, I haven't. How do you do, Phillip?" Margo shook hands with Phillip and exchanged a nervous glance with Jeremy, and she took a sip of her drink.

Phillip gave Margo an effusive hug and said in his most affected voice, "Dahling, you were divine! I know exactly what you mean by 'Easy to be Hard!'"

Margo almost choked at his comment. Coming up to breathe, she stole a glance at her dad, whose attention had mercifully drifted to the bar. She took the opportunity to play slap Phillip and whisper to Jeremy, "This guy is perfect for you!"

"Your father is too much, girl," Jeremy said, pursing his lips.

"Don't remind me. I am so sorry." she apologized. The men shook their heads as if with compassion. Then Margo turned to her mother and said, "Let's go, Mom."

Her mom was glaring at her husband's back. "There he goes, back to the bar." The nervous voice; the shaking head.

"I know."

Before they could get halfway across the room, Margo was stopped by Alan Rubenstein who reached out and squeezed her upper arm as she tried to race by him. Precisely as he had done at least four previous times, he said, "Marvelous job, my dear!" and kissed her on the cheek. "Duty calls!" he whispered in her ear as he maneuvered her into the midst of three bejeweled and beaming middle-aged women.

"Excuse me a minute, Mom," Margo called over the shoulder.

Margo's mother followed after her father and Margo turned to the giddy subscribers. They tittered about the naughty songs and how stunned they were at the line of "bare bums" facing them in the Army induction scene. "We were in the third row, for Heaven's sake!" squealed one as the trio bubbled into giggles.

Margo grinned as the ladies recovered. She answered their predictable questions with as much graciousness as she could muster. After a minute or two she glanced away, hoping to see what her parents were up to.

As she searched the room, her eyes were arrested by the piercing gaze of an impossibly handsome older man who was staring at her. He had longish jet black hair with flecks of gray at his temples. His eyes were just as dark with thick eyebrows arching above them. He was dressed all in black and cradled an amber colored drink with ice. He resembled a hunky Italian movie star at the Venice Film Festival. Margo felt a tingle in her stomach and was sure she was blushing. He smiled, nodded and started to walk toward her. Margo finished up with the ladies, thanking them again, very aware that Casanova was hovering just behind her right shoulder. She turned to him and he extended his hand.

Margo held her breath, consciously smiled and shook his warm firm hand. With a move worthy of James Bond, he put his drink down and placed his left hand over hers. Margo shivered and thought, *I'm in a movie!*

"I enjoyed your performance tonight, Ms. Laughton. And your work in *Much Ado*. I'm a bit of a fan."

His voice was deep and controlled. *Was he a singer? A Shakespearean actor?*

Margo hoped she wasn't making a stupid face or drooling. She bit her lower lip and when she said, "Thank you," she was surprised that she sounded composed. She added, "I'm flattered," and felt her heart beating madly.

He held onto her hand. "I'm Father Gilbert Angelo, and I teach at St. Bart's up the road. Drama Department."

Margo nodded, forcibly holding onto her smile. *He said Father,* she thought quickly, *He's a priest!*

The Cinderella inside of her collapsed; her ball gown turned back into rags. Her mind scrambled to make sense of the scene. St. Bartholomew was the Catholic College across town. It had a well-regarded Drama Department that had spawned several famous Hollywood actors. Margo shook her head slightly to rearrange her brain cells and focus in on what the priest with the smoldering eyes had to say.

Fr. Angelo finally let go of her hand to reach into his jacket pocket and pull out a yellow piece of paper. It was a flyer of some sort. He unfolded it.

"You may have heard that we have a professional touring company that performs all over the country. I don't know what your plans are for the coming year, but I was wondering if you would consider auditioning for the St. Bart Players."

"Oh, I've heard of them!" Margo chirped. She'd been jealous of that private college and its ready-made touring company that eased the transition from college to the professional world. It was a great experience – doing plays all over the the U.S., seeing the country and getting a solid professional credit on the resume.

"But I didn't think people outside of St. Bart's could audition."

"Normally we use our own graduates exclusively, but occasionally actors from other colleges audition, by invitation only." He nodded and smiled. "We're doing an odd duo of plays next year and we need actors with versatility. *As You Like It* and *You're a Good Man, Charlie Brown*. Not many actors can do Shakespeare and sing, as you can. To be frank, I'm directing *Charlie Brown* and I believe I've found my Lucy."

Margo took the flyer from the priest and read the audition notice. *Okay,* she thought, *I'm Judy Garland in "A Star is Born."*

She was about to blurt out, "Yes, oh yes! I'd love to! And thank you for sparing me from moving to New York and getting eaten alive right now!" But when she looked up from the flyer, she was surprised to see Harry putting his arm around Fr. Angelo's shoulders.

"Gil!" he bellowed. "Do you have to go to confession after seeing this play?!"

"Undoubtedly," chuckled the priest. "Great job, Harry! And you've got quite a leading lady here."

"I do indeed! Congratulations Margo!"

"Thank you, Harry." She meant it. "Thank you so much for the opportunity." Then she heard the voices of her parents emanating from the bar. This time she extended her hand to the priest. "I will definitely audition for the Players, sir. Thank you so much!"

"See you there, then," and those brown eyes twinkled at her under his thick raised eyebrows. He turned to Harry and Margo pivoted away, refolding the flyer and placing it carefully into her purse. She put a hand on her chest to still her heart, and then walked through the crowd to the bar in time to hear:

"Goddammit, woman, can't you just leave me alone?"

Her mother's head was cocked and she was speaking to her husband out of the corner of her mouth. "Now, honey, I think it may be time to go."

"Go? Hell! We just got here!" He turned back to the bartender. "Another!"

Margo's mother took hold of her husband's arm and attempted to escort him away. He suddenly roared like a bear in a trap and yanked his arm away, forcibly slapping his wife across the jaw with the back of his hand. It made a horrible cracking sound and people nearby gasped.

Margo's mother whimpered and held her jaw. A crowd of rubberneckers had formed around the couple. Margo pushed her way to her mother.

"I'm okay," she said, "Just get him out of here before it gets worse."

Margo felt the familiar adrenaline rush of disgust-rage-fear. The instinct to get out, save face and make peace took over. She put a firm hand on her father's back.

Quietly she said, "C'mon, Dad. Maybe it *is* time to go . . ."

Her dad spun around. "What the hell is it with the women in this family? I'll go when I'm goddamned ready to go!"

"Dad! You've had enough! Now let's go!" Margo's sister's voice boomed loudly above the whispering spectators. She walked into their midst and took firm hold of her father's upper arm. Amazingly, her dad's bravado crumbled and he let himself be drawn from the center of the crowd to the doors and out.

Margo and her mother followed them out, heads bent low. Once outside the building, the family stopped and listened to Bridget's instructions:

"Mom, take him to the car. I'll be there in a minute. And *I'm* driving home. No arguments."

Margo's mother dutifully obeyed and led her now docile husband to the car.

"You haven't been around. You haven't seen them." Bridget spoke matter-of-factly as she stared at her departing parents.

"I know. I've been so busy. I'm sorry." Margo put her hand on her sister's shoulder.

"I don't mean to blame you, but it's been horrible."

"You were great in there," Margo said with real admiration.

"Listen, dear older sister of mine. When you were home, you and mom used to clean up after him and make it look to the whole world like we were the perfect family. I can't do that."

"It's not that we . . ."

"I've been on the verge of calling the police about them half a dozen times in the last month. And I'm kinda sorry I haven't done it."

Margo's throat tightened up and she felt tears gathering at the edges of her eyes.

"I should've done something years ago. Years ago. He shouldn't still be hurting her." Margo heaved a big sigh and let the tears fall. "Or when Mom first called me. Shit, you shouldn't be having to deal with this."

Margo saw that Bridget was crying too. The sisters embraced.

Margo pulled away and watched her dad who was having a cigarette in the parking lot. Her mom must have already gotten into the car. "Maybe I should move back home after graduation."

"Don't you dare." Bridget scowled. "The best thing you can do for them is live your own life. Concentrate on yourself. And get away. Go to New York. Do what you want to do. That's what I plan to do. As soon as I can."

Margo studied her sister's face. "You're amazing."

"Yeah, yeah, yeah. I'm just a realist. Now get back inside and greet your public. I'd better take them home."

They hugged again and Margo watched her walk to the car, get her dad inside and pull out of the parking lot. Her mom waved feebly from the back seat as they drove away.

She blew her nose, wiped her eyes, making sure she wasn't smudging her mascara, and turned to go back inside. A shadowy figure in the doorway startled her.

"Are you okay?" he asked, emerging into the streetlight. It was Doug.

"No. But I will be." She stood stock still, struggling to keep her tears in check.

"And I thought you came from the perfect family," Doug said gently. He walked over to her and put his arms around her.

Margo couldn't keep her tears bottled up anymore as she relaxed in Doug's compassionate embrace. She buried her face in his shoulder and sobbed. He stroked her back and rocked her softly.

"If only I'd done something years ago. If only I hadn't tried to keep the thing such a big fuckin' secret." Her voice was husky as she gasped for breath.

"Shh. Let it go." Doug rubbed the back of her head and kissed her forehead.

It felt so wonderful to let someone comfort her. She concentrated on the smell of his musky cologne mixed with his make-up remover. And she held tightly onto her little purse where she was sure that a yellow piece of paper was glowing like starshine.

CHAPTER TWENTY-THREE

During the run of *Hair,* Margo was grateful for the routine of doing a play. With classes during the day and the play at night, Margo didn't have much free time to worry about the crises in her personal life. She was secretly relieved to be too busy to do anything about her family. Plus, Bridget was right, she told herself to alleviate the guilt, she had to live her own life.

"My own life, what the hell is that?" she asked her reflection. She'd gotten to the theatre early, almost an hour before curtain, and sat in front of her beloved make-up mirror for the last time in her college career. "I graduate in a month," she said, brushing her hair, "And this cozy cocoon of a college theatre department will be behind me."

She wondered how hard the life of a professional actor would be, really. The stories were horrible. Several of her acting teachers had begun their classes with the words, "If there's anything else you can do with your life, do it." She anticipated years, maybe even decades of struggle, working odd jobs, getting occasional acting parts, long stretches of nothing. Maybe even ultimate failure, something she didn't let herself think about too much.

She was so grateful for the St. Bart's opportunity she could weep. She already had her monologue and song ready for the audition the following week. And, even though she didn't want to count her chickens or jinx anything, she felt pretty certain there was a part waiting for her. Heck, it was a priest who told her that she was his Lucy. Priests don't lie! She would be doing professional acting work right out of college. It was a dream come true. She would be moving to New York with more confidence and professional experience under her belt.

Then there was the guy thing. She'd spent four years in college and had neglected to secure a husband, or even a boyfriend. As her friends were fond of saying, "Where are the mixers after college?"

Since the horrible scene between her parents on opening night, Doug had been sweet again with Margo. She had needed the comfort and she was grateful for it. She was beginning to feel a revival of interest in him, but she couldn't find the twinkle in his turquoise eyes that told her that her affection was being returned. The dullness there now told her that if she hoped for this relationship, she was doomed. So, she cried on his shoulder and let him comfort her, but she was painfully aware that this closeness was temporary and would probably fade away with the last bit of applause as the curtain fell on *Hair* for the last time tonight.

Studying her reflection again, she thought about the many nights she'd transformed her face into someone else's in this mirror. Beatrice in *Much Ado*, Amanda in *Private Lives*, Tzeitel in *Fiddler*, Arlie in *Getting Out*, and other smaller roles through the past four years. All these women with complicated, interesting, involved lives. Margo painted the blue peace sign on her cheek and felt like a fake. *All I want to do is crawl into someone else's skin and live her life,* she thought. *What about my life?*

She smiled at the colorful, cluttered, decorated make-up room reflected in her mirror where her colleagues in art would soon be gathering. She felt close to tears. She loved these crazy theatre kids so much. She would so miss everyone after tonight. And after graduation. She remembered a line from the Broadway musical *Chicago*: "I love you and you love me and we love each other. And that's because none of us got enough love in our childhood. And that's show biz, kid."

Then she felt foolish for her melodramatic thoughts – she was hardly a show biz veteran. Just a college senior about to graduate with a degree in theatre. How could she have hardened show biz regrets already?

She was simply a big zero in the "real world." A college graduate with no professional experience. A virgin with no sexual experience. A student with no life experience. She had spent four years developing her mind and her craft and she felt like she was emerging without an identity. She had even succeeded in eliminating her one distinguishing familial trait – the Laughton protruding proboscis. She looked intently into the mirror and goose bumps rose on her flesh. She didn't recognize the image staring back.

She pulled her make-up smudged towel-bib from her throat and threw it onto the table with disgust as she rose to get dressed. Rounding the corner to the dressing room, she remembered that she had neglected to check her props when she arrived this evening, so she turned from the dressing room door and made her way upstairs to the props table that sat in the wings. She trusted the props master, but she considered it an actor's job to check her own props before a show. If she suddenly found herself without a prop she needed, she would be the one looking stupid in front of an audience. It had happened to her only once, and that was enough.

As she neared the butcher-paper-covered table with the outlined props laid on it, she heard something from behind the stage. It sounded like a dog whimpering. She followed the sound and it changed to sniffling. Someone was crying somewhere behind or below the stage.

She bent down to peer under the raked stage, and she saw shoulders and a huge head of black hair shaking with sobs. It was Tony, the newest member of the out-of-the-closet club, and Margo didn't want to bother him. She turned to sneak away when he whipped around and said, "Who's there?"

Margo froze and winced. "It's me, Tony. Margo." She crouched down to see him. "I didn't mean to intrude. I was just checking my props and I heard this noise and I wanted to find out what it was. Sorry."

Tony shook his head and wiped his nose. "That's okay. Fuck. What do I care what anyone thinks?"

Margo waited for a second. "Do you wanna talk, or should I . . .?"

"Maybe I need a fuckin' hug," he said.

"What?"

"Fuck this play, that's what I say! Fuck everyone in it!" Tony started to get up, but he misjudged the height of the platform above him and whacked his head hard on a crossbeam. "Oh, fuck me!" He held his head in pain and began to cry again.

"Tony, oh Tony." Margo crawled under the stage. Despite his sarcastic words, there was something so little boyish about him, she really did want to hug him. She put her hand on his shoulder. "Are you all right?" she asked, wincing again.

"No, goddamn it, I'm not all right." He continued to hold his head in his hands. "I've been crying for an hour because I'm not sure I'm gay, and I just got conked on the head."

Margo choked out a feeble, "Oh."

"Am I getting a bump?" He held his head toward her.

Margo reached into his bushy hair and, sure enough, felt a bump rising on his scalp. "Yep, feels like a bump. Do you feel dizzy?"

"No. But I did see stars. Pretty cool actually. Kinda like a Bugs Bunny cartoon when someone gets hit over the head with an anvil. I almost heard little birdies tweeting."

Tony actually laughed for a second and Margo felt relieved. She asked cautiously, "Why do you think you're not gay? You seemed really sure when you announced it."

"Well, actually, I am pretty sure. Ninety-eight percent sure. I mean, okay, I'm gay." He rubbed the top of his head. "What I'm not sure of, is that I was really ready to come out."

"Oh."

"I didn't know what it would be like, you know. I mean, I felt perfectly safe telling the Tribe, especially the guys who were in the Improv and all."

Margo nodded.

"In fact, I felt so good, I just picked up the phone and called my folks. And well, they weren't exactly as receptive as the Tribe." He rolled his eyes. "We're Italian Americans, for Chrissake. Mama Mia!"

"Catholic?"

"Of course. All of a sudden, everyone's crying and I'm going to hell! I've been able to deal with it with the play and all because everyone's been so supportive. But tonight's closing night and I don't know how I'm going to deal with all of this without the Tribe!" He started crying again. "I'm freaking out!"

"So you think you should have waited to come out?"

"I needed to do it someday, I know. I guess I don't even know what being gay means to me yet, so when my mother asks me questions, I don't know what to say." He was playing with his shoelaces. "Plus, I really hurt them. I should have waited until I knew exactly how to break it to them slowly and softly. But I was so pumped up after the Improv, I had to come out!" He looked at Margo as though to see if she understood.

Margo was afraid to ask her next question. "What happened in the Improv that made you so sure about coming out?"

Tony looked at her with his head cocked. "You mean no one's told you yet?"

Margo shook her head, hoping that she was finally about to get a glimpse into the Black Box of the Improv.

"Well," Tony sighed, "All I can say is that I fell in love."

"With Jeremy?" Margo had noticed Tony and Jeremy hanging out together more.

"With Jeremy, with Peter, with Robert, with Steve, with *myself!* Hell, even with Doug! Fuckin' Doug. I wonder what his trip is!"

Margo tried to hide her shock at that last bit of information. "So what exactly did happen in the Improv?"

"I shouldn't tell you, if no one else is talking."

Margo begged, "Please."

"Okay, I'll tell you this much: It was Harry's typical huggy-feely get-to-know-you shit, and then it turned, uh, more intense. At first, I was really scared, but Harry helped us all let go, and once I did, it was fuckin' wild. It felt like anything we did was okay. It was the first time I felt it was okay for me to be . . . what I am." His eyes filled up with tears again. "Are you getting what I'm saying?"

"I think so. Maybe." Her mind was filling up with all kinds of wild images. But when she tried to picture Doug in the middle of that, she knew it couldn't have been as crazy as her imagination. She asked Tony softly, "Are you sorry that it happened?"

He was silent as he thought about her question. "No, not really. I learned stuff about myself, like Harry said we would. I just wished there was more time to, uh, I don't know, to process what happened, I guess." He shook his head. "I think I got a false sense of security from the Improv and the world just ain't like that. My family ain't like that, that's for sure. I shoulda waited to come out to them."

Margo nodded her head. A piece of the puzzle had fallen into place. Harry's improvs were like therapy, but unlike therapy, there was no safety net. No opportunity to "process" things, as Tony had said. The situations generated lots of heat from the performers, but at what cost?

Back at her make-up mirror for final touches, Margo was newly agitated. She glanced at Tony out of the corner of her eye as he applied make-up to cover up his tear-swollen eyes. Tony was a strong man with a gift for humor. He would survive this personal ordeal, despite the pain he was feeling now. But what if someone weaker than Tony had met with the same pressure? Someone not so secure in their identity. In their sexual identity. Margo was having a renewed interest in what happened in 1969 and was suddenly dying to know what the person sitting in seat K5 tonight was going to learn from the subscriber in H101.

CHAPTER TWENTY-FOUR

Harry's pre-performance speech warned against "closing night syndrome." He cautioned the cast against letting the pace drag, adding special "moments," and other grandiose behavior just to savor the last opportunity to be in the skin of a character, upsetting the balance of the play. He reminded them that for one more night they were the Tribe – a supportive, creative ensemble of talented people with a message to share.

Hearts were heavy as the cast held hands and bowed heads for the last time together. There was some sniffling in the circle and Margo wondered if Tony's tears would be triggered again.

Harry finished up his closing night speech:

"I want to say again what a marvelous, remarkable and hard-working cast this has been. In my 22 years of directing college theatre, I don't think I've ever encountered a group like you."

Andrea, who held Margo's right hand, whispered out of the side of her mouth, "I bet he says that to all his casts." Margo smiled. Harry went on:

"You have been free and courageous and trustworthy. We have had some wonderful experiences together. People outside the Tribe will never be able to understand what we have shared. It is not their place to know how we achieved what we have achieved. This play is simply our gift to them. The process has been our secret. Let's keep the magic to ourselves."

"Hear hear!" someone shouted. The Tribe laughed. Andrea squeezed Margo's hand. Margo squeezed back and nodded.

"I want to wish the best of luck to those of you who will be graduating and for whom this is your last play here. I feel honored to have worked with you. Brandy, Tony, Jackson, Suzanne, Michael, Barry . . . and, of course, Doug and Margo. My Berger and Sheila. Best wishes to you all."

Thank yous were mumbled. Margo smiled ruefully. The others hooted and applauded approvingly.

"And for those of you who will be returning next year, I encourage you to audition for my next play. I will be directing David Rabe's play *Streamers*, which you may know is a brutal play about young men in Vietnam. Sorry ladies, I guess I won't be working with you next year."

Some of the idiot women sighed a disappointed "Oh!" Some of the guys grunted "Yeah!"

Margo felt the blood drain from her face. She'd read some David Rabe – a savage writer whose plays were something actors could really sink their teeth into. Harry was going to direct *Streamers*. Harry was going to direct a play about a dozen 18-year-old boys who discover themselves in the context of a war. Harry was gearing up for the time of his life.

"But enough about the future. Tonight is your night. It's time once more for the Age of Aquarius. So go out there and share the story one more time. Beads, flowers, freedom . . ."

"Happiness!" the Tribe shouted, finishing his line. Buoyant laughter filled the green room. Hugs and high fives abounded. Then the Tribe ran up the stairs to the stage and one more night of hippy madness.

Margo wasn't sure if it was her imagination, or if this night really was different from all the others. The play felt more ominous than it had ever felt. The fun stuff was still there, and the audience was rolling in the aisles as before, but the heavy parts of the play were stronger and more meaningful. It wasn't just the Tribe; the audience also seemed to be reacting more to the darker elements of the play. They were more electrically charged. Occasionally, someone would yell out from the audience, which was totally groovy in the context of the play. It was just odd and a bit unsettling. There was a very audible shout of anguish during one of the war scenes. It gave Margo the chills. *Maybe it was a Vietnam vet reliving his horrors*, she thought.

Margo couldn't help feeling her own version of closing night syndrome. Rather than milking her songs, it took the form of carefully watching everyone perform their parts and cherishing the specialness of each one of them.

Jeremy's voice and gentle goofy humor made her heart melt. His Claude lived and died powerfully on the stage. When he sang "Where Do I Go?" Margo closed her eyes and wondered where any of them were going.

Andrea's "White Boys" was as juicy and funny as ever. The audience hooted along with her and her face was bright with the joy of performing a song perfectly suited to her talents.

Jackson's anger and pathos were chiseled and brilliant. Margo saw him as a real leader, winding himself in and out of the Tribe as he motivated the black performers. At the end of "Abie Baby" when he said in complete indignation, "Shit, I'm not dyin' for no white man," he shot Margo a fierce look that was full of fire and challenge. She had no idea what he intended, but the memory of it burned in her chest.

Margo especially watched Tony. During his solo bit in the non-patriotic tribute to the flag, "Don't Put It Down," Margo thought she saw him getting choked up again. He folded a huge American flag with mock seriousness, but he was handling it as though it held deep meaning for him. She remembered that Tony's brother had fought in Vietnam and wondered if the family was military or particularly patriotic. That would further explain his reluctance at having admitted his sexual identity to his parents.

Finally, Doug seemed electrifying to her. She admired each of his songs and wild man moves. She howled when his hair flew out behind him as he swung on the rope over the audience during "Donna." She laughed when he belly-flopped into the arms of Tribesmen as he descended to hell in "Going Down." She felt decimated when he rejected her, sending her into "Easy to be Hard." Finally, during "Good Morning Starshine," he came over and they held hands for the first time in the run. Margo felt the light, happy lilt she had felt when she was falling in love with him only weeks before.

She took mental pictures of each of these people and pressed them in her heart album. Each person seemed vivid and beautiful. A magnificent creation. She felt privileged and honored to have shared this time and this stage with them.

Margo loved the words of "What a Piece of Work is Man," which authors Rado and Ragni borrowed from *Hamlet*. They resonated in her heart when she heard them sung:

"What a piece of work is man, how noble in reason, how infinite in faculties, in form

and moving, how express and admirable in action, how like an angel in apprehension, how like a god! the beauty of the world; the paragon of animals."

Standing facing the audience and singing "Let the Sun Shine In" for the last time, she was replete with the knowledge that she was Sheila. She was the mother of the Tribe. The nurturer, the care-giver, the matriarch.

She took her last bow on the stage of Hancock Theatre and felt the torch pass to the younger women. She was finished. She could move on. She could go and leave this place behind.

Or could she?

CHAPTER TWENTY-FIVE

Margo had just removed the last break-a-leg card from her mirror when she remembered Jen. "Oh shit," she said out loud, as she ran up the spiral staircase to the stage and onto the now bare set which was ugly and not magical at all under plain work lights. She stood on the apron of the stage and scanned a completely empty house. Even the ushers were done picking up the discarded programs. "Jen!" she called out once.

From the ceiling, a lone follow-spot operator yelled down, "Everyone's gone, Margo. Show's over."

"Thanks!" she yelled at the ceiling. "And thanks for working the show."

"Best I've ever seen."

Margo smiled and waved and returned to the make-up room to gather her things and bum a ride to the cast party. She was resigned that she'd have to wait until tomorrow to find out if the subscriber in H101 had shown up, and if he had been willing to talk. Part of her hoped not.

The closing night party was a cut above most college closing night parties and the flavor of *Hair*, of course, dominated. Brandy hosted the party at the house she shared. Her housemates must have agreed to be gone for the evening. She really was quite a cook and there was actual food at the party, along with the traditional keg and cheap champagne to toast the play. She had decorated the house with a psychedelic theme. Some classic 60s records were spinning loudly and Tribe members were gyrating in clumps.

Having brought their own stash of joints, it wasn't long before quite a few of them were stoned. Many preferred getting drunk. Others worked on getting a food high. Margo sucked on Diet Coke.

People were chatting and laughing in small groups all over the place, with plenty of face sucking and body stroking. Occasionally a couple would leave the main floor together and return with a special glow about them. It was a party that would have made any hippy proud.

Margo allowed herself to become nostalgic as she reminisced about the play and her college years. She didn't want to think about the future, duty, responsibility, family, Harry. She wanted to be a normal college kid and live in the present for this one last evening.

Andrea wanted to bend her ear about changing her major to theatre and they explored the topic for several minutes. Andrea had been profoundly changed by *Hair*. She tried to articulate something Margo struggled to put into words herself: "You know, playin' a character who is so *not me*, I feel the most *like me* I've ever felt – totally me – and totally everyone else – or all people – or somethin'. Connected. A part of it all. Human, y'know. Gahhh! I'm not makin' any sense!"

"You're making perfect sense," Margo affirmed.

"It sure as hell beats Early Childhood Education. I don't think I wanna work with snot-nosed kids." She put down her beer and scanned the room. "I really wanna dance. But it don't look like my man Jackson is going to do any askin'." Jackson was stuffing his face at the smorgasbord table. "You wanna dance?"

Margo always felt self-conscious when she danced, but Andrea gave her a pouty face so she said, "Sure!" And the two women got up to boogie to Sonny and Cher's "I Got You, Babe," singing along.

It turned out to be fun. Because the music was all 60s, people were doing the twist and the monkey and the swim and the pony. Margo loosened up and got into it. She knew she looked good in a royal blue mini-dress she had found for the occasion. A choker peace sign was in place around her neck, and she had left on her Sheila make-up. She felt like one of those sexy go-go girls that used to be on "Laugh-In." She and Andrea laughed and danced and began to sweat together. Her actor's third eye told her that men were watching them.

She wasn't surprised when one of them came over to join them. It was Jackson and she assumed he was going to bump her away to dance with

Andrea. Margo was surprised, however, when he slid a strong arm around *her* waist and began to dance provocatively with her. Jackson had a big grin on his face and she had to smile back. She really did like him. And she loved that actors could "fool around" on the dance floor and even act sexual without it really meaning anything. In fact, glancing nervously over Jackson's shoulder, she saw Andrea wink at her. She relaxed and danced and enjoyed herself.

The music changed to a slow dance and Jackson put his arms around Margo's waist. Margo shyly put her arms around Jackson's neck and felt herself pressed up against him. *My parents would be choking if they saw me now.* She was putting it together in her own head. *This is Jackson, not Doug. This is a black guy. This is a very sweet and talented black guy. This is a very sweet and talented and gentle man. This is . . .* she didn't want to think about it anymore. She closed her eyes and let herself feel the dance.

Jackson's hands held her back firmly and they swayed together easily. A couple of times Margo felt him squeeze her tighter, and she responded by tightening her hold around his neck and snuggling closer. He pulled away a little and she thought, *Oh my God, is he going to kiss me?* But he didn't kiss her. Instead, he said, without any joking, "It was really great doing this show with you. I'm glad I got to know you before we graduated. You're a hell of a woman. I just wanted to tell you that."

Margo was stunned. No one had ever called her a "hell of a woman." She was trying to think of how to respond when suddenly from over her shoulder she heard, "Get your hands off o' her."

It was Doug and he was well on his way to being drunk or stoned or both.

"Hey, cool it, White Boy," said Jackson, who maintained his hold on Margo.

"I said get your black hands off her." Doug was getting threatening. His southern accent was more pronounced than usual.

Margo was shocked at his attitude. "Doug! Leave us alone. We're just dancing."

"Dancing, my ass! I was watching you. He's just trying to get into your pants to get back at me, Margo. I know his type."

Jackson stopped dancing. "That's enough, Doug. We're just dancing. And I don't give a fuck about you. I mean that."

"Watch your mouth, nigger!" Doug said as he tried to shove Jackson back.

Suddenly, Andrea leapt into the fray from across the room. "Hey, cut it out. This is a party!" She got between the men. "Leave 'em alone, Doug. And you watch *your* mouth."

Margo didn't know what to think. "Doug. What is going on with you?"

"Nothing, man. I just don't like seein' his black hands all over you." Doug stopped and looked around. He seemed suddenly ashamed by the commotion he was causing and backed off. "Fuck, never mind," he said as he spun around and left the room.

Jackson, Margo and Andrea left the dance floor and sat down in a corner together.

"What was that all about?" Margo wanted to know. "Is it my imagination, or have you guys been on the warpath for a while now?"

"Ever since the Improv," Andrea said, glaring at Jackson. "He told me about part of it."

Jackson was staring at the floor.

"Tell her what happened, Jackson."

Jackson locked eyes with Margo. "I didn't want to tell you because you and Doug . . . shit, I wasn't supposed to tell anybody because we promised and all, but I am so fuckin' sick of that racist."

"Doug?" Margo couldn't believe it. "Doug has always been so sweet and gentlemanly."

"You did just hear him call me a nigger, did you not?"

"Yeah, but he's drunk, isn't he?" Margo didn't want to believe it.

"So what? That white boy is from the South and to him I'm just a nigger."

Andrea butted in. "Just tell her what happened." She looked at Margo. "Listen to this."

Margo was listening. Finally, someone was going to tell her about the men's Improv.

Jackson shook his head, rolled his eyes, let out a big breath and began:

"At first it was like the other improvs, you know, we did a little warm up and held hands and vowed not to tell anyone what was gonna happen. Then Harry explained that we would be exploring the 'darker' parts of the play and that some ugly things might happen, but he said don't get freaked because it's an exercise. You know, just let go and don't judge and see what happens . . . shit he always says." Jackson let out another big breath and smoothed his hair down with his hands. He went on:

"Okay, first we're supposed to find our anger, so we did this name calling thing where we wrote a list of the worst names we'd ever been called and gave it to a partner and that partner had to yell the names at us over and over. And then we switched, the other person got yelled at by the other person. You know what I mean?"

Margo nodded. "What names did you pick?"

"Oh you know, the traditional ones – nigger, colored, boogie, jigaboo, coon. And man, it was horrible hearing someone yell those words at me. It got me real mad. Anyway, then I had to yell words at Jeremy like homo and fag and all. And *that* was weird! Bein' on the other side of the mud slingin'. And I could tell it hurt him. He got kinda teary eyed.

"So the feeling in the room got real tense. Everyone was feeling sore and angry and vulnerable, I guess. And that's when Harry divided us between whites and blacks."

"What?" Margo was surprised.

"Listen to this," Andrea said to her.

"Yeah. He told the white guys to hang out for awhile and he took us black guys to the back of the Black Box behind the curtain. He had a roll of tape and he told us to take our pieces of paper with the ugly words on them and tape them to some place on our bodies. On the skin. And then we were supposed to put our clothes back on over them. He went to talk with the white guys while we worked on taping the paper to our bodies. Some of the guys taped the paper on their stomachs, some on their arms. Me, I decided to be weird and I said, 'Kiss my ass, fuckin' words!' and taped the list to my behind. And then I pulled my pants up over it.

"Then we heard Harry tell us to come out from behind the curtain. The white guys were on the other side of the room and they were kinda glarin' at us. Now you know how the ratio of whites to blacks in the play was kinda two to one? Well, it seemed like the white guys had paired up and each pair was assigned to one of us black guys. Once we were out from behind the curtain, the white guys started comin' at us, two guys to each one of us.

"We saw the look in their eyes and got real scared. I didn't know whether to try to run away or to stand my ground. I stood there and glared back and tried to figure out what was happening. Some of the other guys ran and I saw two white guys run after each one of them. I looked back at the white guys and I could tell that Doug and Peter were assigned to me. They were both staring at me with this menacing look. I'll never forget it. Doug, in particular, was lookin' really nasty, like he wanted to barbecue me and eat me for dinner. He was actually kinda smilin'. It was a nasty look."

"Oh shit," Margo said.

"Oh shit is right. I didn't know where to go or what to do. I could hear fighting going on around me. Some of the white guys had gotten some brothers down on the floor and they were wrestlin' or something. They were shouting those horrible words at us. I could hear, 'Nigger, nigger, nigger' all over the room. Doug and Peter were still approaching me real slow and I don't mind telling you I was terrified. I felt cold and like I was shivering from my toes to my ears. I didn't know where to go or what to do. And they kept coming, like in slow motion.

"Then Doug said, 'That's right, Nigger. Don't move. We're gonna getcha.' That's when I bolted and tried to get away. But they were too close and they kinda jumped on me. Doug first. And let me tell you, that sweet southern gentleman turned into white redneck trash real fast, or else he's a better actor than I thought he was, because he was a fuckin' asshole. He even started talking with a southern accent! He and Peter had me down and they were calling me all the worst names you can think of. Then they were tearing at my clothes, pulling my shirt up over my head, and then my undershirt. 'Where is it? Where is it, Nigger?' Doug kept saying. Then I realized what they were doing."

"They were looking for the paper!" Margo said in sudden understanding.

"Right. They were looking for the paper. And, of course, I had been an idiot and taped it to my behind. Let me tell you, I was regretting that choice at that moment!"

Andrea laughed. And Jackson smiled at her.

"Anyway, while I was on the floor, I could see that the white guys had gotten most of the papers off the brothers and they were yelling the words, screaming them at the brothers while pinning them down, or whatever. That's when Doug told Peter to pick me up. Well, as you know, I am not a small man and Peter wasn't strong enough to lift me by himself, especially since I was fighting him so hard. So Doug called in the reserves and three other white guys came over to help. By this time, everyone in the room was watching my little drama and I was screaming and fighting like a goddamn bull.

"I mean, I had these four white guys tryin' to pick me up and hold me while this white racist bastard was saying shit like, 'Quit squirmin', Nigger, you're only hurting yourself.' I tell you, I had enough rage in me for all my ancestors who came over on the slave boats and who picked cotton 'til they died. I was cursin' and fightin' and thinkin' about what it would be like to be on an auction block or be whipped like Kunta Kinte in *Roots*, you know?"

His eyes teared up.

"Shit, I don't mean to cry. But it was horrible. And the worst, I think, was the look in Doug's eyes. It was hatred. But it was more than that. He kept smilin'. Grinnin'. Like he was enjoying hurting me. Like it was a sport. He wasn't himself, I tell you. Or maybe he was more himself than ever. I don't know. But it was evil, man. Fuckin' evil. And that's what really got me. The evil that makes men enjoy hurtin' other men."

He paused to blow his nose. Margo bit her lip and shook her head. Andrea stroked his shoulder.

"Anyway, they finally got me on my feet and by this time, all the white guys were crowded around, encouraging Doug and shoutin' ideas at him. 'Maybe it's on his huge black dick.' 'I think he taped it to his big black ass.' Stuff like that. I was being held by four white guys and Doug turned to the crowd and said real matter-of-fact like, 'Well, I guess we gotta take off his pants, don't we?' The white guys cheered and Doug came over and undid my belt. Then he grabbed my pants and pulled them down real fast. My underpants went down too and I'm standin' there buck naked with my pants around my ankles. The white guys were laughin' and Doug grinned at me and said, 'Well, well, the rumors are a lie after all. His dick is actually quite small isn't it?' The white guys thought this was real funny and they laughed and laughed. Then one of them saw the paper on my ass and ripped it off. They passed it around, taking turns with the words.

"So I'm standin' there, buck naked, being pinned by these white guys and they're yellin' the worst words you can imagine at me. I was so mad I wanted to kill them all."

He was shaking with rage.

"Where was Harry during all of this?" Margo asked.

"Jesus, I have no idea. It was only at the end that I saw him sitting in the audience and just watching us like we were a play or something. Because once the name calling was dying down, he spoke from his seat and ended this part of the Improv. He told the white guys to let me go and I pulled my pants back up. Then he congratulated us on our work and made us all hug each other. That was weird, let me tell you. I did not want to hug any of those white boys, I can tell you that. They were all acting like it was some big acting job they all just did. But I can tell you that that wasn't all acting. Those boys enjoyed being the KKK. They got off on it. Especially Doug. It was like he always wanted to act like that, but because he was born too late he never got a chance. Well, he had a chance in that Improv, and he was fuckin' scary."

Jackson stopped and shook his head. "The thing is." He paused and took a big breath. "The thing is, as horrible as it was, it did help my character. I mean, I've never really felt that kind of racist hatred. I've never felt so violated. I grew up in a nice middle-class suburban neighborhood in the north. My family never really identified with the down-trodden blacks, you know? I mean, we came from slavery, but we worked hard at putting that behind us. My mom didn't even want to watch *Roots* because she didn't want to identify with that time. But that Improv put it all into me. It fired me up. I can see now what my brothers and sisters have been through, and I think, no, I know it made my character in the play better and more real. So even though it was a scary, shitty thing, I'm not sure I'm sorry it happened. 'Cause it woke me up, man. It woke me up."

Margo reached out to hug Jackson. Andrea joined in and the three of them hugged and rocked each other.

When they broke apart, Margo asked, "So was that the whole Improv?"

"The whole Improv?!" Jackson gaped at her with incredulity. "Hell no! That was just the beginning!"

167

CHAPTER TWENTY-SIX

"**I**f that was the whole Improv," Jackson went on, "I would just be hating Doug right now. I mean, I don't like the man, but I also feel sorry for him. Because what he went through was even worse than the shit I got dealt." He paused and shook his head. "And I think it fucked him up, man. I mean seriously."

Margo wasn't sure she wanted to hear what happened after all.

Andrea looked at her. "This part I haven't heard yet."

Both women turned to hear what he would say next. He was silent. They waited. Jackson seemed like he was about to talk, then he looked away.

"What happened, Jackson?" Margo asked.

He shook his head. "I don't think I can tell you this."

"Why? Because of the fuckin' vow?" Andrea was mad.

"No. C'mon, I told you stuff already. Fuck the vow." He shifted his body. "I told you my stuff because it happened to me. But I don't think I should be telling you what happened to Doug." He rubbed the back of his neck. "It just ain't right." Margo and Andrea gaped at him. "I can't do it. I need a drink."

He started to get up and Margo caught his sleeve.

"Can I ask you one thing?" she asked.

"Sure," he said, sitting back down.

Margo held onto his arm. "If I decide to do something about Harry, would you be willing to tell what happened in the Improv?"

"What do you mean, 'do something about Harry?'" he asked.

"I don't know yet. Maybe try to get it so that he doesn't direct any more plays."

"How would you do that?"

"I don't know. All I'm asking is that if I do, would you be willing to tell what happened in the Improv?"

Jackson paused. "I'm not sure. It would depend. But, yeah, probably. At least what I told you about the black and white shit."

"Okay, fair enough." Margo released his arm.

He got up. "You want something to drink?"

"Uh, yeah. Diet Coke, please?"

"Don't go wild now, Margo. Andrea?"

"Uh, sure. A beer?"

Jackson left.

Andrea asked Margo, "So what do you think?"

"I'm not sure. I mean, what happened to Jackson was pretty horrible. But I don't think it was out of the bounds of what a 'daring' improv can be."

"And, as he said," Andrea added, "It helped his character. Shit, it awakened him to the black experience."

"Yeah. But we still don't know what happened to Doug. Or Scott."

"Who's Scott?" Andrea asked.

Jackson returned with the drinks. He passed them out and was about to sit down again when Doug came over.

"Hey, man," Doug said extending his hand. "I'm sorry. I really am. I'm real sorry about using the N word. That's not me, man. I mean, it's in me, my family history and all, I'm sorry to admit." He got real quiet. "But it's not me. Not really. I'm trying to be better than that. I'm a little drunk and I guess I got a little jealous."

Jackson hesitated, then took his hand. "No big deal, man." He looked at Margo.

Doug looked at Margo too. "Sorry, Margo. Please forgive me." He bowed to her.

"It's okay, Doug. You're forgiven, I guess."

There was an awkward silence.

Doug coughed. "Uh, Margo. Would you like to dance with me?"

Margo turned to Jackson and Andrea. Andrea shrugged. Jackson nodded.

"Sure, Doug." But she wasn't sure.

Doug helped her up and escorted her to the dance area. The Beach Boys' "Good Vibrations" was reverberating and Doug started movin' to the groove. After the conversation she just had, Margo didn't feel very groovy. But she started to do a little self-conscious twist.

It was late in the evening and the party was winding down. Couples were becoming cozier, some people had already left, and bloodshot eyes were plentiful. The dance area was still rockin', though it was less goofy and more sexual. Lust was in the air and time was growing short for hooking up with a willing partner.

Margo's head was swimming with the story Jackson had just told her. She watched the man dancing playfully in front of her and tried to imagine him screaming "Nigger!" and pulling Jackson's pants down. His magnificent eyes were suddenly twinkling their turquoise starshine and his infectious smile was tickling her funny bone. She could not put this sweet silly clown together with the image of the racist redneck Jackson described.

She was also dying to know what had happened to him. Both Tony and Jackson had mentioned Doug in their stories. She remembered Tony's words, *"Fuckin' Doug! I wonder what his trip is!"* There he was, with his blond hair flying, and she wondered herself what his trip was. He did say he would tell her what had happened in the Improv after the play was over. Well, the play was over. What if she just asked him?

The music stopped and Margo was about to ask if they could talk when Doug moved close to her, took her in his arms and started to kiss her neck. She held herself rigid and heard his hate-filled words once more in her mind, *"Watch your mouth, nigger!"* She imagined him ordering guys to strip Jackson naked and yelling at him, *"Nigger, nigger, nigger."* But the words changed to "Margo, Margo, Margo," as Doug's lips reached her ear. "You are so beautiful." She was bewildered. And so tired. Her legs felt like they wouldn't hold her up much longer. *What time is it?* She could smell the beer on his breath. *He's a racist and an alcoholic,* her observer proclaimed, *but so's your old man.*

Doug's lips met hers and Margo felt herself get wet with desire, despite her efforts to maintain her values. When the music came back on, it was "Last Dance." *Shit,* thought Margo, as the sultry voice of Donna Summer sang with desire.

She glanced over Doug's shoulder in time to see Andrea and Jackson leave together, his arm over her shoulder. The room was emptying and Margo wanted to give in. So badly. Just this once. Just for tonight. To stop thinking, stop analyzing, to stop being such a goody-two-shoes. She was about to graduate from college. This really was her last chance. She let her herself respond to Doug's kiss.

Margo felt Doug's hands work their magic all over the back, down onto her buttocks and beneath the mini-dress onto her thighs. The tips of his fingers tickled her "down below" and she felt herself ripple inside. Despite what she'd heard about Doug that evening, despite her knowledge that this relationship would not last the night, Margo knew she wanted this man to take her and have her within the hour.

In front of the university's graduate library, there is a statue of a noble hog. The school's mascot. Legend has it that if ever a virgin were to graduate from the university, the hog would fly. Margo decided that the hog wasn't going to fly that year. When Doug groaned, "Where can we go?" she replied, "My place."

They could barely keep their hands off of each other enough to allow Doug to drive them to Margo's dorm. Margo felt her whole body shiver with yearning and a little fear as she let herself desire and anticipate finally losing her virginity. She stroked Doug's crotch and felt the bulge there. He growled and smiled. She almost giggled, but maintained her composure.

Once inside Margo's room, they were both suddenly shy. Or at least not so mindlessly rapturous. Doug put the brakes on and changed the tempo of his seduction. Margo had installed a dimmer switch to her harsh overhead light. Doug lowered the light to a golden glow. Margo lit a candle (only briefly recalling Harry's ghastly candles) and tuned the radio to a soft rock station. Then Doug bowed to Margo, took her hand, and resumed his dance with her.

Margo felt absolutely charmed. He didn't just force his way with her, but wanted to make sure she was properly romanced. Suddenly, her austere shoebox of academic rigidity became a cozy den of delight. Her cheap curtains looked elegant in the candle's flicker. Large shadows played on the wall like love spirits. Her stuffed tiger appeared to be grinning at her from across the room. Margo smiled back, then nuzzled her face into Doug's shoulder. She adored this feeling of heightened sensation as it mixed and mingled with her passion for the man who was holding her and kissing her so gently, so grandly, so earnestly.

She wanted him to hurry up. She wanted him to linger. Finally, finally, he reached up under her dress again and stroked her. Margo shuddered with his touch. And then she remembered she had forgotten to tell him something. She was suddenly embarrassed, but wanted him to know, so she pulled away a little and said softly:

"Doug, um, I'm a virgin."

Doug kept kissing her like he hadn't heard. Then he said, "I wondered." He pushed back a little and gazed into her eyes. "Do you want to?"

She was trembling. She nodded.

He said, "I'll be gentle." And he kissed her softly. Then whispered, "And don't worry, I have protection."

Margo almost giggled again, but managed to squelch it. Okay. Everything was full steam ahead. She figured it was her turn to do something so she began to unbutton his shirt. She kissed his throat and his chest and for a second she remembered the last time she had done that. She remembered the hard, sticky hairs and the sweet taste. She almost paused in her seduction, but managed to put it out of her mind as she pulled his shirt out from his pants and removed it from his body.

Doug pulled away and looked at her intensely. Then he grasped the bottom of her dress and pulled it up and over her head and off of her body. It dropped to the floor and Margo was standing there in her bra and stockings, a little embarrassed, until he took hold of her and pressed her to his bare chest. He unfastened her bra easily from the back. *A pro,* Margo thought. But her thinking ended when she felt the divine tickle of his blond beard on her breasts as he kissed and sucked on her nipples. First one, then the other.

Margo wondered if she was losing consciousness. It seemed like the two of them were transported by magic to complete nakedness on her bed. They kissed and sucked and stroked and squirmed and did all the things that lovers do and Margo felt like her desire could grow no larger. It was pulling her, possessing her, demanding her, screaming in her. She wanted him. She wanted him like nothing she had ever wanted in her life. She wanted him NOW.

She wondered why he didn't just enter her. She thought maybe she was doing something wrong. She reached down and felt his penis. She expected it to be hard and full. It was limp and squishy. She was disappointed. Clearly, something wasn't working. She remembered reading something in a book and began to kiss Doug on the chest, moving down to his stomach, and finally his penis. She licked his penis and, taking a breath, put it in her mouth. She relaxed when she realized she didn't mind the taste and she began to suck and use her tongue on it. Doug's pelvis moved under her and she heard him moan. She also felt his penis respond and get harder and bigger, filling up her mouth. She felt satisfied by her abilities and kissed her way back up Doug's chest until she was lying beside him.

Doug reached for the rubber and fitted it over his penis. He pulled himself on top of Margo and kissed her deeply, feeling around below. Margo was spinning with anticipation and desire and she kissed him back, breathing heavily in between kisses. Doug continued to feel around down there, but he didn't penetrate her.

Margo continued to kiss and stroke Doug's back and feel his weight on her, but she wondered what was taking him so long. She didn't want to break his concentration, but she thought maybe he was waiting because she was a virgin. Maybe he wanted to make sure she was absolutely ready or something. So she whispered,

"Go ahead."

He felt around a little more, but nothing.

Margo put on what she thought was a Lauren Bacall kind of sultry voice and said, "I'm ready. Do it!"

Still nothing. And the fondling stopped too.

Finally, Doug rolled off of Margo and lay on his back beside her. Margo looked at his face. It was tortured. Then she made herself look at his penis. It was shriveled. The stretched out condom hung on it like a used balloon.

Abruptly, Doug sat up, swung around, put his feet on the floor and stumbled away from the bed. He put his hand on the wall across the room, sank into a crouch, and then just sat on the floor, facing the wall. His arms were around his knees and his head was down.

Margo didn't know what to do. She suddenly felt very naked and a little cold. She got up slowly, pulled a blanket around her body and walked over to Doug. She knelt down next to him, put her arms around his shoulders and held him. He shuddered a little. Margo was surprised to see that Doug was crying.

She felt terrible and tried to soothe him. "It's okay, Doug. It's okay."

He didn't move. He didn't turn to her. They stayed there together, her holding him from behind while he struggled not to cry.

"It's because I'm a virgin, isn't it?" she said miserably.

He turned around, took her face in his hands and said, "Oh, God, no." He shook his head. "Don't think that. Don't ever think that." He took her in his arms and they held each other. "It's me. I'm the one who's fucked up." And he cried on her shoulder.

Slowly, they made their way back to the bed. Margo pulled up the covers and they snuggled down into them, holding each other. Doug cried and Margo stroked him and told him he wasn't fucked up, he was okay, he was more than okay, he was wonderful.

Finally, Doug pulled away and said,

"No. I'm not wonderful. And I'm not okay. I'm very fucked up, Margo. I mean, I like you. I really like you. But I don't know if I can make love to you. Or to any other woman ever again." He rubbed his nose with the back of his hand and looked very much a little boy. "I think I'm a fag, Margo. A fuckin' fag. Oh, goddammit." He turned over and cried with his back to Margo.

Seconds passed as Doug sobbed and Margo watched his back shudder. She wanted to scream and curse and smash someone in the face. But all she did was say, very quietly:

"What happened in the Improv, Doug?"

CHAPTER TWENTY-SEVEN

Doug's crying subsided and he turned around to look at Margo. He reached out and pushed a hair out of her eye.

"Well, I can't lie here naked with you and tell you what happened, that's for sure!" He got up, found his jeans and put them on. Then he walked over to Margo's desk chair, pulled it out and sat in it. "Do you have anything to drink?"

Margo got up too, found an oversized sweatshirt to put on and walked over to her mini-fridge. She was embarrassed that it held no beer or any other alcoholic beverage. "Just Diet Coke and orange juice," she apologized.

"May I have some orange juice, please?" Doug asked like a perfect gentleman.

"Of course!" Margo poured him a large glass, placed it on the desk in front of him, then went back to sit on the bed and waited for him to tell his tale.

Doug held the glass in both hands and took a couple of gulps. He placed the glass back on the desk and stared into the middle of the room. Then he began.

He told her the story of Jackson and the other blacks. Margo didn't stop him from telling her what she already knew because she wanted to hear it from his side. She had to give him credit. His version wasn't very different from Jackson's. He was disgusted by his own behavior and didn't want to excuse it as an acting exercise. He admitted to growing up in the South where "nigger baiting" was still a game enjoyed by many. He said it was fun for him to be able to do it one more time. As he said this, there was evil in his eyes and it frightened Margo. But she sat and listened to him without moving a muscle.

After the men felt their racial anger and their separation, they hugged and made up and Harry said they needed to feel their bonding and connection. Half of the men lay down on the floor in a circle, feet on the inside, heads on the outside. The other half stood inside the circle and walked around sort of like musical chairs. When Harry clapped his hands, the walking men were to stop, find the man lying closest to him and lie down on top of him. Then they were to breathe together and to feel each other breathe, head to toe. Harry said they were to feel the other person's spirit and life energy, feel their history and their essence. Doug had no idea how to do that, but he tried. It was important to him that he try everything to the best of his ability. The prostrate men breathed with the supine men for a few seconds then, when Harry clapped again, they got off the guy they were on and did the musical chairs/bodies thing again.

Doug said it was no big deal, in fact, he really thought he was getting hold of the "essences" Harry was talking about, until he realized that some of the men weren't just breathing together. There was groping and whatnot going on and when Jeremy got on top of Doug, he started to touch him. Doug whispered fiercely, "Cut it out!" And heard Jeremy suppress a snicker. Doug wanted to punch him out. But he stayed where he was until Harry gave the signal to get up, because he was a good actor and wanted to do the Improv just right.

That wasn't so bad and when it was over Doug thought, *Okay, that's that.* But that was only the beginning because now that the men of the Tribe had experienced anger and separation, and then connection and togetherness, it was time to establish the Tribe's leader.

Doug took another big slug of orange juice, dribbling some down his chin and into his beard. He wiped his chin absentmindedly, sighed and continued:

"First of all, I don't get why we had to establish me as leader. I was *already* leader 'cause I was Berger. But, Harry said we had to establish it among the men and I had to really feel it. Then he brought out the red ball."

"The same red ball we used when the women were in the Improv?"

Margo asked.

"Uh huh, same ball. Anyway, it was time to test the leader, me. Harry stuck me in the center of the circle of men and, just like at the women's Improv, the men started throwing the ball at me. Oh, did I tell you that we had all taken off our shirts by this time? Well, we had. So that damn ball is hitting me and stinging me all over my back and chest and arms. I mean, most of those guys can *throw*. But I'm acting like the big tough leader.

"See, all the time, Harry is saying stuff to me like," Doug adopted a solemn Harry-like voice, "'Berger, you are the leader of the Tribe. You are the strong one, the powerful one. You can endure anything.' Shit like that."

Doug's Harry impersonation was pretty good and Margo couldn't help but laugh. Doug smiled and shook his head. Margo was glad to see him relaxing. He went on:

"So I'm taking it and taking it and I'm listening to Harry and it's starting to sink into me. I mean. The ball doesn't hurt anymore. No matter how hard they throw it. I do feel mighty and powerful and shit. I am not kidding you. It's working. I'm feeling like some kind of big, tough, invincible leader. And I think the other guys are noticing this. Harry did, I'm sure.

"He stopped the ball throwing and congratulated me on enduring the blows of the other men. It was clear that I had leadership potential. There were just another couple of 'tests' I had to pass. So I'm feelin' like Hercules – you know, bring on the tests!"

Margo raised her eyebrows.

"It's a guy thing, Margo."

"I didn't say anything!"

"It was that look."

"Sorry! Go on."

"Anyway, there were these tests. I had no idea what Harry had in mind, but I was really Berger by this time. And Berger didn't give a shit about any tests. So I didn't give a shit about any tests. You know how it is."

Margo nodded, but wasn't sure that she did. In all the improvs she had done, she had never really "lost" herself to her character. She wasn't sure if an actor was supposed to ever get truly lost in a character. Whatever, she didn't. She always maintained an outside eye that kept her detached and observing during an improv. Clearly, Doug didn't. He apparently got lost.

"I guess because every guy wants to be leader, every man feels jealous of the leader. Angry towards him. Well, I was supposed to endure the anger of each of the guys. Let each of them hurt me in some way."

"Oh my God."

"I know it sounds horrible, but it really wasn't. I mean, Berger didn't care. He was into the pain. It was like he was proving something by being able to endure it. You know, it's like those Kung Fu masters, or those guys who sleep on a bed of nails. You gotta get past the pain, Grasshopper."

Doug snorted. Then paused. He stared into space and seemed to be recalling the episode so that he could describe it. Margo was wondering about this scene where one by one each of the men inflicted some pain upon Doug. It was unthinkable. It certainly wasn't something women would do. And meanwhile, Harry sat and watched?

Doug coughed, then said, "There was a box of stuff that Harry brought out. The guys could use something from the box, or use their bare hands. Whatever they wanted. But they only had one chance each to hurt me. Then they had to like bow before me and declare me leader, saying stuff like, 'I pledge my allegiance to thee, Berger, powerful leader of the Tribe.' Shit like that.

"At first, I got punched and slapped. One guy kicked me behind the leg so that I fell down to my knees. They waited until I got back up before going on."

Margo shivered and pulled the bedspread up around her shoulders.

"Then, I guess so that they wouldn't seem to be copycats, the guys started rummaging in the box. That's when it became like real torture. One guy stuck me with a pin, another took Harry's candle and dripped hot wax into my stretched out hand. It really burned. But I didn't cry out. I didn't make a sound. I just stared straight ahead and was in a kind of trance. I mean, it really was awesome."

Doug rubbed his thumb on the palm of his hand. Margo buried her grimace in the bedspread.

"Until Jackson. Fuckin' Jackson. It was like he was lookin' for a way to get back at me. In the box he found two metal clips. Kinda like for holding paper together, you know?" Margo nodded. Doug took a big breath. "Well, he took the metal clips and he clamped them onto my nipples. And he left them there. He fuckin' left them there. And I didn't think I could take them off without admitting that I was hurting. So I stood there and took it. The metal clips pinching my nipples and hurting more than almost anything I'd ever felt. And I looked down and my nipples were bleeding!" His eyes began to tear up at the memory.

"And I'm standin' there, putting up with all this pain, and I can't help it, but tears start to fall out of my eyes. I'm thinkin' 'Goddammit! Goddammit! Stop cryin'!' But I can't help it. It's like the metal clips and seeing the blood from my nipples – that was the final straw and I just fell apart." He wiped his hands over his eyes. "This is when I'm thinking, 'Shit, I failed, I'm no goddamn leader at all.' And I'm thinkin' they're all gonna make fun of me and Harry's gonna kick me out of the play and God knows what else. And that's when everything changed!"

Margo sat up and hugged her arms around her knees.

"All of a sudden, Harry got up and yelled out how great I was. How I had endured such tortuous pain and held it all in. He told them to remove the clips and they did. Then Harry came over to me and hugged me and comforted me and it felt so good. Like my dad or something. And he told the guys to join in. Tell me how great I was. Tell me what a great leader I am. So before I know it, I'm being hugged and patted on the back and cheered and the guys are saying things like, 'Shit, you're really strong!' 'I've never seen anyone endure pain like you!' 'I don't think I coulda put up with what you did!'" Doug's eyes got bright. "And, I tell you, I felt great. I felt proud of myself. I felt like the king of the universe!"

He stood up. "Then Harry got them chanting for me. 'Berger! Berger! Berger!' And he told them to make a parade for me. I was a hero! And that's when the guys came up with that procession thing that you saw when you were there. They hoisted me on their shoulders and marched me around the room chanting and cheering. I was laughing and howling like a coyote. It was fantastic." Doug had his arms out wide. "I was a hero."

Margo smiled and shook her head with disbelief.

"Then Harry said it was time for the men to show their love for me. He said, 'Berger has endured great hardship. He is our leader. We must love him. We must adore him.' They put me back down on the floor and I stood there, hugging and high fiving guys. Like a football hero. It felt great." He sat back down. "Then the guys made a circle around me and Harry told us all to take off our clothes."

Doug stopped and looked at Margo as if to ask if he should go on. Margo held her breath, then asked cautiously,

"And you all did?"

"Yeah sure." Doug shrugged, "Why not? I figured something like this was going to happen. I guess I was kinda waiting for it. Plus, it was an improv. You don't question things in an improv!" Margo wanted to counter that but kept her mouth shut. Doug got real quiet. "Maybe I was looking forward to it. I don't know.

"Anyway, so we're all standing there naked and Harry tells me to lie down on the floor. And he gives something to Jeremy. Claude. He says, 'Take this, Claude, and decorate your leader.' Or something like that. I'm figuring it's paint, you know, like for Indians. We are a tribe, you know. So I'm lyin' there waiting for Claude to paint me with war paint or whatever. And he comes over to me and starts to dribble this stuff onto my body. He's got some kind of jar and a stick or spoon or something and he dips it into the jar and dribbles stuff on my body. The guys all take turns and before you know it, I'm covered with this gooey, sticky liquid."

"Honey!" Margo suddenly said.

"Yeah. It was honey. I figured it out after awhile. Anyway, I'm beginning to freak out realizing I'm being covered with honey, but I'm holding myself real still and strong, you know?

"Then Harry says, 'Berger is covered with poison. Poison! He will die if it isn't washed from his skin. Men of the tribe – you must be willing to sacrifice yourself for your leader. Are you willing to sacrifice for him?' And they all yell, 'Yes!' And they probably thought Harry was going to bring out wash cloths or something, but then he says, 'Men of the Tribe, you must lick the poison off of your beloved leader!'"

"What the hell?" Margo gasped.

Doug stared straight ahead and said, "It took a second, then one by one they knelt down over me and began to . . . lick the honey off my body. One by one they all licked me. They licked my face and my chest and my arms and my feet and . . . and at first I was disgusted and I couldn't believe what was going on. But Harry was there saying things like, 'Berger, you are the great leader. Your men adore you. Look what they're willing to do for you. Feel their love. Feel their devotion. They are willing to take the poison into themselves for you. They are willing to die for you!' And so I'm trying to get over feeling sick to my stomach and to get into this and feel their love and shit. And I close my eyes and feel the licking on my body, all over my body and . . . all of a sudden, I start to get excited." Doug's eyes filled with tears again, but he didn't seem to notice. "I mean, it felt great. Sexy, you know. And, and I could feel myself getting hard. I couldn't help it.

"I was Berger and everyone loved me and I loved them. I was filled with love and I was feeling real horny and then while I was being licked on my arms and my chest, one of the guys started licking my cock." Doug stopped and rubbed his eyes with his hands. He went on. "I opened my eyes, but I couldn't see who it was because there were heads in the way, licking my chest and stuff. So I put my head back down on the floor and I let it happen. The guy took me in his mouth – and, you know – and . . . and, Jesus, I came. I came like a volcano. I came right into this guy's mouth. Fuck. I came into a guy's mouth!"

He buried his head in his hands and began to sob. But he kept talking:

"And it felt great. Greater than any time I'd been with a woman. And I've been with lots of women."

He stopped and looked up. "Margo, I am not a fag. I swear to God, I am not a fag. But that felt so goddamn good. Shit, I don't know what to think." Doug turned away.

Margo didn't know what to say. She waited. Then she dared to say, "Then what happened?"

Doug looked at her hard. "I don't think I can tell you anymore. It's just that – it just got worse from then on. Like my explosion carried over to the others and everyone got horny and, uh, and they all acted on it."

Images of naked guys in the Black Box filled Margo's head. She saw Harry, sitting on one of those folding chairs with his hands clasped in front of him, smiling and smiling like an evil Buddha, all puffed up and pleased with himself and his power. And getting turned on. She wanted to throw up.

"And the sick thing is," Doug went on, "I don't even know who it is that sucked me. I never did find out who it was. And I can't get it out of my head. Even tonight while you were sucking me, I was thinking about him and wondering where he was and if I would ever feel that way again. I'm sorry, Margo. I wanted to make love to you. But I couldn't. I can't. And I don't know if I'll ever be able to love a woman again. I don't know." His sobbing overcame him and he sat there with his head in his hands, rocking back and forth and back and forth.

Margo sat on the bed and watched him. When his sobs subsided a bit, she slowly walked over to him, reached out and touched his shoulder. He sat bolt upright and pushed her hand away saying,

"Don't touch me. I'm a really sick man, Margo, don't touch me. And don't say anything. Please."

He got up, put on the rest of his clothes and stumbled out without looking back at her.

It was now Margo's turn to cry.

CHAPTER TWENTY-EIGHT

When dawn broke, Margo's eyes were open. She had spent a fitful couple of hours trying to sleep, but her sleep was filled with dreams of naked men being licked and sucked on by other naked men, naked black men with papers stuck to them while the word "nigger" sounded and sounded like a church bell, and bleeding nipples with metal clips clamped to them.

She got up to make herself a cup of coffee and sat back down on her bed, knees pulled up, watching the sun rise through her cheap curtains. There was no romance left in her dingy dorm room. It was just a dreary way station for a serious student that would soon be vacated for the next student who had earned a "single" by having put up with years of college roommates. Her stuffed tiger looked like an inanimate beat-up rag doll again, and the cinder block walls of her room looked strictly institutional this morning. She took a sip of coffee and wondered how many theatre students would be needing psychotherapy after graduation.

Eventually she got up and gazed out her window. Across the grassy mall outside she could see the graduate library and she could just make out the legendary statue of the noble hog in front. She saluted the hog and wished it a good flight. It seemed like she would graduate a virgin after all.

She went to take a shower, got dressed and copied an address out of her *Hair* notebook onto a slip of paper. Then she went for a long walk. During the night she had made a decision and, hopefully, this one trip would be all that it would take to accomplish the task she had given herself.

It was probably insane, and she was pretty sure that she wasn't thinking straight. But she felt that she had to at least try it. For starters.

Her walk took her to a suburban neighborhood adjacent to the university campus. Student apartment buildings gave way to rental houses which gave way to nicer one-family dwellings which gave way to lovely upper-middle-class homes with sprawling lawns and manicured bushes, some of which were flowering. It was quiet and cozy in this well-established neighborhood where a few families were getting themselves off to church, and here and there a bathrobed individual reached out the front door for the Sunday paper.

The walk was long, but Margo used the time to clear her head and think. Think what to say, how to ask. She hoped that logical reasoning would work. Once he knew the dangerous effect he had on students, he'd quit, wouldn't he? Deep inside, she really didn't think so, but she knew she had to begin her task here.

When she neared his home, it was almost 11:00 a.m. She felt that was a safe time to call upon a person, even if it was a Sunday. She walked up to the front door and rang the bell.

She heard scuffling inside, the muffled sound of, "God, who could that be?" And finally the door opened. Margo expected to see a frazzled Harry, his tuft of hair especially disheveled, wearing a set of rumpled pinstriped pajamas and carrying a raggedy teddy bear. She was surprised to see a good-looking woman in her late 40s who obviously cared about her looks. This was the kind of woman who put on her make-up and fixed her frosted hair the instant she got out of bed. She wore a white and gold running suit with gold thong sandals, and her nails were impeccable. Margo was so stunned that this was Harry's wife that she was speechless.

Finally, the woman spoke, "Yes? Can I help . . .?"

A teenage voice from inside the house yelled, "Who is it?"

The woman continued, "Oh, hey, aren't you the actress? The one in *Hair*? We saw it last night. Marvelous production! You were wonderful!"

Margo snapped out of her trance, "Yes, thank you. I'm Margo Laughton." She extended her hand. "How do you do?"

"Well, come on in," the woman said, opening the door for Margo. "I'm Judith Adler, Harry's wife. I'm so pleased to meet you, though I must say I'm surprised to see one of Harry's students here at the house, and on a Sunday morning too."

"I'm sorry to bother you, but I must speak with Har—, uh, Dr. Adler. It's kind of urgent."

"Oh, okay. I'll go get Harry. He's just having breakfast. We were all up late last night! As I'm sure you were!" And the lovely woman departed.

Margo sat down in the living room. She looked around at its spotlessly clean and elegant simplicity. After having been in Harry's office, she had trouble imagining him living in this uncluttered, beautifully appointed space. Then Margo turned and saw a wall of eerie eyeless faces, and she realized she was indeed in the home of the masked one.

A barely cognizant teenage boy rounded the corner and stopped, surprised, when he saw Margo.

"What're you? Seventh Day Adventist?" he asked.

"No, I'm an actress. I was in *Hair* and I need to talk with Dr. Adler." Margo was starting to feel really stupid for coming to Harry's house. She should have waited until Monday and gone to his office. "Are you his son?"

"Yeah. We saw *Hair* last night. It was okay. Which one were you?"

"I played Sheila."

"Which one was that?"

"The lead."

"Oh yeah." And he walked out.

Margo knew Harry had a wife and a kid, but somehow she hadn't imagined his existence to be like The Brady Bunch. She really wanted to get up and leave and was wishing strongly that she hadn't come, when Harry appeared, just as unkempt as she had expected.

"Margo dear, what are you doing here?"

"I need to talk with you, Harry." Her voice cracked a little.

"What about? Are you all right?" He seemed concerned. Like a father.

"Yes, I'm fine. But other people aren't." She hesitated. "I need to talk with you."

Harry's demeanor changed slightly. His eyes got harder and his fatherly posture became defensive.

"Let's go into my office," he said. And he led the way to the back of the house. At the end of a hallway was a closed door. Harry opened it and Margo stepped in. Yep, this was Harry's place all right. This was obviously the one room Harry had been permitted to decorate. It was just as filthy and cluttered as his office on campus, with papers strewn about, books left open and piled here and there, and more of those damn masks staring at her from the walls.

They took seats as expected – Harry behind his desk; Margo in a chair beside the desk. Harry sat back, laced his fingers across his stomach and waited. Margo was shivering with fear. And she was so tired. What the hell did she think she was doing? She didn't know where to start.

Harry said pleasantly, "I hear you have an audition for the St. Bart's Players. Good luck with that."

"Oh. Thanks." That threw her off. She took a deep breath and began. "Well, uh, Harry, I'm here because I wanted to tell you that I've heard about what went on in the men's Improv and some of the men are really upset about it and I think it was some pretty horrible stuff to put them through and . . ."

She hated how she sounded so uncertain. Not very imposing. She was about to go on when Harry raised his hand.

"You know what went on in the men's Improv?" he asked.

"Yes."

"So, the men have been talking?"

"A little." Margo was lamenting her decision to come here. She wanted to rewind the tape, leave Harry's house and just go back to her dorm. She did not want to 'tell' on the men. She did not want to betray their trust.

Harry cocked his head and glared at her. "Where are they?"

"Huh?"

"Where are the men? Are they out on the lawn waiting to come in here and accuse me of some wrongdoing, or are you all alone with some high and mighty cause that is based solely on rumors and has been puffed up by your own fertile and prejudiced imagination?"

Margo wasn't sure how to answer that. "I'm on my own. Right now."

"And what, exactly, have you heard about 'the men's Improv?'"

Margo inhaled and went for it, recounting the highlights of both Jackson's and Doug's tales. She added her encounter with Tony and emphasized how upset, no, out of their minds, each of these men were as a result of the Improv.

She ended with, ". . . I wanted to discuss with you the possibility of . . ."

". . . of me not doing any more improvs?" he interrupted.

". . . of you not doing such *dangerous* improvs . . ." she corrected.

"Dangerous?!" Harry's voice rose.

Margo couldn't believe she was still talking. She hated confrontation. She wondered if some of Sheila's blood was flowing through her arteries.

"Or . . ." She sat up straighter, stared him right in the eye, and channeled her inner Sheila, ". . . maybe you should stop directing plays at this university."

There. She said it. It was out in the open. She waited for the blow.

Harry didn't move. Margo could detect no crack in his façade, no slight shifting of his body to indicate that he was even remotely uncomfortable with what she was saying. She had no inkling of what his response would be.

"First of all, young lady," he began, in an irritatingly patronizing tone, "you are not the first naïve student to accuse a college professor of, shall we say, inappropriate behavior. And I must say I am disappointed. I'm very disappointed in you, Margo. I had you pegged as a real pro. I thought that you, of all of my students, would be going on to great things as an actress. But now I can see that you are vengeful, misguided, narcissistic . . ."

"Narcissistic!?" Margo blurted out.

"Yes, narcissistic. To think that you would want to bring down a tenured professor with a great deal of respect in the university community as well as the community at large. Margo, do you really believe that causing a scandal just to get your name in the papers will advance your cause as an actress? I didn't peg you as one who seeks publicity stunts. But I can see I was wrong."

Margo couldn't believe what she was hearing.

"No, Harry. That is not my motive. I didn't want to do anything about you. I just wanted to graduate and move on from this place. But after hearing Tony and Jackson and Doug . . ."

"Ah, yes, Doug. You like Doug, don't you?"

"Yes."

"Are you doing this to impress him? Is that it, Margo?"

She hated to hear him use her name. "No, Dr. Adler. I'm not trying to impress anyone. I'm trying to protect people."

"Protect whom?"

"Future students. Future acting students. The cast of *Streamers* next season, who will trust you and enter into your improvs and not realize that they're about to be abused by a perverted voyeur who poses as a college professor."

"Is that how you think of me? A 'perverted voyeur?'"

Margo hung her head and said softly, "I think you are a troubled man who needs help."

"So you're the big hero – protecting the student body, getting the sick professor the help he needs. What makes you think that anything that went on in the Improv was so sick or wrong?"

"The men . . ."

"Oh sure, the men are telling tales. Well, did it ever occur to you that the men might be exaggerating to impress you? I've noticed both Doug and Jackson showing an interest in you. Isn't it possible that they're trying to gain your sympathy or devotion by telling you of the trials they've endured?"

Margo shook her head. "It wasn't like that."

"Oh no? Well, tell me. How did Doug tell you his story? When did he tell you?"

Margo felt her blood drain away. It was like he'd been spying on them. "He told me last night. After the cast party."

"*After* the cast party?"

"Yes," she hesitated, "We were . . ."

"Oh, and perhaps you two were having sex? Wasn't he just trying to impress his lover? A little pillow talk?"

Margo couldn't stomach this distortion of Doug's feelings. "No! In fact, he was ashamed because he couldn't, he couldn't . . . and he told me about the Improv to explain why . . ."

Harry smiled evilly. "Ha! He couldn't get it up and he blamed me?! Oh, that's good! That's rich! I know men grasp at straws in the bedroom, but blaming an acting exercise for impotence? Now I've heard them all!" He laughed a big, hearty, booming laugh that ricocheted around the small room and hurt Margo's head. "Did it ever occur to you, my dear, that the man is simply not attracted to you? Or that he was too drunk? Or that he suffers from some psychological or physiological problem? Or is it less painful for you to believe that *I'm* responsible for his lack of performance? Margo, let's look at who needs help here."

Margo swallowed to keep her morning's coffee down where it belonged. What the hell did she think she would accomplish here anyway? She started to get up.

"Wait a minute, young lady. You've made some serious allegations here.

Don't you think you owe me the courtesy of hearing my side of the story?"

She sat back down and met his gaze.

"First of all," he began, "you know as well as I do that nobody is forced to do anything in an improv. I give suggestions and it's up to the actors to decide what to do about them."

"But it isn't that simple! Actors think that they have to do the things you suggest for their 'acting.' And they trust you not to harm them. Plus, actors are afraid that if they don't do what you suggest, you'll kick them out of the play or blackball them in the Department."

"I'm sorry to be speaking while you're interrupting me."

Margo almost gagged.

Harry continued, "Secondly, college actors have to push through their inhibitions to reach new levels of experience. This is a painful, sometimes embarrassing process and some actors regret certain things they do. But modern actors are required to do a lot of things that most people would find embarrassing. And you, of all people, cannot deny that *Hair* worked."

"Yes. It was a great production."

"It was a great production. It was more than great. It was a breakthrough for most of the actors. And that breakthrough would not have been possible if we hadn't broken through some walls and boundaries through improv. I'm sorry. But that's how it is."

"The end justifies the means?"

"The end justifies the means." Harry cocked his head. "It's an art, Margo. You don't get to art without having to go through pain."

Margo was at a loss for words. Harry had turned it all backwards. She stared into space trying to sort out her feelings and what she should do, or not do, when Harry leaned forward and spoke again:

"And let me say one more thing, Ms. Laughton. If you spread rumors about what went on in my improvs, I will see to it that your acting career ends here. As you may know, I am well connected in the theatrical community. I have a long reach." He folded his hands on his desk. "If you pursue this little project of yours to destroy my professional life, the reputation you ruin may be your own."

Margo felt paralyzed. As she looked into Harry's cruel eyes, she felt the empty sockets of a dozen masks glaring at her.

"Now, get out of my house," he said quietly. He did not offer her one of his famous hugs.

She got up carefully, and found her way out of Harry's office. As she sped down the hall and toward the front door, she felt Harry's wife and son watch her go. She didn't know if Harry was behind her. She walked out of the house, down the front steps and out into the street without breathing. She was several blocks away before she felt that she could slow down. Then she stopped and threw up into some manicured bushes. She wiped her mouth with the back of her hand and trudged on. When she reached the edge of the campus, she held onto a telephone pole and bent over as if to throw up again. She could only gag and then she spat. She stood back up, holding onto the pole because she felt dizzy. She saw some colorful pop art on the pole and when her eyes focused, she realized it was a poster for *Hair*. She remembered that she hadn't gotten one for herself so she removed the poster, careful to pull out the staples so it wouldn't tear. She wanted a memento in case it was the last play she would ever be in.

CHAPTER TWENTY-NINE

Back at her dorm, there was a dramatically scrawled message on the message board on her door: "Where are YOU?!?!? See me the INSTANT you get in!!!!! Jen." Margo threw the rolled up poster on her bed, and then went down the hall to Jen's room.

Jen's door flew open one second after Margo knocked.

"Get in here and listen to this!" Jen pulled her friend into her smoky room. "Where have you been? I've been dying to tell you what happened last night!"

"Well, there was the cast party. Then Doug and I, well . . . and then I went to see Harry this morning. Stupid, stupid, stupid. I'm so fucked up."

"You what?! Doug, what? Harry?! On a Sunday morning?"

"I went to his house." And Margo told her the whole story. She told her about her encounter with Tony, the cast party and Jackson's story, her attempt at love making and Doug's story, and finally the humiliating tale of her visit to Harry's house.

Jen was silent as Margo spoke. When she finished, Jen got up and hugged her.

"Oh, you poor thing. He is such a bastard! I hate that man, Margo." Jen let her go and started to pace. "I hate him. Fuckin' hypocrite! He *has* to be stopped. No telling how many college actors he's fucked up in the head. Maybe even killed."

"Maybe. But I don't think I want to be the one to stop him."

"No, no, no. Don't say that. Not when we're so close." Jen sat Margo down and sat down very close to her. "I met Mike Matthews last night."

"You did? Whoa. He was there, huh?"

"Oh, yes, he was there. Good ole H101. I recognized him right away. He really doesn't look much different from his college pictures."

"What happened? How did you meet him?" Margo's interest helped dissipate the fog of self-disgust and self-pity clouding her mind.

"First of all, I just watched him." Jen sat back and lit a cigarette in her typically dramatic fashion. "I watched him throughout the entire play. He was glued to it. I mean, it was a good production, but not that good."

Margo raised her eyebrows.

"If you can't take a little criticism, you shouldn't be in show biz." Jen waved her cigarette at her friend. "Anyway, he seemed riveted to Doug. Watched everything he did."

Margo interrupted, "Remember how Doug looks like Scott Warren?"

"Of course." Jen seemed insulted. "I am not oblivious to that fact! So he's watching Doug and getting all caught up in the play and I notice he's really studying the slides. Especially the ones of the campus."

Margo's mind was clearing. "Because he was a student here at that time."

"Right. He's seeing the slides like they're pictures of his college days. And I can see he's starting to fidget. Finally, there's this slide of a protest rally or something here on campus, and in the middle of it, there's this guy giving the camera the finger and looking like he's saying, 'Fuck you!' Well, when Mike saw that, he just about jumped outta his seat. He actually let out a yelp. Kind of a moaning yelp."

Margo's eyes were wide. "I remember that. I distinctly remember that! Someone yelled at that slide. Why do you think he yelled?"

Jen's voice lowered and she spoke slowly. "That slide was a picture of Scott Warren and it was taken the day he died."

Margo got the chills. She was all ears and listened to every last drop of Jen's story.

"After the play, as he was getting ready to leave, I hopped across the aisle, blocked his way, and introduced myself."

"Did he know who you were?"

"Oh yeah – he'd gotten the letters. He tried to push past me to escape up the aisle, but I grabbed his sleeve and begged him to at least hear me out. His eyes were all red like he'd been crying, and he pulled away to rub them and I thought he'd bolt. But he settled down and agreed to talk with me. We went to an all-night diner and Mike spilled his story of what happed to Scott Warren."

Mike and Scott were close. They'd gotten to know each other well in soul-searching acting exercises, as well as in a friendship that spanned three intense college years.

Mike described Scott as a brilliant but confused young man. He had a macho image, had been a high school varsity athlete and was popular with the girls. Mike even thought he had a black belt in karate or judo. He was from an army family and was expected to follow in his father's boot steps. But Scott's macho image was faltering. When he changed his major from Political Science to Theatre, his father practically disowned him. He was happier than ever, but felt like he was disappointing everyone. He was determined to show them that a real man could be an actor. He used to walk around imitating Steve McQueen or Sean Connery – two actors he found especially masculine.

Finally, Scott told Mike he was having trouble with his girlfriend, Shelly. Shelly thought all actors were "faggy" and asked Scott if he was now a fag because he was in theatre. Then he admitted to Mike that he had wondered the same thing about himself. He had even begun to have performance problems with Shelly and it was killing him. Mike remembered him crying when he told him that. He also remembered being excited because he was gay and really liked Scott.

Scott and Mike both got cast in Harry's *Death of a Salesman* as the brothers, Biff and Happy. The two actors were thrilled to be given such great parts, and to be acting together. They worked long and hard on their characterizations, having frequent dinners together to discuss things. Mike admitted he was falling in love with Scott. It bothered him that Scott was still going out with Shelly, but he hoped there would be an opportunity to show his love soon.

Then came the improv. Harry's improv, designed to get the brothers, Biff and Happy, bonded. It was vintage Harry, with conflict, struggle, nudity, "brotherly comfort" and finally male sexuality that both the actors participated in, seemingly willingly, even eagerly. However, when the lights came back up in the Black Box, Scott ran from the room, barely getting his clothes back on.

Mike wasn't sure what happened after that. Evidently, on the way back to his dorm, Scott encountered a massive campus protest and he got swept up into it. He even got hit on the head by a cop who tried to detain him. That's when he flashed the bird and screamed "Fuck you" at a campus newspaper photographer who was snapping pictures. He apparently did some LSD at the protest too. At least, that was the official reason given for his suicide.

Scott's father had insisted on an investigation and an autopsy. He wanted to know if the cop's blow to his son's head was responsible for his leap. They found traces of LSD. Scott wasn't the first student who thought he was a bird while tripping on LSD. Case closed.

But for fifteen years, Mike knew the real reason Scott jumped. And Mike had felt responsible. He knew that he was in love with Scott and had wanted to be sexual with him. The improv was the perfect opportunity, but Scott wasn't ready. He was too fragile. Mike should have known. He blamed himself. Even though Harry was there and watching the whole thing and didn't stop it, Mike blamed himself.

"And that's why he never said anything about Harry and the improv." Jen concluded. "He thought he was responsible for Scott's death and he was scared he'd go to jail or something!"

"Unbelievable!" said Margo, exhaling audibly. "He really didn't think that Harry was at all to blame for setting up the situation? For encouraging them? For not stopping them? For watching them?!"

"Apparently not."

Margo shook her head. "You know, Mike was a victim of Harry's, um, improprieties as much as Scott Warren was. So how did you leave it?"

"Well, I didn't have all the juicy facts that you gathered during the night, but I told him our fears about *Hair*'s improvs and I told him we were going to try to get Harry to stop somehow."

"Did he say he'd be willing to tell his story?"

Jen paused dramatically, raised one eyebrow, and declared, "Yes."

CHAPTER THIRTY

Margo marched into the office of the current head of the Theatre Department, the beloved Dr. Cimino, bright and early on Monday morning. Dr. C was the picture of the contented college professor nearing retirement. He wore a plaid jacket and a bow tie under his pleasantly pudgy face. Thin wisps of white hair circled his head like a halo and he appeared positively jolly to be sitting up straight at his tidy desk at 8:00 a.m. on a Monday morning. Theatre people tend to be night owls. He was the only theatre professor with office hours from 8:00 to 10:00 a.m.

"Margo dear! What a surprise! My heavens, what are *you* doing here? Of all people, you, of course, have a perfect A in my course! You will graduate with honors. What in the world can I do for you?"

"I'm not here about Theatre History, Dr. C." Margo shut the door behind her. "I need to talk with you about something else."

"Of course, of course. Please sit down."

Margo sat in front of the desk and, without a pause, told the tale. She omitted the details, skipping to the meaty parts. She finished by making her summation:

"Dr. Cimino, I feel strongly that Harry should not be permitted to direct any more plays here at the university."

Dr. C was quiet for a good long time. His grin had vanished and his expression had morphed from confusion to shock to what Margo thought was sorrow. His posture slumped slowly. Finally, he spoke:

"Now Margo, there have been rumors about Harry for years. Even way back when he was a graduate student here." He paused. "But no one has come forward with such vivid descriptions of what goes on in his improvs."

Margo sighed in relief. Dr. Cimino went on:

"But frankly, Margo, I'm having a great deal of trouble believing it all."

Margo was jolted from her satisfaction.

"First of all, the boy who killed himself – they did an autopsy and found that it was drugs." He took off his glasses and cleaned them with a handkerchief. "Harry has some unorthodox methods, I warrant you, but I doubt his improvs are as inappropriate as you described. I'm sure the men are telling you stories, Margo. Harry's a tenured professor, you know. If his methods were as objectionable as you say they are, someone would have said something a long time ago."

"But that's just it!" countered Margo, "Students have been afraid to say anything. They're ashamed or afraid to be blackballed in the Department or ruin their acting careers or something. Or even afraid it was their own fault, like Mike Matthews."

"Mike Matthews." Dr. Cimino shook his head. "No, I don't remember him." He started neatening up a pile of papers. "At any rate, Margo, I don't think there's anything I can do, even if your stories are true. Harry's a tenured professor."

Margo was stunned. "But you're the head of the Theatre Department!"

"Yes, but technically, Harry is my equal. No. You'll definitely have to go higher up the ladder than little ole me."

"Do you mean you can't help me?" Margo found herself speaking louder, as though Dr. C was hard of hearing. "Who should I talk to?"

"I really don't think I should get involved at all. And my advice to you is to drop this. It will only lead to bad things. Let this go. Graduate and move on, Margo."

Later in the day, Margo's discussion with Dr. Stockerton, the third leg of the Theatre Department's tenured professor triumvirate, was even more frustrating.

"Margo, your allegations are ridiculous. Where are the men, after all? You are just spreading rumors because you are a vain and vindictive bitch who wants to get back at a Theatre Department that didn't cast you in enough plays to suit your star struck image of yourself."

Margo was speechless at that assault. What the hell was Stockerton talking about?

"Furthermore, if we try to limit what directors do in their improvs, pretty soon someone will come in and want to fire me for my improvs. No, we must give directors artistic freedom."

And he threw her out.

Standing outside of the offices of the hallowed professors of the Theatre Department, Margo clenched her fists. How could Stockerton think that she, of all people, was a vindictive bitch who wanted revenge? After how hard she had worked, how much she had put into this Department? And, what does he mean that someone might fire him for *his* improvs? He leads the most uninspired improvs ever. No one would fire him; they would just be bored to death. He was a bigger asshole and egotist than Margo had suspected and Dr. C was a coward. They both just wanted to protect their own asses. Forget about the students! She was sorry she'd wasted her time with either one of them.

She turned to leave the dingy hallway and was paralyzed by the sight of the pear-shaped professor of performance waddling down the hall. He seemed to pause in his gait when he saw her too. He walked past her without a greeting. Margo could smell his body odor mixed with men's cologne as he went by. She felt repulsed and, once he was safely entombed in his office, she ran out of the caliginous theatre building and into the sunlit day.

Filled with doubts, she walked with her head down trying to decide what to do. She desperately wanted to take Dr. C's advice and just drop it. Why not? No one was asking her to do this. And why should she anyway? If Harry had been doing this for decades, why had no one else ever tried to stop it? Why her and why now? And how could she ruin a man's career? Nothing that bad had happened to *her* after all. If the men were upset or wounded, they were the ones who should come forward. Not her. She should just walk away and graduate. In just two weeks! Graduate and move on, like Dr. C said. Graduate and . . . Shit! What time is it?

She looked at her watch then heard the chapel bells in the distance . . . Noon! It was already noon and she had a 1:20 appointment at St. Bart's to audition for her first post-college professional job!

She sprinted to her dorm, changed clothes, picked up her make-up kit and hair brush and threw them into a bag with her sheet music and photo-resume. She barely made the last cross-town bus that would get her to St.

Bart's on time. On the bus, she closed her eyes and focused on regaining whatever scrap of composure she had left. She did her make-up as the bus jolted along – waiting to do her eye-liner and mascara at red lights. She attempted to tame her hair.

When she got off the bus, she felt disoriented by this quieter more ivy-covered part of town. She consulted a campus map that was posted on a notice board. The theatre building was on the other side of the campus. She had to walk quickly along a tree-lined avenue where an occasional helicopter seed spun to the ground. A couple of squirrels chased each other around and up a tree trunk chirping loudly, their tails twitching as they raced. Margo felt lighter and freer. Students walked past her on the sun-dappled sidewalk. They nodded and smiled. They looked somehow cleaner and nicer than students on her campus. More expensive clothes, perhaps? Did they have better dentists and dermatologists? She was only a few miles from her college, but it felt like another country. Where she wasn't the enemy of the people.

Reaching the theatre building she had a couple of minutes to spare. She did a vocal check, singing a couple of bars of her audition song quietly. She was relieved to discover that she still had a voice. Part of her was completely shaken by the events of the last couple of days, by the entire process of *Hair*, she realized. But if four years of college theatre had taught her anything, it was how to put her personal life on hold while she performed. Trust your technique. Trust your training, she told herself. She walked to the door of the theatre and literally wiped her feet on the big gray door mat before entering.

On the bus ride back to her school, Margo allowed herself to relive what had been a wonderful audition experience. She rested her head on the seatback and felt the warmth of the sun on her face as she recalled shaking hands again with the handsome Fr. Angelo. He had greeted her with a broad smile, and introduced her to the group of people who were hearing the auditions. She sang, and her big voice filled the small theatre. She was pleased that her vocal instrument was there for her. And her comic monologue made them laugh out loud. She could sense that they were sitting up and paying attention to her. She was new to them, not having gone to their college, and they appeared interested in her.

They asked her to read from both plays, and sing again – this time from *You're a Good Man, Charlie Brown*, the song "Happiness." When she was finally done with her audition, she walked down the stairs of the stage and up the aisle where she was stopped by Fr. Angelo. He handed her a paper and said, "Callbacks are this Thursday. And this is a rehearsal schedule and more information about the Players and the commitment the tour requires. We'll be calling you."

She smiled and closed her eyes. She had had a glimpse of what the future would be like. Life after college would be lovely. Connecting with new directors, new actors, new artists. She felt like she was emerging from a four-year-long incubation in an ill-fitting egg. The last line of the song, "Happiness" was stuck in her head:

"Happiness is anyone and anything at all
 That's loved by you."

Margo glanced up and saw the chapel bell tower of her college. She loved her college, she loved acting, her art, and she loved her fellow actors – past, present and future. She arched her back to stretch. And made a decision. Yes, she would leave her college, but she would not leave Harry there too, to abuse the next generation of student actors. To hell with Harry! She would find a way to stop him.

CHAPTER THIRTY-ONE

Back in her dorm room, Margo dug into the bottom drawer of her desk and found the campus directory all students get in the fall. She opened to "Administration." She needed to know who was at the top of the administrative ladder on which theatre was the bottom rung. She considered the Chancellor of the University himself, but she was leery of talking with another man of academia. Looking a little bit down the list, she made her pick. Dr. Theresa Gilligan was Dean of the Division of Arts and Humanities. Margo called her office and made an appointment to see her. After stating that she wanted to discuss a professor's sexual misconduct, she was given a slot in Dr. Gilligan's busy schedule the following morning.

The rest of the day she attended a class, worked on an anthropology paper, studied for final exams and tried to eat dinner. She decided she needed to have Doug and Jackson on her side. Maybe Tony too. She called Jackson first. He was enthusiastic about helping. He said he'd gladly talk about what happened to him at the Improv. He did not, however, want to talk about what happened to Doug or the others. Tony, on the other hand, refused to say another word about himself or the Improv. He hung up on her.

Finally, Margo got up the courage to call Doug.

"Doug, it's me, Margo." Silence. "Are you there?" Pause. Pause.

"I really don't want to talk, Margo."

"No no no – don't hang up, Doug. This isn't about us."

"Okay, what?"

Feeling like she had about half-a-minute before he'd hang up on her, Margo launched into what she was doing, why she was doing it and finally asked if it was okay with him if she told his story for the sake of helping fellow students.

There was another long pause.

"I don't know, Margo."

"Doug, do you want other students to go through what you went through?"

"Well, I've been thinking about it, and I really think it did make me a better Berger." He paused again and actually chuckled, "That sounds funny – a better Berger. You want fries with that?"

Margo shook her head and smiled. She was grateful for a touch of levity.

"Okay, sure. A better Berger. But what about Doug? And all the future Dougs? What about them?"

Silence on the line again. Margo held her breath. She really thought he had hung up and she was about to say something when she heard his tentative voice.

"Okay. Alright. You're right. I get it. One condition."

Margo held the phone tighter. "What's that?"

"That nothing, I mean nothing, ever gets out into the newspapers or anything, because my mom would be devastated if she knew about all this."

Margo nodded, "Agreed." And before he left, she said quickly, "One more thing!"

"Jesus! What else, Margo?"

Margo closed her eyes, "Listen. I will do everything in my power to make it so that you don't have to talk about what went on. But, if it comes down to it, would you, uh, 'testify' on what happened to you in the Improv?"

"No, Margo! Absolutely not!" Doug let her have it, "Fuck, Margo – testify? What is this? A god-damned trial? Fuck no!"

"Okay, okay. I doubt it will come to anything like that." She decided to play her trump card. "But I have to tell you about a boy named Scott Warren." She told Doug the story.

"Imagine," she finished, "if you weren't as emotionally strong as you are. If, maybe, you were depressed or on the edge. I mean, shit, think how upset you were when, you know, things didn't work out with us. Can't you see how someone could be thrown over the edge by what happened to you?"

Doug was silent. Then he said quietly, "Yes."

Margo wondered if he had been contemplating anything so drastic. She hurried on. "That's why we have to stop Harry from directing any more plays. Your story will have more impact if you tell it."

"Maybe."

"Will you do it?"

A long pause. "I'll think about it."

The next morning Margo made her way to Dr. Gilligan's office in one of the red brick Colonial buildings on the main quad. Margo walked up the long staircase and past the white columns that framed the huge carved wooden door, and felt like David going to meet Goliath. She had no idea what Dr. Gilligan would be like.

After several uncomfortable minutes in the waiting area, Margo was ushered into the Dean's almost homey office. Unlike Harry's cramped little lair, this office had a high ceiling, plush carpeting and two comfortable armchairs.

Dr. Gilligan got up from behind her immaculately shiny desk and reached out to shake Margo's hand. She had light brown hair with gray streaks pulled into a bun. A few hairs had escaped and softened her wide make-up free face. She wore pearls with her navy blue military-styled suit, with pearl stud earrings to match. Her hazel eyes searched Margo up and down through gold-rimmed bifocals. She looked like a combination of someone's mom and a rear admiral.

As Margo sat down in one of the armchairs, she felt both at ease and on edge. She glanced at a photo on the Dean's desk. It was a younger version of Dr. Gilligan with, Margo counted, four children, three of them boys! *Pot of gold!* Margo thought.

Dr. Gilligan spoke first, "How do you do? Margo Laughton, is it?"

"Yes, ma'am," Margo replied. *Military brat training,* she thought.

Dr. Gilligan got right to the point, "I understand you are here to accuse one of our professors of sexual misconduct." Margo winced at the word "accuse." "I'm listening. Please tell me about the situation."

Margo perched on her chair. She began the tale of Harry and the men.

For the most part, Dr. Gilligan listened to Margo without interruption.

She made some notes on a yellow pad, but mostly kept her eyes on Margo while she spoke. Her face held a serious, concerned expression, but very little other emotion. She nodded occasionally and asked for clarification a couple of times.

Margo hadn't prepared her remarks at all. At first, she thought she would just mention the highlights, maybe just the *Hair* improvs she knew about, maybe avoid the most lurid details of Doug's ordeal. But once she started, she couldn't stop. She figured she might not get another chance to talk. She told it all. In vivid detail. And she told what she suspected about Scott Warren's suicide too.

As she spoke, Margo was beginning to think that Dr. Gilligan would be a disappointment too. Dr. Gilligan remained impassive and seemed to simply listen. *Maybe I'm a total idiot, or some kind of conservative wacko,* Margo thought as she talked. *Maybe this kind of behavior happens all the time and is actually sanctioned by the University. Maybe it is okay to do anything for Art.*

When she finished, Dr. Gilligan appeared to study her notes and silence enveloped her for a few seconds. Margo waited and looked at her hands, folded in her lap. Finally, the Dean spoke. Her voice cracked a bit as she began.

"These are serious allegations. Certainly, if a professor at our university is doing this kind of thing he must be stopped immediately."

Margo felt relief wash over her like a shower after a tough game of rugby. Finally, someone who understood and would do something!

"But how can we be certain that these things actually happened?" Gilligan asked, "Not that I don't believe you but, as you say, you were not actually there. It's hearsay."

"Some of the men are willing to talk if they have to."

She nodded and wrote something more on her yellow pad.

Margo broke the silence and blurted out, "I hope you understand. I don't want to harm Harry in any way. I don't want to ruin his reputation or the university's, and I don't want this getting in the papers. I just want him to stop directing plays."

"Are you certain that he doesn't abuse students in his classes?"

"Yes. I've taken his acting classes. No one I've talked to has ever said anything bad about his classes. Just the plays he directs."

"All right then. While it's true that I have certain authority over Dr. Adler and the other professors in this Division, I am not certain what the best course of action is on something like this. I may need to hear from others who were involved in the improvs. And I need to research the 1969 suicide. I'm not sure a connection can be made there. Tragic as it is. Let me think about all of this. I'll be in touch."

They both stood up and Gilligan came out from behind her desk to shake Margo's hand again. "Thank you," she said, "This was not an easy thing to do."

Margo didn't feel like she'd said enough. She added quickly, "I may be able to produce the actor who was involved in the 1969 suicide. His name is Mike Matthews . . ."

Gilligan nodded. "You've done your homework, young lady. Thank you."

Back out onto the steps of the red brick building, Margo still wasn't sure that she'd been emphatic enough. She wasn't sure Dr. Gilligan got the point. She had seemed too calm, too unemotional. She wondered if the Dean would really do anything, or just try to sweep it under the rug, which had probably happened many times with Harry during the course of his career. *"Even way back when he was a graduate student here,"* she remembered Dr. C saying. But she guessed it was all she could do for now. She walked to the library do so some studying. She felt some weight had lifted from her shoulders and she found herself humming "Happiness" as she walked along.

There were two messages waiting for Margo when she returned to her dorm. One was from St. Bart's. It said, "Callback Thursday 7 p.m." with a number to confirm. She smiled and her heart did cartwheels. The second one said, "Call Dr. Gilligan at home tonight," with the number. Her home number. Margo's heart then did a belly flop.

First Margo called to confirm the callback. She got a machine and left a message and a THANK YOU! Then she called the second number.

A woman answered, "Hello?"

"Hello, Dr. Gilligan, it's Margo . . ."

"Hold on!" the voice said. Then Margo heard a loud, "Mom!" and the voices of children in the background.

Then Margo heard another line being picked up and a similar-sounding woman's voice yelled away from the receiver, "I got it up here! Hang up, please!" Click, and the children's voices turned off.

"Hello, sorry, that was my daughter, this is Dr. Gilligan."

"Uh, hello, this is Margo Laughton returning your call."

"Oh Margo, good. Thank you for calling back. I've thought a lot about our meeting and discussed it with another colleague. We would like to set up a kind of informal hearing. I want some of the other administrators to hear the story, and I want to hear the men tell their versions. I have reserved a private conference room for this coming Monday at 10 a.m. Can you make sure that each of the men will be there?"

"Yes, ma'am," Margo said with more confidence than she felt.

When she hung up, Margo's head was throbbing. A "hearing." A private hearing, but a hearing nonetheless. She was confident that Jackson would be there. And she decided to invite Andrea to talk about what happened to her. But would Doug talk? She had less than a week to convince him. And what about Mike Matthews? She marched down the hall to Jen's door.

Before knocking she froze as a question entered her mind, "Would Harry be there?"

* * *

The callback on Thursday evening was a joy. Despite the roller coaster of emotions Margo was riding, she was able to focus her energy and perform well. She sang with ease and flair. She read with heart and humor. She wondered if maybe it was better to audition with a mind full of distractions – maybe she wasn't able to over-think things and screw herself over.

She also read scenes with other actors up for roles. She definitely clicked with a couple of them, including a short and quietly funny actor trying out for Linus. He reminded her of Woody Allen. They read a scene together and got laughs. The whole atmosphere felt fun and carefree. She felt like she could do no wrong here on this stage with these people who seemed delighted with her. She was, to her own amazement, amazing.

Fr. Angelo saw it too and took her aside at the end of the audition.

"If it were up to me, I'd cast you as Lucy right now. But this is a two-play tour and the two directors must consult before the final decision." Margo tried not to smile too broadly and simply said, "Thank you" as she shook his hand. In her mind, she was packing her suitcase for the tour, thrilled to be getting out of town and postponing New York for a year.

CHAPTER THIRTY-TWO

Andrea, Jackson and Margo met in front of the colonial building that housed the Offices of the Deans on the following Monday at 9:45 a.m. They commented on each others' appearance and laughed nervously. They had each chosen to wear conservative clothes, like this was a courtroom drama. Jackson even had on a jacket and a tie. They had never seen each other dressed like that; it was quite a switch from their hippy duds. Doug was late and Margo was getting worried that he wouldn't show up. Andrea reminded her of how often he was late to rehearsals and Margo felt better.

The real concern was whether Mike Matthews would make it. He was committed to being there, but was very busy with his work, he had told Jen. Furthermore, his car was in the shop. Jen had offered to go pick him up. She'd left two hours ago. Margo had her fingers crossed hoping that he would be there.

At 9:55 the well-dressed trio decided to enter the building and find the conference room. Doug would just have to make his own entrance. They felt strangely formal as they passed casually dressed students in the halls.

When they reached the waiting area outside the conference room, Dr. Gilligan was there to meet them. Margo introduced Jackson and Andrea to her. Margo also explained that Doug was late but she was sure that he would be there, and that Mike Matthews would be there too, but maybe not until eleven or so. Dr. Gilligan nodded, then spoke in a confidential way.

"Before we go in, let me tell you who's in there." The three students listened intently. "I've invited Dr. Maria Hermosa, Assistant Dean of Student Affairs, and Dr. Samuel Pinchet, Director of the School of Communications." Margo was disappointed. Pinchet was a boob; a poster child for the Peter Principle. Dr. Hermosa she did not know. Dr. Gilligan went on, "I've also invited the two senior professors in the Theatre Department, Dr. Cimino and Dr. Stockerton." Margo lowered her head and exhaled. "I know, Margo, you told me how little they regarded your story, but they should be here for this, as you must know." Margo nodded, as did Jackson and Andrea, whose eyes were widening.

"Finally," Dr. Gilligan continued, "I felt I had to invite Dr. Adler."

"What!" Margo blurted out.

"I'm sorry, Margo. I only felt it was fair that he hear the allegations and be permitted an opportunity to defend himself."

Margo was worried about Doug, "It's going to be hard to tell what happened with him sitting right there."

"I realize that, but please do your best. This is an informal hearing, not a court case. No one is forcing you to say anything you don't want to. But I urge you to be completely honest."

Andrea seemed anxious, "But I'm just a sophomore and I just switched my major to Theatre. I'm going to be blackballed right out of the Department."

"Nothing of the kind will happen," Dr. Gilligan assured her. "Let's go in."

They entered the forbidding conference room and Margo realized they had dressed appropriately. Around the room hung paintings of frowning academicians in gilded frames. A long mahogany table gave off a deep rich shine and reflected the small gold chandeliers which hung above it, and the tray of water glasses which sat upon it. Only the worn and stained gold carpet betrayed the room's age, and the lack of funding allocated to renovation at the university. On one side of the table sat the cast of characters that Dr. Gilligan had described. Dr. C seemed strangely sad and Dr. Stockerton appeared to be glaring at Margo. Margo heard the word *"Bitch!"* in her mind as though telepathically transmitted there by his baneful brain.

Finally, at the foot of the table sat Harry. He appeared neat and tidy in a well cut suit that Margo was sure his wife had picked out for him. He didn't look up as the students entered the room, but seemed preoccupied with picking at his fingernails.

Dr. Gilligan sat at the head of the table and gestured for the students to sit along the presently vacant side of the table. Margo sat beside Dr. Gilligan, Andrea sat beside her, and Jackson sat in the middle of the table closest to Harry. There were two empty chairs nearest to Harry, for Doug and Mike.

Dr. Gilligan began by saying, "I've just spent some of the most unsettling days of my career. Since Ms. Laughton first spoke with me last week, I have done my own research and consulted with several colleagues and an attorney. I still do not know what to think on this disturbing matter, so I have gathered you all together today to hear from all sides."

She then introduced each of the people present and explained why they were all there. As Margo looked across the table at the assemblage of academicians, she felt her confidence drain away. She knew that Andrea and Jackson would do a good job of telling their stories, but she didn't think that would be enough to sink Harry. They had to hear from Doug and Mike. She glanced at her watch. It was ten past ten and Doug still wasn't there. She wondered if he was chickening out after all. And she prayed silently that Mike and Jen would arrive safely and in time to testify.

In the middle of Dr. Gilligan's introduction, the door opened and Doug walked in. "Sorry I'm late," he said and he moved to an empty seat. It wasn't until he was halfway there that he saw Harry. Margo could see his step falter and she knew that she would hear about this later, but he kept going and sat down, nodding to Jackson and Andrea. He didn't look at Margo.

Dr. Gilligan repeated a shortened version of her introduction and finished by saying: "As you all must agree, this is a serious matter. However, this is an informal investigation, not a trial." *It looks pretty formal to me*, thought Margo. "The nature of this hearing is strictly confidential. What is said in this room stays in this room. Is everyone agreed?"

There were nods and affirmative statements all around the table. Margo and Andrea shared a glance – the words sounded familiar to them.

Stockerton had a question: "Are we at liberty to ask questions of the students?"

"Yes," said Dr. Gilligan, "However, remember that we are here to hear the allegations, not debate them. Please make sure your questions are for clarification, not argumentation."

Dr. Gilligan turned to Margo and asked her to summarize her allegations. Margo hated the word "allegations." It was like "rumors" or "lies."

She gave a brief introduction to her "allegations" for the benefit of Drs. Pinchet and Hermosa. She described for them what an "improv" was and how it was used in the context of a play's rehearsals. She said that she believed that Harry's improvs were inappropriate and went beyond the bounds of decency and art. That he'd been conducting these improvs for years and that many students had been harmed by participation in them. She told them that she did not wish to tarnish his professional reputation or to have him dismissed as a teacher; all she wanted was that he would no longer be permitted to direct plays at the university. Finally, she said that rather than explaining second hand what happened in the improvs, the students who actually experienced them would do the telling. She passed the ball to Andrea and sat back to listen.

Andrea was great. In a matter-of-fact, detailed way, she described the women's part of the Improv and how it led to her shirt coming off and her fear of being raped, even gang raped.

When she seemed to have finished, Stockerton asked, "I want to be clear. You were not actually raped, were you?"

"No," said Andrea.

"And you did, in fact, behave sexually with 'Berger.' You seduced him, as you say?"

"Yes," Andrea admitted, "But it was, you know, like a game. It was part of the Improv. And Harry pushed me to do it."

"Harry pushed you? You didn't think you could say no?"

"No. I didn't." Andrea looked at the table. "Harry is very persuasive."

"I have a question," said Dr. Hermosa. "Were you aware that there is nudity in *Hair* and that in a rehearsal you might be expected to take off your blouse?"

Andrea appeared stunned at the question. "Well, uh, yes, I knew that there was nudity in *Hair*, but it wasn't like that in the Improv. It was like, you know, an orgy or something, like things were all crazy and out of control and I felt . . . scared. I guess."

"But everything you did, you did willingly, did you not?" Dr. Hermosa persisted.

"Yes. Kinda. I guess so." Andrea admitted sheepishly.

"And how old are you?" Dr. Hermosa asked.

"Nineteen."

Dr. Hermosa nodded and made a note on her yellow legal pad.

Harry said nothing.

The temperature in the room was getting warm. Margo felt a trickle of sweat run down her side.

Jackson spoke next. He was strong and calm. He told his story of the racially charged part of the Improv with clarity and dignity. Margo was riveted by his words. Only toward the end did she notice Doug just beyond Jackson, squirming in his seat. Of course, Jackson was painting a rather unbecoming portrait of Doug as a racist. Suddenly, she wondered if this depiction of Doug would harm the believability of *his* testimony.

It was clear that Jackson made an impression on the panel of professors and administrators. Racial issues were hot on the largely white campus and the times were such that no college campus wanted to be accused of inciting racial tension. There was a respectful silence after he finished. Then Stockerton piped up again:

"May I ask how your performance was affected by this Improv you describe?"

"Uh, well, it did help me get at my black anger."

"Would you say that the Improv helped you? That the character of 'Hud' – is that the name? – was more focused, indeed, more in touch with his blackness than before the Improv?"

"Yes, I would have to say that was true."

"So, given the choice, knowing how the play came out, can you say that you're sorry that the Improv happened?" Stockerton glared at him with eyes squinting.

Jackson cleared his throat and spoke slowly. "I'm sorry the Improv happened the way it did, but I'm not sorry about the results in terms of my character on stage."

The atmosphere around the table seemed to shift. Jackson had hit on the main issue. Is it permissible to do "anything" in rehearsal if the actor gains something from it? Dr. C was tapping a finger on the table and glancing off to the side; Dr. Hermosa was frowning and making some more notes on her legal pad; Harry was smiling.

Margo wasn't really worried. She had thought something like this might happen. It was the testimony of Doug and Mike that was crucial. She looked at her watch. 10:45. Hopefully Mike Matthews would show up in a quarter of an hour. In the meantime, it was Doug's turn.

Before he began, he asked if Jackson and Andrea could leave the room. He didn't want to have to tell his story in front of them. Dr. Hermosa made a note. Margo wondered if she was writing "RACIST!" on her pad. Jackson and Andrea got up and left, whispering to Margo to call them after it was over. Margo nodded.

Doug's face was shiny from sweat and he was breathing heavily. Margo suspected he was uncomfortable sitting near Harry with just one chair between them, and she wished she could have rearranged the seating. Harry stared at Doug, but Doug was avoiding even a glance at him. This made him sit awkwardly in his chair, which made him appear even more miserable.

Nevertheless, his southern composure won out and he began eloquently, describing how excited he was to be in a Harry play, to be in *Hair*, and how willing he was to do anything Harry said. He said Harry was like a guru to him and he wanted to squeeze all he could from the master. And how he truly believed that an actor had to be willing to do anything for his Art.

He began to describe the Improv, going back over Jackson's story a little, then he began to falter. He repeated again how much he admired Harry and wanted to do anything he said. He glanced at Harry as he said that. Harry wore the expression of a disappointed father. Margo thought she even saw him shake his head the tiniest little bit.

Doug looked away from Harry and down at his hands which were laced together on the table. He paused for a long time. He wiped his forehead with a handkerchief and undid the top button on his shirt. He took a drink of water and cleared his throat. He tried to talk, but nothing came out. It was as if he was suddenly struck dumb. Margo wanted to slap him on the back to start him up again. Finally, he got up, looked at everyone, shook his head, and walked swiftly out of the room, slamming the door behind him.

Margo got up and ran after him. He was quite a ways down the hall by the time she caught up with him. She grabbed him and turned him around to look at her.

"Where are you going?" she demanded.

"I'm sorry, Margo. I can't do it. I can't tell it." He pulled his arm away from her and fled down the hall.

"Can I tell it?" she called after him.

He turned around, put his arms out while walking backward and shouted, "Tell them whatever the fuck you want, Margo!" He turned and ran.

Margo let him go. There was a big knot in her chest. She put her fist there and thought for a second about what to do. Then she turned around and went back into the conference room.

Everyone seemed lost and confused. Except Harry. Harry smiled at her when she came back in.

Margo took her seat and everyone settled back into the table.

"Doug feels he is unable to tell you what happened. So, with your permission, I will tell you what happened to him in the Improv."

"Were you there?" Stockerton asked with a sneer.

"No, I was not. But Doug told me what happened. And I was there to witness the effect the Improv has had on him and his sexual identity."

The room was silent at that last statement. Margo told the story, beginning in her bedroom after the cast party.

When she finished, she was pretty sure she had convinced them. Drs. Gilligan and Hermosa looked seriously upset. Dr. Pinchet, the boob of the Communications Department, actually looked sympathetic. Dr. C looked distraught. Even Stockerton held his tongue, for the moment. Only Harry, undoubtedly feeling the noose around his neck, spoke up:

"Quite a story, my dear, but that is all it is. A story. A dramatic story, I warrant you, but a story nonetheless."

"Are you saying, Dr. Adler," Dr. Gilligan asked, "that you did not encourage students to cover Doug Mulloy with honey and lick it off of his naked body?"

"No. That did happen," he said. Dr. Hermosa actually gasped. Harry hurried on. "But it wasn't as sordid as Ms. Laughton has described. First of all, he wasn't naked. His shirt was off and that was all. Also, he had honey only in the palms of his hands and the men each took a tiny lick. They actually found it funny and I wondered if the exercise was foolish." He laughed charmingly and there were a couple of relieved smiles around the table.

"Secondly, the violence you described, Margo, was hardly as dramatic as all that. I suspect Doug was trying to impress you with his feats of prowess." A chuckle or two from the table.

"Finally, never, never, never, has an improv of mine become so grotesquely sexual. A boy ejaculating on the floor of the Black Box Theatre? Ridiculous! I would most certainly forbid that kind of activity, no matter how much the students wanted to do it."

Margo tried to interrupt, but Harry kept talking.

"Ever since the 60s, students have been obsessed with their own burgeoning sexuality. And in theatre, we struggle daily to maintain the bounds of common decency. After all, actors are supposed to be free and uninhibited. I do not personally believe, however, that 'uninhibited' means acting on every animal urge that happens to come over you. Many times in an improv, students will find ways to behave in illicit ways under the guise of a 'character' they are portraying. It is a way to experience some vulgar fantasy of theirs and call it 'Art.' But I am careful to call a halt when I see this kind of behavior going on.

"Of course, this time I was directing *Hair*, and the opportunities to explore sexuality seemed obvious. I also believe there was an inclination, among the males of this cast, toward homosexuality. When the men were alone in the Improv, several of them began to explore this. Doug Mulloy was one of them. When I steered the 'exploration' away from homosexual activity, they became livid, especially Doug. I believe this is why Doug has concocted this story and enlisted you, Margo, in his scheme to bring me down. He knew you were a strong woman and you would follow this through where he could not. And you've done well, my dear. You are sincere in your desire to do the right thing. If only you weren't fueled by a pack of lies."

Margo glanced around the table and saw hostile eyes appraising her – Stockerton, Dr. C, Pinchet, even Hermosa, she thought. She felt betrayed on all sides, by Doug, by Harry, by the University, by Theatre. For once, she had taken a firm action in response to an injustice and it was coming back to destroy her. She didn't want to consider that those around the table believed Harry, but their expressions told her that her worst fears were coming true.

Dr. Pinchet asked, "I'm not clear here. Are you saying that the men wanted to have homosexual experiences in your improvs and you stopped them?"

"Basically, yes." Harry answered, sanctimoniously.

"Okay. I'm clear now." Pinchet responded.

Dr. Gilligan asked Margo quietly, "Will none of the men come forward to say what went on?"

Margo shook her head. "Jackson might. But the others didn't want to talk about it. They all took vows of confidentiality when the Improv started and they won't talk." Dr. Gilligan glanced at Dr. Hermosa.

"So," Dr. Pinchet interjected again, "What we're left with is your word against his?"

That about summed it up. The table got restless.

Stockerton, of course, took the opportunity to offer his two cents, "What we're left with are a couple of stories of perhaps embarrassing, perhaps upsetting activities in the course of an improv, but I don't see that any abuse went on. Or that any of the students, who were legally adults, mind you, were adversely affected by what went on. The young black man actually said the Improv helped him." He shrugged his shoulders and gave a so-what-are-we-doing-here? expression.

Margo felt defeated. Her illustrious college career was ending in a humiliating episode which might, in fact, ruin the acting career she'd been preparing for. She wanted to turn back the clock to a week ago and forget that she'd ever initiated this travesty.

She was about to apologize to them all for wasting their time when there was a rapid knock on the door and in flew Jen and a handsome forty-something man.

Jen sputtered something about traffic and getting lost and she gave a blustery introduction of Mike Matthews, then finished with, "Well, I guess I'll be out here," and she darted out, closing the door behind her.

Mike Matthews stood just inside the doorway and greeted the tableful of stunned faces.

"Hello, as you heard, my name is Mike Matthews. I apologize, but I was hung up at work. I believe you have been waiting for me."

CHAPTER THIRTY-THREE

"Please take a seat, Mr. Matthews," said Dr. Gilligan, "Would you like a glass of water?"

"Yes, please."

Dr. Gilligan poured a glass and handed it to him. Margo felt like an angel had just stepped into the room. She glanced beyond him to Harry and was gratified to see a look of real distress etching his face.

Dr. Gilligan again introduced the group around the table. Mike reached across the table to shake hands with Dr. Stockerton and Dr. Cimino, his old professors. He did not shake hands with Harry.

When Margo was introduced to him, he took her hand as though to shake it and put his other hand over it.

"It's nice to finally meet you," he said quietly.

"Thank you for being here," Margo replied, gripping his hand.

Dr. Gilligan then addressed him: "As you know, Mr. Matthews, we are here to determine whether Dr. Harrison Adler has been conducting theatrical improvisations which are sexually abusive. I believe you were a student actor who was in one of Dr. Adler's plays and you were involved in one of his improvisations?"

"Yes, I was."

"When was this?"

"It was the fall of 1969. The play was *Death of a Salesman*."

"And you believe that you were abused in an improvisation which was conducted in the course of rehearsals for this play."

"No. I do not believe I was abused." There was a murmur around the table. "I believe, however, that the improv was abusive and resulted in the suicide death of my acting partner, Scott Warren."

"You cannot prove that!" Dr. C spoke up for the first time during the hearing. He stood up and pounded his index finger into the table top. "That was one of the greatest tragedies of our Theatre Department – a talented student committing suicide. But he was a troubled kid and he was into drugs! The autopsy proved it!"

Dr. Gilligan remained calm. "Please sit down, Dr. Cimino. Let us hear what Mr. Matthews has to tell us."

Mike Matthews spoke clearly and confidently:

"First, you must know that I've thought about this so much over the past fifteen years that I remember it like it was yesterday."

He took a deep breath and began. "Scott Warren and I were really good friends. I met him in my sophomore year when he switched his major to theatre. We got to know a lot about each other in acting classes and our friendship grew out of that."

He had a quiet demeanor and a gracious attitude. Margo noticed that Dr. Hermosa was nodding and she looked thoughtful.

"He knew I was gay. He was one of the first people I came out to."

Dr. Hermosa's expression went from thoughtful to painful. Margo looked away from her.

"And I knew that he was having trouble with his parents, his girlfriend and his identity. His parents were furious at him for dropping Poli Sci to go into theatre; his girlfriend called him a 'fag' for being an actor; and he was having trouble with sex. He told me that he was this big jock and real macho and all, and I think he was having doubts about his heterosexuality. We did not actually discuss that. I didn't think he was ready to deal with it.

"We both got cast in Harry's *Death of a Salesman* and we were thrilled. It's a tough play and we were excited to be playing the brothers, Biff and Happy. We did a lot of talking about the play after rehearsals, working on our acting journals together, things like that. And I think I was falling in love with him."

Dr. Stockerton was making furious notes on his legal pad. Margo tried to read them across the table, but couldn't.

"We were both looking forward to our big improv with Harry. It was an opportunity to discover more about our characters. We were dedicated, devoted actors who wanted to be fully immersed in our art.

"When we got to the Black Box Theatre that day, Harry was already there and the room was really dark. I think he had one candle lit. It was creepy."

Drs. Gilligan and Pinchet nodded their heads. They had heard about the one candle from the others.

"Harry told us that the improv was designed to get us bonded as brothers. We started out by sitting on a couple of stools facing each other and telling each other about ourselves. Harry asked us questions like: What being a man meant to each of us, what was our biggest fear, things like that. Then we did some trust exercises that were no big deal – falling backwards into each other's arms and so on. I don't think I need to explain that."

He looked at Dr. Gilligan. She shook her head.

"Then it got more, uh, intimate." He paused and said, "We had to strip naked."

He glanced around at the stunned faces at the table and shrugged, "It was the 60s." He exhaled loudly. Margo looked at Harry. He was staring straight ahead with no emotion on his face.

Mike continued slowly, "Okay, so we were naked and Harry told us to put the stools together and sit back to back on them. Then Harry got out these ropes and tied us together. Hard. The ropes were tied tightly with a lot of knots. I couldn't even move my arms from behind my back."

Harry made a move as if he was going to talk. Everyone looked at him. He shook his head as if saying, "excuse me" and resettled himself in his chair. Mike went on:

"The object of the improv was to work together to get free of the ropes. Well, we worked and we worked and we struggled, but the ropes were really tight and they hurt. After a few minutes, it didn't seem like we were ever going to get free so Scott said something like, 'Geez, Harry, these ropes are too tight. What's this supposed to prove anyway?'

"Well, Harry just about went through the roof! He screamed, 'Don't break! Don't ever break!' meaning, don't break character. This was an improv, we weren't supposed to step out of it to comment on it or anything. Scott, I'm sure, felt humiliated. He was trying to be this great actor and he was getting yelled at by a great director. Plus there was the fear of being booted from the play if you didn't do what a director told you to do." He looked around the room as if to see if the group understood him. There were some micro-nods. He continued:

"So we get struggling with the ropes even harder. And by this time the ropes are really cutting into us and we're getting all sweaty and I'm wondering what the hell this has to do with *Death of a Salesman*. I mean, *Death of a Salesman* is about this poor, sad traveling salesman named Willy Loman and how his two jock sons don't want to end up a big, fat failure like their dad. So why the hell were Scott and I tied together and trying to get free? Pardon my language." He took a sip of water, then went on:

"That's when Harry started taunting us."

"Taunting you?" asked Dr. Gilligan.

"Yes. Insulting us. He was being Willy Loman and showing his disgust with us."

"What kinds of things did he say?" asked Dr. Hermosa.

"I remember him staying things like, 'You're both a couple of shits. You'll never amount to anything. I am so disappointed in you both. Failures. Look what I raised. Failures!' And while he's saying this I'm thinking, Shit, this is not what Scott needs to hear right now. He already has a father calling him a failure, he doesn't need it from Harry too.

"That's when I hear what sounds like Scott sniffling or crying. Well, Harry loves that and he yells at him, 'Babies! You're both crybabies. Too chicken to stand up for yourselves and be real men. I'm so ashamed of you.'"

Mike's voice was getting more animated.

"Then Scott yells back at him, 'Fuck you!' or something, and Harry says, 'What's that, Biff? Talkin' back to your dad? The man who raised you and worked his whole life to put food on the table?' But Scott keeps going, 'Get us out of these ropes!' he says. And he jerks really hard to one side and we lose our balance. We tip over off the stools and land on our sides. I hear Scott yell, 'Shit, my elbow!' and Harry shouts back, 'Watch your mouth, you asshole! My sons, a couple of faggots!'"

Margo saw Dr. Hermosa wince. Harry was gazing out the window. A ray of light illuminated his sweating pin head.

"Scott yells back at him, 'Faggot, my ass, faggot!' and Harry gets real intense. He walks over real close to us and says, 'What did you say, faggot?' Then he leans over and says real quiet, 'You've got one of the best bodies I've ever seen, Biff. A real athletic specimen. I bet all the guys on the team want you.'

"Scott is pulling really hard on the ropes now, but Harry keeps talking, 'Those pecs are to die for,' shit like that. That's when I get into it. I could tell he was getting to Scott and I wanted him to stop. I say something like, 'What the hell are you doing, Harry?' and Harry becomes the stern professor again, yelling at *me* now, 'Stay in the improv. Don't break.'

"So I'm thinking, okay, this is what he wants, he wants us to get at our anger and outrage and it's working. Acting is so cool. This is what it's all about. And I can tell that Scott is back into it too because suddenly we're really working together with the ropes, using our hands and our arms and sliding our backs against each other and twisting from the hips to loosen the bonds. And Harry's saying things like, 'That's it! That's my boys. Working together. I love you both so much. I love you. I love to see your bodies working together. Strong athletic bodies. I raised you right.'

"And I say, 'You sure did, Pop.' And we're squirming and moving and the ropes are loosening and we both give a big mutual jerk and suddenly we're chest to chest instead of back to back! Lying on the floor, tied together, chest to chest. Naked and, uh, front to front.

"And Harry's still talking to us, 'You're both so powerful. So connected. There's nothing like the tie between brothers. You know everything about each other. You understand each other's darkest secrets. You love each other. You protect each other. You think about each other all the time. You love each other.'

"Well, I'm blown away because it's like Harry is reading my mind. Scott is starting to cry really hard now and I'm thinking that it must be true for him too. I'm so excited. And Harry keeps going, 'Who have you ever trusted more than each other? Who loves you more than each other? No woman will ever love you as much. No woman will ever completely understand you. No one understands how helpless and vulnerable you really are. But you can tell each other.'

"So I say, 'I do trust you, Biff ('cause that's his character's name). I do, you're the greatest.' And Scott says, 'Oh Christ, Happy. I don't even know who I really am.' And I say 'You're my idol. I'm so proud of you.' 'But I've let so many people down,' he says. And I'm dying because I know he really feels that, so I say 'No, you haven't. Mom thinks you're the best. And to me, you can do no wrong. I love you, Biff. I honestly love you.' By this time the ropes are pretty much off and Scott is really crying and saying something like, 'Dad's right. I'm a failure. I've let everyone down.

I'm no good.'

"I couldn't stand to hear him say that. I started to hug him and say, 'I love you, man. I love you. I mean it. I love you.' And before I know what's happening, I start to kiss him. At first he resisted, but then he gave in and kissed me back.

"It was wonderful. It felt so good, in the dark, all hot and sweaty. And this man that I loved so much was loving me back. And I was overjoyed. I wanted him. I wanted him so much. Once we started, I couldn't stop. I'm not sure if he resisted. He seemed to be so with me, so into it."

Mike paused and Margo thought she saw that his hands were trembling.

"And I've gone over and over this in my mind every day since it happened. But I think I raped him. Part of it was mutual. I do believe that he wanted it." He paused, his mouth held open. "But when it finally came down to it, I raped him. And when the lights came up in the Black Box, I could see the disgust and horror on his face.

"Then he bent over and started bawling like a baby. This is when Harry came over and sat next to him and cradled him in his arms and told him everything was okay, saying, 'You did great. It was a great improv. You really reached a new part of yourself.'

"Scott pushed Harry away and said in a nasty voice, 'Don't you touch me, you faggot!' and he snatched up his clothes. He dressed furiously, saying 'A new part of myself! Shit! This was *not* a new part of myself! This was fucked, man. I am not a fag!' I tried to hug him, but he pushed me away too and ran out of the Black Box." Mike paused for a second to catch his breath. "I never saw him again."

Mike closed his eyes.

"I know the coroner's report said that Scott's suicide was because of some LSD he took at a protest rally later that day. But I know the real reason Scott jumped from that ninth floor dorm window." Mike opened his eyes and put his hands flat on the table in front of him. "He couldn't live with what he'd learned in that improv. Maybe it was something he needed to learn about himself eventually. But the way it happened was wrong. With Harry baiting him and for Christ's sake WATCHING it all. And that's why I'm here today. For fifteen years I thought I was responsible for Scott's death because I forced him to have sex when he wasn't ready. But I see now that it was Harry who created the scenario that allowed it all to happen. It was Harry who encouraged it and watched what was going on. And it was Harry who didn't stop it. I don't know what makes him think he's some kind of god who can make people do things so he can watch and get his rocks off or something. But it's wrong. It's not Art or Theatre. It's just wrong. And he has to be stopped before he hurts anyone else."

The late morning sun was making the room sweltering. A fly buzzed busily against one of the windows. There was no other sound in the room for several long seconds.

Finally Harry faced the table. He cleared his throat and spoke:

"Mike, I am sorry about what happened to Scott Warren. That boy was emotionally unstable, and if my improv caused him to hurt himself, it is tragic. However, there was LSD in his blood. We cannot prove anything about why he chose to take his own life. But let me make something perfectly clear," he turned to the table, "I do not force any of my students to do anything. I give suggestions and watch them create and explore and break through inhibitions that would otherwise keep them trapped in mediocrity. After one of my improvs, my actors are fearless to express themselves. My plays prove the value of the work. The purpose of theatre is to hold 'the mirror up to nature,' ladies and gentlemen. And I'm afraid that sexuality is a part of nature. It is a part of our modern lives. Actors who graduate from my plays are equipped to perform in today's theatre."

"But Dr. Adler," Dr. Gilligan said, "you say that you do not force your students to do anything. But do you stop them when things seem to be getting out of hand?"

"What is 'out of hand,' Dr. Gilligan? Our world is violent and it is sexual. Art reflects that. True artists of the theatre must be willing to explore that. In my improvs, we do that. Don't blame me that the world has become sick and confused. I'm to be congratulated that I can get my actors experiencing all of this in a controlled environment."

"But, do actors really have to *experience* things in order to play them?" All heads turned to Dr. Hermosa who was glancing at her notepad. "Isn't that why they call it 'acting?'"

A brief silence followed her question. Then Margo heard a muffled chuckle.

Harry looked like he wanted to speak, but stopped with his lips held pursed.

Dr. Gilligan cleared her throat. Then she said:

"First of all, Dr. Adler, perhaps these students were not being 'forced' to do things they didn't want to do. And I understand that they are all legally adults. However, I heard it mentioned several times that they felt pressured to follow your suggestions and not to 'break' as I believe Mr. Matthews said. I believe they trusted you. Indeed, as their professor and director, you are in a position of power and I believe they had a right to trust that you would not put them in any danger – emotional or otherwise. When you saw things become indecent, I believe it was your duty to stop them."

Harry lunged forward and blurted, "I think 'indecent' is . . ."

Dr. Gilligan held up her hand, "Let me finish." Harry sat back in his chair. "It is difficult to determine what is indecent and what is daring or even artistic. I would encourage some input on this, but let me say that from what I've heard today, I am willing to state that what went on in your improvs was, indeed, dangerous. And I believe it was abusive. Students were damaged. Perhaps seriously. One perhaps fatally, though without a suicide note that is impossible to determine."

"Dr. Gilligan, if I may," Stockerton was on his feet, "surely a professor of Theatre cannot be held responsible for how a student reacts to an exercise that is designed to stretch him beyond his inhibitions so that he can approach Art . . ."

"Dr. Stockerton, I am tired of hearing the words Art and Theatre elevated to the level of the sacred. This is not a theoretical discussion about the limits of sexual propriety in Theatre or Art. We are discussing the conduct of a professor at this University in the Division of Arts and Humanities of which I am Dean."

Stockerton sat down. Margo suppressed a smile.

"As I listened to what was being said here today, I realized that I was not just listening as a dean or a professor, but also as a mother. I have three sons and I want to believe that if I send them to this University, or any school, they will be educated, enriched and even stretched past some of their inhibitions. But if what I heard today had happened to one of my sons, as a mother, Dr. Adler, I would be wanting your head."

Harry swallowed and was silent.

"As a Dean, I must insure the safety of our students while preserving the reputation of our University. You are a tenured professor here at this University, Dr. Adler. You are held in high esteem here and in the community at large. You have a family and a home and a reputation.

"I understand the students who have spoken today would prefer that none of what they said becomes public knowledge. They have been abused enough by what has happened to them. Public humiliation would only hurt them more."

No one spoke. Margo could hear that fly buzzing at the window. Dr. Gilligan appeared to be at a momentary loss for words. Finally, she shook her head, and addressed the table quietly:

"I am going to need some time to sort this out and come up with a decision. Drs. Hermosa and Pinchet, please stay for a moment so we can arrange another time to meet and discuss this.

"I will be in touch with the rest of you . . . thank you . . ."

As Dr. Gilligan spoke, Margo glanced out the side of her eye at Harry. She was surprised that he looked calm, even relaxed. He was gazing at Dr. Gilligan almost like a little boy looking at his mother. She wondered if maybe he was glad that he had finally been caught. That it was all finally out in the open. Or was she just projecting? Over his head, the dust in the air was being illuminated by rays of light filtering in through the grimy windows. She sang silently to herself, *"Let the sun shine, let the sun shine in."*

Finally, Dr. Gilligan reminded them that the proceedings had been confidential and they were not to be discussed outside of this room. Everyone nodded thoughtfully. Margo smirked at the irony. *Just like a Harry improv,* she thought, *Nothing goes outside these walls.* She was compelled to glance at Harry one last time and her heart jumped. He was staring directly at her with a malicious glare. This was not over.

CHAPTER THIRTY-FOUR

That evening Margo sat in Jen's room, enjoying a cold Diet Coke while she retold the events of the hearing. Jen was an appreciative audience – applauding at the testimonies of Jackson and Andrea, hissing and booing at the comments from Stockerton, shaking her head at Doug's retreat and throwing wads of paper at a stuffed elephant whenever Margo mentioned Harry. She also marched in a little victory parade, tooting on an invisible trombone around the room, to celebrate her own heroic delivery of Mike Matthews just in time for him to talk. When Margo recounted Mike's story, Jen teared up a little. Finally, for Dr. Gilligan's final words, Jen actually put her hands together and said, "Thank you, God!"

"Jen!" exclaimed Margo, "When did you suddenly get religious?"

"I'm not, but, man, it sure feels like Good overcoming Evil, or something like that." She shrugged.

"Well, it's not over yet . . ."

Jen interrupted her, and put on her best John Wayne impersonation, "And after saving Drama Town, Sheriff, you get to ride off into the sunset on a national tour while I stay here in this hole to rot for one more semester!"

"Shut up!" Margo threw a pillow at her and laughed.

Suddenly there was a knock at the door.

"Margo, are you in there?" Rebecca from down the hall peeked her head in, "Phone for you."

Margo got up quickly. "Thanks!"

Jen gasped, "It's got to be Gilligan! Shit, this is it! Good luck!" Jen gave her two thumbs up as Margo gave her a "Yikes!" look and ran out the door.

About a minute later, Margo walked back into Jen's room and closed the door behind her.

Jen was banging on her desk like a drum roll.

Margo felt her face drain of its color and she leaned back against the door.

Jen stopped drumming and waited. "Well . . . what's the verdict?" Her voice cracked, "Don't tell me . . ."

"I didn't get it," Margo said with a trembling voice. She sat on Jen's bed and put her hands on her mouth.

"Didn't get what?" Jen looked confused.

"The tour. I didn't get the St. Bart's Players Tour."

"Oh man, Margo, I'm so sorry! But, I don't understand," Jen came over and sat next to her, "You said it was practically a done deal and . . . Oh shit! Son of a bitch!"

They looked at each other and said together, "Harry."

* * *

A week later, Margo was back in Dr. Gilligan's office to hear her decision. Margo did not feel warm and fuzzy about the meeting. When she shook hands with Dr. Gilligan, there was no comforting warm smile, just an officious, "Thank you for coming." Then, "Please, sit down." Margo sat in the nice armchair again. Dr. Gilligan sat behind her desk. Margo thought she looked more like the rear admiral than the mom at that moment.

"Margo, I wanted to talk with you one-on-one so that we can be absolutely certain that this matter has been handled to your satisfaction, with the utmost care, concern and confidentiality for all involved. I have agonized over this, and consulted with my colleagues . . ."

And probably a team of attorneys, Margo thought.

"And I want you to know that Dr. Adler will not be directing any more plays at this university."

Margo nodded. She didn't know how to respond. Dr. Gilligan waited, but when Margo didn't speak, she continued:

"Dr. Adler will be permitted to continue teaching and he will retain his status as full professor here. However, if there are any more complaints from students, further action will be taken."

Margo thought for a second, then said, "Will there be any kind of announcement?"

"Well, as you said, the students affected do not want any publicity on the matter. Nor, I admit, does the University."

I'm sure, Margo thought.

Dr. Gilligan went on, "So, no, there will be no formal announcement, per se. But at some point, it will become clear that Dr. Adler has 'retired' from directing plays on this campus."

"Very good," said Margo, feeling simply numb after the entire episode. She was about to get up to leave when she felt a sudden surge of something. She stared directly into Dr. Gilligan's eyes and declared, "And just so you know, no matter where I am, as long as Harry is here, I will be paying attention. If I ever hear of Harry directing another play at this University, I will do something to stop it."

Dr. Gilligan nodded. Margo thought the Dean was convinced, and a little shaken.

On the way out of Dr. Gilligan's office, Margo caught her reflection in a decorative mirror. She thought she saw Sheila smiling back at her.

* * *

Margo trudged through the last couple of days of her last semester of college in a fog. She was done with her theatre classes, so she didn't have to go into the theatre building ever again. After practically living there, she felt somehow exiled.

She had a couple of strange dreams about Doug and Harry and Scott Warren and Mike Matthews. She wondered over and over if she should have done more – called the newspapers, or a lawyer, or insisted Harry get fired or arrested or something. Did she make it too easy on Harry and the Theatre Department and the University?

But why was it up to her anyway? Harry didn't really hurt her. Why was she always the protector? The one who took care of the people being hurt?

Walking alone by the noble hog after finishing her final final, she paused to examine his prodigious snout. "You tell me," she addressed the hog, "Why did I stick *my* big snout into Harry's business anyway? I could have just graduated and moved on. And I could be on my way to a national tour.

Why did I have to be a hero?" The hog did not answer.

She saw Doug one last time, at graduation. They sat close to each other, one person apart, in alphabetical order of graduating seniors in the Theatre Department. He had shaved his beard and cut his blond hair. She thought he looked preppy enough to join an investment banking firm. He stared straight ahead and never met her gaze. Her playful, wild, irreverent Berger was gone.

With the last of her boxes piled into the back of her parents' Ford station wagon, she was driven home by her newly-sober-again dad and oh-so-proud mom who was thrilled to have her oldest daughter home for a few weeks before she moved to the big city. "Your room's all ready!" her mom almost squealed. "We have so much to talk about!"

Margo's dad launched into a story about how he was able to fix a neighbor's lawnmower. Just by listening to it, he could tell exactly what was wrong and had the perfect part right in the garage. "It works like new," her mom chirped in. "Damn right it does!" her dad proclaimed, "Started right up. And I sharpened the blade too."

"That's great, Dad," Margo said.

"Works like new," her dad said again.

As they drove away from the campus, with her *magna cum laude* diploma in her hand, Margo gazed at the sky from the car window. She thought she saw a noble hog flying overhead.

THE END

AFTERWORD

Thank you for reading *The Improv*. I am not first-and-foremost a writer, but I felt I had a story to tell and I crafted the means to tell it with the help of many helpful reader friends and one professional editor.

Lots of questions came up for early readers and you may want to ask some of the same. I'll answer a few here, then provide a link to my website where you can find more answers, and give me your feedback.

Q: You say this is a "novel based on a true story." What's true and what's not?

A: Most of the rehearsal activities in *Hair* are true, including the main parts of the big men's Improv – the violent attacks on Berger (and there were more; I'll tell you about that in a bit), the licking of the honey, the adoration of the leader stuff. Also, the improv between Margo and Doug in Harry's office did happen. The improv where Scott Warren and Mike Matthews were tied together back-to-back in chairs did happen to a duo of actors in another play.

The suicide of Scott Warren did not happen. I invented that story line to imagine how far the damage from the improvs could progress. I wrote the initial draft of this novel in the early 1990s, as an act of vomiting up what had happen ten years earlier, then put it under my bed for almost twenty years. I wasn't sure it was a story people would care about; I especially wondered if Scott Warren's suicide was going too far.

In the intervening time, the light had been turned on in "Black Boxes" all over the world – from the chapels of the priest pedophiles to the locker room of Penn State. Tragically, on September 22, 2010, Rutgers freshman Tyler Clementi jumped off the George Washington Bridge after being web-cammed by his roommate while "making out" with another man.

Suddenly, I knew that the suicide of Scott Warren, who had been watched by Harry while "making out" with another man, was utterly believable, and that sexual abuse on college campuses is, in fact, a reality that can no longer be ignored. I wanted people (especially young people) to know that this can happen in a drama department too – any place where people of power can impose their twisted will on innocent others. When my mother-in-law pulled my first draft out of her storage area and asked, "Do you want this back?" I reread it and got the chills, realizing how timely the story had become. I spent eighteen months revising it.

Characters' names have been changed, some are entirely fictional, some are conglomerations of several people. Jen, for example, is a mixture of four of my college friends, including one who had been raped and then participated in a Rape Investigation Practicum.

Margo is based on me. I did play Sheila in *Hair*, I did participate in the improvs, as I wrote, and I did manage to be the whistleblower to stop this director from directing any more plays at the university.

Q: What happened to Harry? How did the University get him to stop directing plays?

A: The fall after I graduated, I got a letter from "Jen." Not a letter really, just a clipping from the college newspaper. Across the top "Jen" had written, "*All's well that ends well . . . – XXOO.*" There was a photo of "Harry" and the title, "Director has new role." The subtitle was: "Associate dean post filled." The article read, in part:

> *Sometimes a rise to power carries with it a price. And "Harrison P. Adler," the newly appointed associate graduate studies dean for programs, has paid the price. He has had to forsake a major interest – directing campus plays – to play another role. . . . [The appointment will] take up much of his time, "Adler" says, and leave little time for much else. For the first time since he came to the University in 1963, "Adler" will not direct any major shows on campus, "I will really miss that," he says.*

The University created a new position for him. And that was that.

Q: Why didn't you write this as a memoir and tell the whole truth? [Or as one reader said, "You need to write this as a memoir and get the bastard."] Alternatively, why didn't you tell it in the first person?

A: I'm not brave enough. In fact, when I left acting and went into TV news, I thought briefly about becoming a reporter, but quickly realized that I do not have the guts to probe into people's lives and tell their stories. I went back to my science roots and became a meteorologist. I feel much more comfortable analyzing computer models and helping people prepare for the weather.

I grew up in a family where my father really did say, "Nothing goes outside these walls" and "Never write anything down." I shook while writing parts of this story, feeling the ghost of my father and the shadow of "Harry" breathing down the back of my neck. Revealing what went on in the privacy of my dysfunctional family and the candle-lit darkness of the Improv felt like a treasonous act. I still feel like I will be punished for telling the tale.

As something of a victim myself, or a victim-witness if you will, this is the best I could do.

I did not want to contact others who were in the play or the Drama Department and ask them to go back to that time and then ask permission to tell their stories. Some of them have died; a few from AIDS. And I simply could not write it in the first person, putting myself so fully back there. This was a close as I could get to the fire that can still burn me from so long ago.

In fact, once I graduated from college, I really severed ties with the place. I moved far away, first to New York City, then to Seattle. I never told anyone, including my family, what had happened during *Hair*. I only kept in contact with a small handful of friends and "Doug" was not among them. I never joined any kind of alumni association, never became a donor, never even went back to see any of the plays. I only returned once – for the retirement celebration of "Dr. C."

Q: What happened to "Doug?" Did you ever contact him?

A: "Doug" today is a successful actor, and he is happily married. He has appeared in several well-known Hollywood films, has had recurring roles on television and makes a living as an actor.

I got back in contact with him through Facebook. I wanted him to read *The Improv* and get his permission before attempting publication. I was shaking when I messaged him and told him about the book. He enthusiastically agreed to read it.

I'll never forget the email I got from him after he read the book:

> *Finished the book and really enjoyed it. You really captured his manipulation and the 'fatherly' mask he wore to hide his perversion. Don't know that you know he had private "rituals" with his Berger that I can tell you about if you feel like you want to add stuff. Congrats. P.S.: I'd rather not explain over email. Call me.*

I did not know about private "rituals."

I was nervous calling him, but I did and, after thirty years, he sounded exactly the same. We spoke for an hour. He was still furious about what happened during *Hair* and angry for letting himself be manipulated by that "asshole."

I took notes, trying to capture his words. Here is the gist of what he said:

> *I used to leave my backpack on the loading dock before rehearsals so I could just leave the room as quickly as possible once they were over. Because if I lingered at all, he would grab me and say, "You know we have to have a ritual."*

> *Then, when everyone was gone, he would close the door, light the candle, turn off the lights, and make me take off my shirt and my belt. You know the metal ladder in the back of the room? Well, he told me to hold onto one of the top rungs, with my back to him. Then he would flog me with my own belt.*

> *He would say stuff like "The leader has to absorb the pain for the Tribe," shit like that. Like you put in the book. "There'll come a point when this pain won't hurt you anymore."*

> *I still feel sick to my stomach thinking about it. I tell you, the thought of him still fills me with pure terror.*

> *And like you put in your book, about watching with a third eye, I kind of came out of myself and watched the whipping as he did it.*

Then, he made me chew on the belt that he whipped me with. I was "eating the pain." You know, it was my favorite belt. I kept it and wore it. For years, I'd take off the belt and see the bite marks. I finally threw it away.

Oh, and when it was over, he would hug me and comfort me. Like a dad. Fuck.

Here's another one. It's like the one in your book with the guys tied together. He tied me up naked with a rope, lying on the floor. I was supposed to struggle to get out. At one point he got on top of me and held onto me to make it harder.

Then he touched my genitals. Honestly, that was the only time he did that. And I stopped it right here. I said, "Hold it!" And he said, "I need to go as far as I can go before you stop me." What the fuck?

"Doug" spoke with frankness and a kind of disbelief about the sadistic acts that "Harry" had done to him. I didn't think that anything more about "Harry" could shock me. But I was freshly repulsed.

I thanked "Doug" for his courage. I told him that I was afraid that he would hate the book, or hate me, because he wouldn't want people to know what happened.

He said, "Hey, like you said, it's a novel based on a true story. A novel! No one needs to know it's me or all that really happened. And it's about time the story came out.

"You know, you said it in your book, I would have done anything to be a better actor and I trusted that asshole. I believed that actors were supposed to do shit like that. Like it would make me a better actor. But I've been in this business for years now and what he did was just bullshit! And at the time I thought if I didn't do it, he'd just get someone else for the part. And I would never get to be an actor. I'm such an idiot!"

I reminded him that we were in our early 20s and he was a guru to us. That he, "Doug," was a victim.

He said, "You know, we were adults, so I guess what he did was legal or whatever. But, shit, he had power over us. I'm real glad you're doing this. If one kid reads this and realizes that he doesn't have to do this kind of shit, it will be worth it."

I added some of what he told me to the book. For example, I thought the licking of the honey was to show the men's love for Berger. "Doug" told me it was a "poison" and they were saving his life by licking it off of him.

I couldn't figure out how to fit the private "rituals" into the text so I've put them down here as a kind of record, I guess. It's not perfect, but it's on paper. And maybe it'll help someone.

So, here it is, the ultimate act of a former Sheila who sang with all her heart:

How can people be so heartless?
How can people be so cruel?
Easy to be hard.
Easy to be cold.

FOR MORE . . .

If you want to know more, visit: www.mjmcdermott.com

Please give me your comments. If you have been in a situation like *The Improv*, if you have been abused or manipulated in an educational or artistic setting, there is a place on the website where you can tell your story.

A portion of the proceeds of this book is being donated to Broadway Cares/Equity Fights AIDS. If you care to donate directly, there is a place where you can do that. Or you can go to: www.broadwaycares.org

ACKNOWLEDGEMENTS:

Thank you to all who read drafts of *The Improv* and gave me comments: Adria Ali, Karen Ali, Janet Anderson, Claudia DeGagne, Alicia Edgar, Alan Eisen, Ann Emerson, Jill Farbarik, Bill Fraser, Ron Fischer, Crystal Hainsworth, Patty Hardy, Catherine Hunt, Emily Kane, Cristie Kearny, Addie Keller, Laura Lea King, Patty King Kuntz, Auoha Kone, Lance & Jan Lambert, Ricardo las Neves, Judy McDermott, Laura Mueser, Perry Norton, Maureen Nutting, Lisa McNiel, Nicholas O'Connell, Ruth Pritchard, Kathy Robinson (and her book club), Karen Russo, Liz Schmidt (and her book club), Jacqui Sinatra, Mary Kay Vadino, Ingela Wänerstrand, Susan Warner and Rachel Zampino.

Thanks to my editor, Nancy Wick of Enlightened Edits, for her expert editing skills and the encouragement I needed to believe that I had actually written a book.

I reached across the decades to my dear childhood friend, Jeanne Sears Bellis, who took the original production photos of my college production of *Hair*. She still had the negatives in her files and used one of them to design the amazing cover of *The Improv*. (With input from my publisher and after a thrilling on-line poll – thank you to all who voted.)

Great thanks to my friend, publisher, website designer and former PTA Co-President, Julia Detering.

Finally, love and gratitude to my supportive husband John and my inspiring sons, Kirby & Patrick.

ABOUT THE AUTHOR

M.J. McDermott is an Emmy-Award-winning writer, actor and meteorologist. After graduating with a degree in Theatre Arts, she moved to New York City to pursue acting. She did some theatre, television (including a day on *All My Children*), and narrated for Buick at car shows all over the U.S. After changing coasts, she earned a degree in Atmospheric Sciences. M.J. is currently a TV weathercaster in Seattle, where she lives with her husband and twin boys.

Made in the USA
Charleston, SC
23 March 2013